HELENA

A Peek into the Past

Nettie Balzer
Helena – A Peek into the Past

njbalzer@sasktel.net

Printed and bound in Canada

ISBN 978-0-9880661-0-6

Cover Design by Christopher Tyreman

**DEDICATED TO
MY GRANDCHILDREN**

ABOUT THE AUTHOR

Nettie (Friesen) Balzer is a mother, grandmother and great-grandmother. She spent eleven years working as a Church Secretary and nearly five years as Director of a Church Women's Group. In 1992 she was given her mother's life story and 22 years of diary entries to translate from German to English. Her mother, Helena Banman, used German script letters mixed with English letters in these pages and when writing letters to her children. Nettie finished translating those pages in time for her mother's 100th birthday and hoped one day to write a Mennonite "Little House on the Prairie" kind of book for her grandchildren. "Helena – a Peek into the Past" is her first book.

Table of Contents

Introduction

Children and grandchildren are not always interested in their family history until they grow older, but it's good to know and understand the backgrounds of those who came before us. For that reason I've written down the stories of my mother, Helena Banman Friesen. Some of her stories were written down in "scribblers" (notebooks) and some were told to her children through the years. She was born in 1898 and lived to be 102 years, however this book only includes the first 41 years of her life.

"**HELENA**" is a book of short fictional stories built around actual events in her life. Some of my relatives may remember things or imagine situations in a different way than I have portrayed them. Many names of people mentioned are fictional, however family names and dates are correct so far as I could determine. I've included some Low German words (along with their translation) and have written them they way they would sound to those of us who speak English. Therefore, some of those words will not be the same as those found in the Low German/English Dictionary.

Although Helena and her family lived in several villages in southern Manitoba while she was a child, I have only included the two she mentions most in her stories: Kleefeld and Neuendorf.

I'm so thankful to my siblings for their memories: Helen and Anne wrote things down for me before they passed on. I appreciated the many phone conversations with Jake, Tena, Chris and Dan. Julius – thank you for inspiring me to write stories when I was just a little girl.

Thank you to my Banman cousins; I appreciate you sharing your parents' memories. Cousins Julie Wall and Nettie Peters took me around the country side where our parents worked and lived on the east side of the Saskatchewan River. Thank you too, Cousin Betty Guenther for your help in researching relatives on your genealogy computer program. Thank you to cousins Marie and Abe Giesbrecht and Elizabeth Wiebe for taking me around to the villages on the west side of the river.

Thanks to my daughters: Verdeen, for encouraging me by taking me to a Writers Workshop in 2011 and editing the first few chapters, and Karen, for editing the whole story for me along with lots of great suggestions to help make the stories flow.

Most of all, I am thankful to God for HELENA, my mother: for her faith, for her example, for her humour, for her love of us and of life. She was the best!

Nettie Balzer

Life in Southern Manitoba

CHAPTER 1

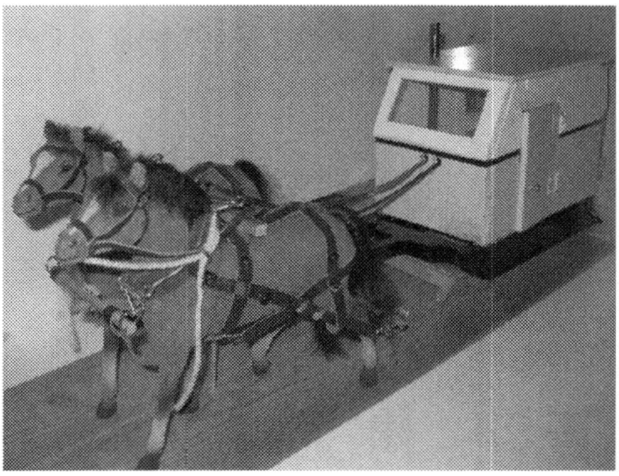

Model of caboose
(Museum at Osler, Sask.,)

The snow drifts sparkled brightly in the morning sunshine beside the trail the horses made as they pulled the caboose (a closed in sleigh). Three year old Helena Banman and her sister, one year old Agenetha, were bundled in thick woollen quilts on a pile of straw on the floor of the sleigh.

Mama Helena and Papa Julius sat on the bench at the front. Papa had a little window through which he could look outside and control the horses with the reins that were pulled through the window. Helena could hear the horses snorting and the harnesses jingling as they trotted along in the snow. It sounded like bells ringing, and the runners of the sleigh made creaking noises on the hard snow.

The family was on their way to Grandma and Grandpa Banman's home in the village of Kleefeld, Manitoba, which was about 10 miles from their home in Neuendorf. Helena liked to go to her grandparents' home because this was the village where she and Agenetha were born. They had only recently moved to the village of Neuendorf and she remembered some of her relatives and other people who lived in Kleefeld so it felt like she was going 'home'. On this trip Mama and Papa were very quiet, except for the clucking noises Papa made with his tongue to make the horses keep on trotting. Whenever Helena peeked out from the blankets, she could see her breath on the cold air.

"Stay under the blankets or you'll get too cold." ordered Mama quietly. But that was hard to do because it was such a long trip and Helena got very tired of staying under the blankets. Agenetha didn't want to lie still either. After much wiggling and playing between them, Papa ordered, "Lig schtell! (Lie still)." Once they settled down it didn't take long to fall asleep.

Photo of house and barn still in use
in the Village of Blumenheim in Saskatchewan.
(Photo used with permission)

Finally they arrived in the village and Helena awoke to the smell of wood smoke and fresh bread as they made their way to the Banman farm buildings. Papa stopped at the house to let Mama and the girls get off the sleigh. He woke the girls, helped Helena out of the sleigh, and after unhitching the horses he led them into the barn. Mama carried Agenetha as they walked into the house.

In Mennonite villages, the houses and barns were built together. The house was at one end, there was a room in the middle and the barn was at the other end. This centre room called the 'gahnk', was especially helpful in cold and stormy winter weather because the farmers didn't have to go outside to look after the animals, and the animals were safe in the barn. The stacks of hay and other feed for the animals, was kept near the barn and some was brought into the loft above the cattle stalls. The room between the house and barn was also used to store firewood needed for the winter and in the summer was a place for the barn clothes and boots so the house could be kept cleaner. Helena and her family walked into the building through this middle room and opened the door to the house.

As she was helped off with her coat, Helena looked around and saw relatives that she knew. There were her uncles, Peter, Jake, and Solomon and her big cousin John. They all looked serious and spoke quietly with one another. After Papa returned to the house and warmed himself by the stove, the brothers and their wives and children went to the bedroom and gathered around a board laid across saw-horses. Helena looked around the room. She tugged at Papa's coat sleeve.

"Papa," she whispered. "Where is grosfoda?" In answer to her question, he picked her up, pointing to a body lying on a board, mostly covered with a sheet. She gazed at her grandfather John Banman's face. It was December 13, 1901 and her first experience with someone dying. Death was not something little children in Mennonite communities were shielded from. In those days there was very little medical help for people and many died young. Grandfather was only 73 years old - but that was old to Helena.

After spending the evening with grandmother Banman and the relatives, Mama, Papa and the girls went to their Klassen grandparents' house for the night. The funeral was held three days later in the Old Colony Church, where many neighbours came to grieve with the family.
Helena sat as still as she could with her mother. The women and girls all sat on one side of the church, while all the men and boys sat on the other. Two men sat at the front of the church, facing the rest of the people. They were called 'vor-singers' (song leaders). One of the men announced a song and after humming a few notes they all began to sing very slowly, drawing out every note and word in a nasal, sad tone. There were no pianos, organs or guitars in the church. Helena was used to hearing this kind of singing, but today with the people looking so sad, it was hard to keep back the tears so she hid her face against her mother's arm.

After the funeral they returned to Grandma Banman's house, where all the women brought buns and made coffee. This was a favourite time for Helena at all the family gatherings! It was faspa time - a light meal of buns and coffee. She was sure there would be a sucka schtek(sugar cube) that she could dip into her coffee. She was getting so hungry, but it wasn't the custom for little children to eat first.

The men were all served, and took their time eating and talking. Next, the women sat down to eat. The older girl cousins helped pour coffee for their parents and the little children stood around with solemn faces. It was hard to wait with a rumbling stomach and the rich aromas of coffee and fresh baking. The chime clock in grandma's parlour ticked resolutely as the adults lingered over their food and conversations.

Helena tugged shyly at her mother's sleeve and whispered, "Me hungat (I'm hungry)." Mama reached into her plate and broke off a little piece of her bun and gave it to Helena. Agenetha was on Mama's lap eating brocken (little pieces of bun soaked in a cup of milk). When the women finished eating, they hurried to clear places for each of the children.

Finally Helena got to have her sugar cubes! Mama gave her a saucer with a little coffee in it, and she carefully dipped the sugar cubes and sucked on them, while listening to her cousins chattering away next to her. The women busily washed dishes in big tubs on another table.

"Have you enough to eat?" asked Mama while she dried her hands. "Papa has gone to hitch the horses for our ride back to our own village."

"Yo (Yes)." Helena answered. She climbed down off the chair and let Mama help her with her coat and a trip to the cold out-house. After saying their good-byes, Papa tucked Helena and Agenetha into the sleigh while Mama climbed in to sit on the bench.

"Wait," called one of Helena's Aunts. "Here are three hot stones from the oven. They will keep your feet warm on the way home." Papa opened the door to the caboose as she handed him a gunny sack with the stones. He put two of the stones on the floor of the sleigh so he and Mama could put their feet on them. Then he wrapped the other stone in a blanket and placed it at the girls' feet. (A gunny sack was a brown bag of woven burlap used for storing grain)

For a while the little girls were allowed to sit up, bundled warmly in the quilts on the straw, but it was dark outside and soon the rhythm of the jingling harnesses and the clopping of the horses' hoofs on the hard snow caused their eyelids to feel heavy and close. They were so sound asleep they didn't even notice their arrival at home or that Mama and Papa had carried them into the house and put them to bed.

Busy Lives

CHAPTER 2

A few months later, the snow began to melt, creating puddles and mud everywhere. Even before all the snow disappeared some of the birds had returned and Helena loved to listen to them sing. The first sound was the caw-caw of the crows and then the robins and meadowlark songs were heard The robins were so pretty with their red breasts and the meadowlarks' song sounded like they were singing 'Fritze Franz keelkyi zup' (Fritz Franz noodle soup).

Helena watched Papa let the cow and her new baby calf into the warm sunshine. She laughed as the little calf jumped and bucked, making little 'maw' sounds. There was new life everywhere in the spring – new kittens and puppies, new colts with long legs trying to keep up with their mothers and birds singing. Everywhere the grass was turning green, little purple crocus flowers were peeking out and the trees had shiny new leaves that were sticky to touch.

Drawing by Nettie Balzer

In the month of May, when the sun had warmed the ground enough, Mama and Papa ploughed the garden. Papa used the ox to pull the plough. Mama led the ox while Papa held the plough and tried to make straight furrows. After the ground was ploughed, Mama carried out a pail of old potatoes from the year before.

"Helena," Mama called. "You can help me get the potatoes ready for planting. Find the smallest potatoes and I will pick out the bigger ones."

Helena carefully picked out the smallest old potatoes. Some had long sprouts growing on them and she had fun breaking them off like Mama told her to. Mama cut up the larger potatoes into pieces. Then, while Papa dug a hole, Mama and Helena put the little potatoes and pieces into the ground so they could grow into potato plants. They also planted carrots, onions, peas, beans, corn, cucumbers, cabbage, and watermelon from seeds her mother had carefully saved.

After following Mama down the rows for a while, Helena sat down and began opening the little bags of seeds. Some of the seeds were very tiny and a few spilled on the ground.

"Helena!" Mama said. "Leave those seeds in the bags – go play with Agenetha!" Helena was tired of gardening anyway and joined Agenetha where she sat on the ground playing with a rag doll.

As the ground grew warmer, the little girls were able to run outside barefoot and loved the feel of the ground - especially the puddles when it rained! When Helena and Agnetha heard children's voices on the village road, they ventured out to see them and played with Annie and Katie Peters for a while.

"Look," Helena called as she walked into a puddle of water. The children joined her and now they stood in the small puddles giggling and watching the mud squish up between their toes, listening to the new calves bawling around the village.

"Miyalles (Girls)!" called Mama later. "Come in for supper." The girls ran back to their house. Mama stopped them at the door with a pail of water and rinsed off their muddy feet. It was milk soup and fried eggs for supper!

In the evening some of the neighbours gathered to visit and talk about their farms and gardens. The men stood around smoking cigarettes and talking about new calves and lambs while the women discussed the progress of their gardens. The adults visited while the children played until bedtime.

After the neighbours drove away, calling "Goude Nacht! (Good Night)," Mama washed the girls feet again, tucked them into their blankets in the schlope benk and had the girls repeat the prayer they were learning; "Furchte Gott, (fear God) liebes kindt (dear child). Gott der Herr (God the Lord) zeet und veis alle ding (sees and knows everything). Amen" (See picture of schlopebenk at the end of chapter 4)

Mama and Papa were busy all summer. Mama weeded the garden while Papa cut the long grass with a scythe to make hay for the cows to eat in the winter. Cutting the grass was hard work.

Papa swung the scythe, creating a rhythm with each step. He stopped often to catch his breath and take a drink of water or cold coffee. Sweat poured off his face and he wiped his forehead often with his handkerchief. After finishing several rows of cut grass, Papa picked up a pitch fork and threw the grass on piles to form hay stacks.

The next morning Papa hitched the ox to a stone boat, stopped at each pile of hay, picked it up with his pitch fork, threw it on to the stone boat and brought it to the barn. After many days of this and always worrying that it might rain, he finally got all the hay pitched next to the barn. The days seemed to fly by and soon it was August, and Helena was another year older.

Scythe used to cut hay. The farmer grasped both handles and swung the blade over the hay. (Scythe at Osler Museum)

Stoneboat drawing by NB

Getting Ready for Winter

CHAPTER 3

"Girls," Mama said one day. "Come to the garden and help me pick beans and peas." As Mama bent over the plants, Helena tried to copy her. Agenetha plopped down in the dirt and pulled the peas off the vines.

"Not so hard, Agnes," Mama said. "You'll tear the plants out of the ground - do it like this." And she showed her how to hold the vine and carefully pull off the peas. But Agenetha (also called Nita or Agnes) was only 2 & ½ years old and soon lost interest as did Helena, going off to play instead.

In the evenings Mama sat outside with her apron full of peas or beans. She shelled the peas and cut the ends off the beans. One of their favourite meals was green bean soup. Many of the beans were left to ripen on the vines and then picked later in fall. Mama laid out the ripe beans and peas on sheets of paper to dry in the sun. In the winter they would be soaked in water over night and then cooked for meals. Helena and Agnes tried to shell peas too, but they loved the sweet taste of the pea pods as well as the peas and ate more than they shelled.

Helena, with Agnes toddling after her, loved to run with her arms outstretched between the rows of corn, listening to the rustle of the long dry leaves. It seemed that the corn stalks were whispering "Come and hide!"

"Come find me!" Helena called to Agnes as she hid in the tall corn. Mama often smiled as she listened to the girls giggling and playing in the garden.

The next vegetable ready was corn, and corn-on-the cob was a favourite meal. Usually when the people in the village had corn-on-the cob, no other vegetables or meat were served.

Some of the cobs were left to ripen on the stalks. Once the kernels had become hard and ripe, they were picked, peeled and left to dry. Then they were rubbed off the cobs and put in a dry place for the winter, when they could be soaked over night and cooked the next day for a meal. Some of the kernels were kept to plant the next summer and some of them were ground into corn flour.

All summer it seemed, the cucumbers kept on growing and sometimes Helena helped to pick them so Mama could make salt pickles and dill pickles. Mama also cut stalks of dill, tying them together with string and hanging them from a nail on the wall. The dill would be used later to make borscht soup.

As the weather turned cooler, Mama covered the tomatoes, watermelons and muskmelons so they wouldn't freeze during the cool nights. Finally, just before the weather got too cold, Mama picked the tomatoes, melons and cabbage heads, pulled all the onions, and brought them into the house. She tied the onion greens together and hung the onions from a nail on the wall. They would keep well through the winter.

Then it was time to dig up the potatoes and the carrots. Mama and Papa dug up the plants and shook the dirt off of the potatoes, digging deeper for those that were far down in the ground. Helena sometimes helped put them into pails to be carried to the root cellar. The girls enjoyed the busy sounds of potatoes plopping into the pails and tumbling into the cellar potato bin. The cellar was a hole dug into the ground below the floor inside the house, with a wooden lid covering it.

Once all the vegetables were safely in the house, Mama chopped the cabbage, putting layers of cabbage and salt into a stoneware crock. After putting a clean plate with a heavy stone on top to keep the cabbage down, she covered it with a cloth. Helena watched mama work.

"Why did you put a plate and stone on the cabbage in the crock?" Helena asked.

"Because it pushes the cabbage down so it will ferment. In a couple of months, we'll have sauerkraut and I can make sauerkraut soup!" she answered. Helena had to wait for the soup, but for now she and Agnes nibbled on the core of the cabbage heads. That was their favourite part of the raw cabbage!

Mama gathered all the seeds she had dried; peas, beans, corn, tomato, cucumber, melon and flower seeds. She put each kind into a small cloth bag, tied it with string and put them all into a tin box which she placed in the cellar. Next spring she would bring them out and plant another garden and the work of growing food for another year would begin all over again.

As the weather cooled, out came the wool sweaters, warm underwear, stockings and zocken (knitted or crocheted slippers). The snow came down in earnest and the wind howled in fury as the snow piled against the house and barn. The frost was thick on the window panes and Helena and Agnes liked to put their mouths against the window, making a circle in the frost with their warm breath. That way they could look outside, until the circle froze over again.

With the fall and early snow, came neighbourhood pig-butchering. The village people gathered at one farm at a time, butchering the pigs, making sausage and head-cheese, cutting the hams into chunks and rendering lard. The ham and sausages were hung in a smoke house to cure them.

Helena loved to follow her parents around even though she was often told to get out of the way. She played with other children and listened to the women visit while they worked.

When everything was done, the neighbours went home, each with a piece of the meat for their evening meal. Tired Mama and Papa tucked the children into bed and got some sleep themselves. The next day they would do it all over again, at another farmer's place!

There were not a lot of trees on the prairie where the village was located, so Papa and some neighbour men got together and travelled north by horse and wagon to cut trees and saw them into short logs. After a few days they returned to the village and the families piled wood logs close to their homes. Papa spent a lot of time splitting the logs with an axe so the pieces would fit into the clay brick stove they used to cook with and warm their house.

Because wood was not plentiful and the fires had to burn all winter, the children of the village were also sent out to the fields to pick up dried cow manure. They brought gunny sacks full in the fall and stacked them in a dry place. Some people had manure presses that shaped the manure into even pieces to fit the stoves. If the firewood was not enough for the winter, the families could burn cow dung to heat the houses and cook their food. Helena was still too young to help with this, so Mama and Papa went out to the fields themselves. They also gathered straw from farmers' fields to burn in the brick ovens and to use for bedding for the animals to sleep on in the barn.

The winter was cold and it was hard to keep the house warm enough. As long as they had the smoked meat, dried vegetables and other vegetables in the cellar they did not have to worry about food. They were able to eat fairly well for the rest of the season. The firewood lasted almost until spring.

Work in the winter was slower with not as much to do. Papa bundled up in his Russian fur coat and cap with ear flaps and went out to feed the animals every morning and clean the manure out of the barn.

Mama also got up early, shivering as she lit a fire in the oven with some straw. Once the straw caught fire she added wood. Then she also bundled up and went to the barn to milk the cow and bring in fresh warm milk before making breakfast.

With the brick stove heated, the room felt warmer. Mama cooked porridge and called the girls.

"Lena (Helena), Nita (Agnes) – get up for breakfast."

Chamber pot (Osler Museum)

The girls got up, pulled the chamber pot from under the bed and used it before they got dressed. (There was no bathroom in the house so a small enamel pot was used for an indoor toilet).

The door opened and a blast of icy cold air blew into the room as Papa arrived for breakfast. He took off his barn clothes, warmed himself by the brick stove, washed his hands and then sat down at the table.

"Kom, Herr Jesu, sei du unser gahst und segne vas du uns bescheret hahst, Amen (Come Lord Jesus, be our guest and bless the food you have given us)," prayed Mama.

After some porridge and warm milk, the girls were ready to play and when papa was done with his coffee the girls bounced on his knee.

Swinging Helena onto his lap, Papa bounced his knees up and down as he recited a silly little poem; "Kickerra kee, de hone est dout. Vua zel vie dem begroven? Hingeram schultenbak ohven". (Cock-a-doodle-doo the rooster is dead. Where shall we bury him? Behind the brick oven). Helena giggled as she was jiggled up and down.

"My turn!" begged Agnes. Papa picked her up, put her on his foot, held her little hands and swung his foot up and down as he recited,"Schokel, schokel schaiya. Oustren ate ve aiya. Pinksten ate ve vitit brot. Schtoav ve nich, dan voa ve grout". (Swing, swing, swing. At Easter we eat eggs, at Pentecost we eat white bread. If we do not die, we will grow up.)

In between meals Mama sat near the brick stove knitting sweaters, socks and zocken. With the short days and early darkness, candles and coal oil lamps were lit before supper. A lantern was lit for the barn when Mama attended to the evening milking and Papa provided the animals with food and straw.

Every Sunday the family went to church to meet with their neighbours, sing hymns and listen to a sermon preached by their minister.

A Surprise

CHAPTER 4

Finally spring came, the snow melted and the weather was warm again. It was time to plant another garden. Papa hitched the ox to the plough and loosened the rich black earth. After raking it smoothly, Mama planted her vegetables. It was hard work and she seemed more tired than usual.

"Helena, go and get your sister." Papa said one nice summer day. "We're going to visit the Peters children at the other end of the village." Helena was excited because she often begged to visit the Peters girls but Mama had been too busy and tired. Now she ran to get Agnes, who was playing with a puppy behind the house.

"Come!" she said as she grabbed the little girl's hand. "We're going to see Annie and Katie Peters!"

Papa hitched up the buggy, swung the little girls up onto the seat and climbed up. He picked up the reins, giving them a snap onto the horses back. The horse trotted quickly onto the road.

"Why isn't Mama coming?" asked Helena.

"She's not feeling well, and I'm going to bring Mrs. Peters over to help her for a while," said Papa.

At the Peters home, the girls ran off to play while Mrs. Peters quickly hurried into the buggy.

Helena, Agnes, Annie and Katie dug their bare toes into the warm moist soil in the garden. They sat in the shade of a plum tree, watching the new kittens play-fighting with each other. Agnes giggled with delight and tried to catch them, but they scampered out of her reach. Annie picked up the little orange kitten and let Agnes touch it. As it started to play with her hand, it scratched and bit her.

"Ow vei! (ouch!)" she said as she jerked her hand back, but she laughed as it rolled onto its back in the dirt.

"Miyalles (Girls)," called the Peters' oldest daughter Elizabeth a few hours later. "Wash your hands and come in for supper."

The girls ran off to the well in the back yard where Elizabeth had hauled up a pail of water. Annie was the biggest, so she scooped up dippers of water for them. The cool water felt so good as they splashed it on their hot faces and hands. Then they ran into the house. Mmmm!! They could smell fried smoked sausage! There were home made noodles and Scmuah Kumpst (stewed cabbage with raisins), and fresh buns!

Swing drawing by NB

Elizabeth came out and said, "Come on girls, how about a ride on the swing?" There was a big tree in the front yard with a long, strong thick rope looped up and tied to a high branch. At the bottom of the loop was a notched wooden board

Agnes was first on the swing board and held tightly to the ropes as Elizabeth gently swung her – not too high. Helena was next and laughed as she was swung higher and higher. It tickled her stomach every time she came down. Annie and Katie took their turns and there was lots of laughter.

After a while, the girls grew tired and Agnes wanted Mama. It was getting late and even though the sun was still quite high in the sky, it was past bed time for little Agnes. Helena was getting a bit worried. It was fun to play with the neighbour children but now she just wanted to go home. They sat on the stoop of the house and looked toward the road. Finally they saw some dust at the other end of the village street and heard a horse trotting and harnesses jingling. When they saw Papa's buggy, they ran eagerly to the road. He drove past them to the house and turned the horse around. Mrs. Peters got off and Papa came to put his little girls into the buggy.

"Why did you wait so long to come?" asked Helena. "You'll see," replied Papa.

When they arrived home the girls ran to the house. As they entered through the door they heard a baby crying. Wondering who was visiting, they looked into the bedroom and saw Mama lying on the bed, holding a crying baby. Mama looked very tired, but smiled at the girls.

"Come and see your baby sister Anna," she said. Little baby Anna had stopped crying and the girls moved closer to look at her. She seemed so small to the girls, but she was perfect! It was July 5, 1902. They were excited and wanted to hold her.

"No," said Mama. "Not yet, but soon. Helena, you're a pretty big girl and you're almost five years old. Will you set the table for Papa and put on some faspa? He's hungry and maybe I'll have something to eat, too." Mama watched from her open bedroom door.

"That's very good, Helena! Now get the butter, buns and cold sausage from the cupboard. When Papa comes in, he'll heat the water for coffee."

"What's this?" Papa asked when he came inside, looking surprised and peeking around the furniture. "Do we have a maid in our house?" Helena giggled, and ran back to take another look at little Anna.

Papa put the water on for coffee and made up a plate of food for Mama. After finishing his food, he looked at Agnes, slumped on the chair, falling asleep.

"Helena," he said. "Take Agnes with you and go to the out house. Then we'll get you both into bed." When the girls came back, Papa had pulled out the "schlopebenk" drawer and unfolded their blankets. He picked Agnes up and helped her take off her dress and climb into the bed. Helena needed a bit of help too and soon they were both sound asleep, dreaming of swinging high up in the clouds while a perfect, tiny baby cried nearby.

A Schlopebenk (Osler Museum). The seat is a lid that lifted and the drawer underneath was pulled out for sleeping.

Helping Mama

CHAPTER 5

For the next week Mrs. Peters or her daughter Elizabeth came every day to help with washing diapers and making meals. In those days a mother stayed in bed for at least a week after having a baby. Helena had to keep Agnes entertained and help Mama wherever she could. Because the house they lived in was not very big, Helena often awakened at night when the baby cried, but fell asleep as soon as she stopped. After a few days the girls were used to the baby and didn't hear her at night any more.

"Helena," Mama often called when she was busy and heard the baby crying. "Go and rock the cradle – I'll be there soon to feed Anna."

The summer was busy with berries ripening and garden peas ready to pick. In the middle of all that work Mama still had to milk the cows, bake bread, wash diapers and clothes and many other things. Some days she was very tired. The little girls began helping even though they were only five and three.

"Here, grind the coffee beans for me," Mama suggested.

"Helena – toss some grain on the ground for the chickens." When Helena first tried to gather eggs from under the hens they pecked her hands and she cried. Mama comforted her and said she could just help feed the chickens until she was a bit older.

The days were filled with all the farm work but some

evenings the neighbourhood men gathered again at Mama and Papa's yard, leaned against the wagon wheels or sat on the ground smoking their cigarettes and discussing their work.

Saturdays Mama washed the girls' only dresses so they would be clean for Sunday church service. The girls would have a quick wash and get into bed.

Sunday mornings after milking the cows, doing the other chores and having breakfast, Papa hitched the horse to the buggy and they drove to church. Just like it was at her grandfather's funeral, all the men and boys sat on one side of the church and all the women and girls sat on the other side of the room.

One of the two men sitting at the front inside the church, announced a hymn. "We will sing hymn number 35," and he began to sing. All the people found the song and joined in singing the slow German words. The singing went on for a long time because some of the hymns had 15 verses or more!

It was often hard for Helena and the other children to sit still because the songs were long and the scripture that was read before the sermon was all in the High German language. At home they all spoke the Low German dialect. They really could not understand what was being said, but as they grew older they learned the songs and how to read and write High German.

After the singing, the Eltesta (bishop) read the sermon for the day. When he finished, all of the people bowed their heads in quiet prayer until they were dismissed.

"Gouden moryen (Good morning)," the people greeted each other. They milled around visiting with many who lived on nearby farms or villages and then enjoyed the buns and coffee the women had brought. It was good to visit.

Back home again the weeks were filled with harvesting the grain and the garden vegetables. The weather became cold again as they prepared for another winter. This winter they didn't have quite as much food because there hadn't had enough rain to grow as many vegetables.

One night Papa and Mama were awakened to a terrible noise of cackling and shrieking chickens in the chicken coop. Hurrying into his clothes, papa ran out with a lantern and saw a coyote running off with one of the chickens. There were several more lying dead.

As he came back to the house, Mama asked him, "Did we lose any?"

"Yes," Papa replied. "There are several dead. It's hard to live here on the wild prairie with so many coyotes and wolves around." Losing livestock happened often to the early settlers.

"That means there will be fewer eggs and with the cows giving less milk I wonder how we will make it through the rest of the winter." Mama wondered out loud.

"The crops were not very good either, so there won't be much money to buy the things we need," Papa said.

“Helena and Agnes," Mama said one spring evening. "I’d like you to go to Mrs. Heiden’s house and borrow some sugar. I want to make some "schmaunt kuken(cream cookies)."

Mr. & Mrs. Heiden were having supper and made the girls wait until they were done. Helena and her sister stood near the door and watched in fascination as Mrs. Heiden cut a piece of bread into four pieces, speared a piece with her knife, dipped it into some syrup and ate it. Being hungry, it made their mouths water and Helena decided that when she grew up she would eat bread with syrup the same way!

In December the family made a trip to Kleefeld for Christmas. Many relatives gathered for a meal of Pluma Mousse (fruit soup) and Schinken Fleisch (ham) at Grandma's house. On Christmas morning the girls were happy to receive some candy and an orange as their gifts. Grandma Klassen surprised them by giving them a rag doll she had made. They were very happy.

Two Grandmas and a Grandpa Visit

CHAPTER 6

The next summer, on August 29th 1903, Helena, Agnes and baby Anna were taken to the Peters place again and when they got home, there was another baby girl! Helena and Agnes were excited to see tiny little Susanna!

Helena was now six years old and was learning how to wash dishes, while Agnes carefully dried them.

"Helena! Please get Anna away from the wood box!" Mama would say. Anna was just over a year old and crawling all over the place. She pulled herself up at the cradle to see the baby and nearly tipped it over.

"No! Anna! Don't pull the blanket off the baby!" Helena called. But Anna was determined to see the world and the oldest girls were busy keeping her out of trouble. Helena and Agnes would rather be playing, but baby Anna was fun to play with too.

The rag doll Grandma had given them was very special to the girls, but sometimes they argued about whose turn it was to play with it. They both wanted the newer doll and not the old one they had before.

"Girls, we only have one new doll so you have to share it," Mama said. One day after hearing the girls fighting about the doll again, Mama got a piece of cloth from an old dress and made another doll. Now there were three rag dolls for the girls and little sister Anna.

The summer brought the garden and field work for Helena's parents. For the girls it meant helping but it also meant long days of sun and play time. Helena loved the sounds of summer: the distant barking of dogs answered by other dogs in the village; the honking of the neighbours' geese – she loved to watch them run and flap their wings as they chased away dogs, cats and chickens; the roosters' crowing and the chickens contentedly cackling to each other as they laid eggs in their nests.

The children often stood at the fence and listened to the cows munching grass nearby and the horses snorting or neighing to other horses in nearby fields. Helena picked grass and poked it through the fence boards for the animals.

The piglets were getting bigger and rooted in the dirt - or mud if there was a puddle nearby. Now with crops and garden vegetables ready for harvest the air would soon be cooler and they would need to wear sweaters or coats.

One morning in early September of 1903 the girls looked up to see horses and a buggy coming toward their farm.

"Mama!" the girls called out. "Someone's coming to visit!" They were excited when they saw their grandparents driving up to the house.

"Ho!" called Grandpa Klassen as he pulled on the reins to stop the horses. "Gouden Moryen!" he said as they climbed down from the buggy. Then the children saw Grandma Banman sitting on the back seat!

"Vilkommen!!' said Mama as she greeted her parents and mother-in-law. Meanwhile Papa had seen the company coming so he drove back to the house from the field with the oxen. Mama led the way into the house and as the grandparents spent some time getting re-acquainted with the little girls and the new baby, mama quickly peeled potatoes and onions. While they were simmering on the stove she called Helena to go to the garden to pick some dill weed and sorrel leaves. Helena and Agnes both ran to the garden and back with the herbs. Mama had some sour buttermilk so she made a big pot of zumma borscht for the family and their company.

After their dinner she led the grandmothers to see the garden and how it was growing. Some of the plants were not doing well but there were lots of potato plants. Papa and Grandpa went out to the barn and the fields to look at the work of the farm.

Soon they were all sitting in the shade beside the house and visiting while eating knackzoat (roasted sunflower seeds). Grandma Banman raised her hand to get their attention and then said, "I want to let you know that I'm going to get married again. The widower, Mr. Peter Hamm has asked me to marry him and we will move to Mexico this fall."

Papa was a bit stunned by this news but could understand that his mother was having a hard time. Widows back then did not have any way of earning money unless their children continued to do the farming and took care of them. This way she would be taken care of by Mr. Hamm.

"Why do you want to move to Mexico?" asked Papa.

"There are quite a few families that want to move. Mr. Hamm has some relatives there and so do I. The wedding will be the last week of this month, September, and then we will leave. It will be hard to leave all of you."

After some faspa, the grandparents left to go back to their homes in Kleefeld. At the end of September the Julius Banman family travelled back to Kleefeld for the wedding and for goodbyes as the girls' grandma left for another country very far away.

The fall of 1903 and the winter of 1904 were hard for the Banman family. It was hard to get wood for the brick stoves of the village. The men again gathered several teams of horses and big hay racks and made their way north to where there were lots of trees. They did not bring back as many logs as they had wanted to. It was slow work with two men needed for each saw, and after several days they finally returned. Then they cut the logs into shorter pieces for the stoves.

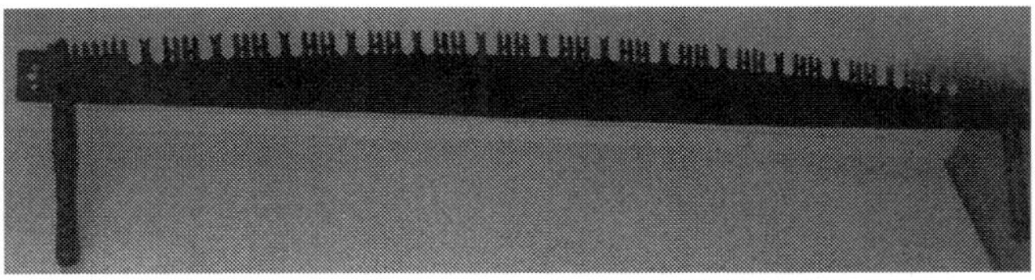

Two-man saw used to cut down trees. (Osler Museum)

On April 16, 1905 another little baby girl came to join the family. When the girls were brought home from the neighbours' they saw little Katherina wrapped in a blanket in the cradle. By now Helena was seven years old, Agnes five, Anna three and Susanna two. There were many chores for the older girls to do and they were often busy helping to keep their little sisters happy, but there was lots of laughter as the little girls ran around the house and played together.

Fun with Cousins

CHAPTER 7

"We're going to Kleefeld to visit Grandma and Grandpa Klassen tomorrow morning," Mama told the girls one evening. Helena and her sisters loved going to visit their mother's parents. The Daniel Blatz family lived on the same yard and it was fun to visit the little girls and boys in that family. Daniel Blatz was Mama's half-brother, so the Blatz children were their cousins.

Wooden wagon drawing by NB

The next morning Mama, Helena, Agnes, and Anna climbed into the wagon and the girls excitedly chattered away. Papa helped Susanna up, and Mama held baby Katherina on her lap. Papa climbed up and as he made the 'clucking' noise with his mouth and snapped the reins, the horse trotted onto the road.

Sometimes the girls sat on the bottom of the wagon playing with each other and sometimes they stood holding on to the sides of the wagon, looking out across the fields and at the houses they passed along the way, or watched the big wooden wheels turning, turning, beneath them. Watching the wheels almost made them feel dizzy! It was a very bumpy, shaky ride as the wooden wheels turned over the ruts and stones in the road. Helena started singing "Ahh h ..." and her voice sounded very funny because of the bumps and shaking of the wagon. Her sisters joined her and pretty soon the noise got to their parents.

"Schtell!" barked Papa. They stopped singing and looked at each other and then it seemed even funnier, so they sat on the wagon floor giggling. Even their giggling sounded funny with the shaking of the wagon and the harder they tried to be quiet, the harder they laughed! Their parents looked at each other and couldn't help but smile.

After a while the ride seemed long to the girls, and they sat on the blankets listening to the rhythm of the horses hoofs clip-clopping along the road. Anna and Susanna fell asleep.

Finally they arrived in the village of Kleefeld and stopped at Grandma's house. Grandpa and Papa led the horses to the barn where they were given some hay to eat and water to drink.

Grandma greeted them at the door and said, "Kombt e-nen! (Come in). Dinner is ready. Let's sit down and eat." The house smelled wonderful! They all bowed their heads in silent prayer and then dug into the food. Grandma's pluma mousse, fresh bread and fried schinken fleisch (ham) tasted so good!

After the good meal, the girls asked their mother, "May we run over to see the Blatz girls?"

"Yes," she replied. "Go and have a good time." That would give her time to spend with her mother so they could visit without interruption. Mama and Grandma got caught up on family news while Susanna played on the floor with a rag doll and Katherina slept. The three oldest girls ran over to the Blatz house.

All of the girls were very shy and stood a short distance away from each other, saying nothing, but only glancing at each other and smiling. The Blatz boys came over to where the girls were and acted silly. Jacob ran to get his father's violin and played a bad screechy tune. The girls giggled and when Jacob put on a pair of funny looking glasses, they all broke into laughter and had a wonderful time playing together. It seemed they had just got started when they heard Mama call them.

"Girls, it's time to go home," called Mama.

"Nay, kev vie nich lenga blieven (No, can't we stay longer)?" begged Helena

"It's getting late," answered Mama. "And we need to get home to milk the cow and feed the chickens and pigs."

Because their mother was so busy with more little ones to look after, the older girls learned to work on the little farm. Helena learned how to milk the cow; Agnes had to gather the eggs and Anna set the table.

Milk and cream separator (Osler Museum)

When Mama put the cream separator together and poured in the milk, the girls liked to take turns cranking the handle and watching the cream come pouring out of the spout into the pail that was set underneath and watch the skim milk pour out of another spout into a different pail.

Mama used some of the cream to make butter. She put the cream into a syrup pail, put the lid on tightly and shook it. The older girls took turns shaking the pail. After a while they could hear a 'bump, bump' sound in the pail and when they took the lid off, there was a lump of butter and some butter milk. The butter milk was poured off and used to make Zumma Borscht soup. Mama added salt to the butter to make it taste good.

Going to School

CHAPTER 8

Now that Helena and Agnes were eight and six years old, they began to attend school in the nearby Village of Schonwiese. Their teacher was Mr. Peter Ens.

Most villages had their own schools. School was often held in someone's home and the children were taught in the German language. Helena and Agnes went to school in the schoolhouse near their parents' friends, the Enses. They learned to read and write in German script letters, learned to read the New Testament and were taught arithmetic.
"Ah, Bye, tzye, Dye, Ei, F, Yye, Ha, E, Yot, Kah, L, M, N, Ou, Pye, Ku, Errr, S, Tye, Oo, Fow, Vye, Ix, E-e, Tzet." This is how the Low German speaking people pronounced the letters and all the children chimed in together to memorize the alphabet.

"20, 1 & 20, 2 & 20, 3 & 20, 4 & 20....." The girls had to learn how to count and how to add and subtract. The German way of counting is different from the way we count in English. The number 'twenty one' would be read as 'one and twenty' in German.

During stormy or cold winter weather Helena and Agnes sometimes had to stay with the Enses for few days. Being shy little girls, this was hard for them. They didn't like being away from their parents.

One Friday evening Helena overheard the teacher say "The weather is very bad. The blizzard is making travel very difficult." The girls thought they would have to stay with the Enses. Helena was very worried and drank lots of coffee to keep from crying. Then they heard horses and someone call "HO! (Whoa)!" There was their father. He hurried into the house, stamping the snow off his feet. The girls were so relieved and hurried into their coats, mittens and caps.

"Here," said Mrs. Ens, handing a cup to Papa. "I've just made fresh coffee. Get yourself warmed up before you get back out into that storm!" While Papa warmed himself, drank the coffee and visited, the girls stood waiting with their coats on.

"I can still make out the trail, but the storm is getting worse. I may have to walk ahead of the horses with the lantern, but I think they will know the way home," he said.

"If it gets too bad," Mr. Ens said, "you are welcome to come back and stay the night." At this the girls looked at one another in dismay.

"Thank you, but I think we will be fine. Besides, my wife will worry if we don't come back in a little while. Come on girls. Let's get bundled into the sleigh!"

They went out and climbed into the caboose. The wind was cold and the snow swirled all around them. Papa strained to see out of the little window and urged the horses on. Before long, they could make out the dark shapes of the village houses as they drove past them to their own house. As they walked into the warm house they were greeted by a very relieved Mama.

At the end of another school day the girls found themselves locked in the school house! The teacher had locked the door and left without checking to see if all the children had gone home. The girls were putting on their coats, hats and mittens when Agnes decided to check outside and see if Papa was there to pick them up.

"Helena!" she called when she tried to turn the door knob, "I can't open it! How can we get out?"

"I'll try," Helena said as she walked to the door. But she couldn't open it either and they realized it was locked. Running to the window and blowing warm breath on the frosted window pane and rubbing it with a sleeve, they looked out to see if papa was there.

When their father came to get them he tried the door and knocked. The girls ran to the door calling, "We're here! The teacher locked the door!"

"I'll try to open a window," he said. After pushing and tapping on a window frame he managed to open it.

"Pull up a chair so you can climb out," Papa told them. The girls climbed up on the chair and crawled through the opening into Papa's waiting arms. After closing the window they made their way to the sleigh and home.

Finally the snow began to melt and the first signs of spring began to arrive. Purple crocuses peeked out of the old brown grass close to small snow banks that had not yet melted. High overhead in the sky they could hear the loud honking of geese returning to their nesting grounds and the robins could be seen plucking long grasses, carrying beaks full of them to the nests they were building.

In the middle of the month of May when the mud in the garden had dried, it was again time to hitch the ox to the plough and get the garden ready for planting.

As Papa hung on to the plough and Mama led the ox, Helena was told to whip the ox with a tree branch to make it move. Sometimes all she had to do was tickle the ox with the branch and the ox would remember to walk forward.

Since the weather was warming up, the cow with her calf, the horse, and the pigs could be let out of the barn to eat the new grass that was growing and for fresh air. The pigs had to be in a pen so that they would not wander away. The cow and horse were tied to a fence post with long ropes so that they could graze nearby.

While Mama planted her garden with the girls' help, Papa began to shovel all the manure out of the barn.

"Eeyoo," the girls muttered as they held their noses. The manure smell was awful and they were glad they were in the garden and not shovelling in the barn! Papa used the wheelbarrow to take the manure to the field where it was dumped. When it was dry and ploughed into the ground along with the soil, it helped to make the plants grow.

The summer passed quickly and soon the girls were back in school, skipping with their friends and learning to read and write.

More Sisters – More Work

CHAPTER 9

On a cold November 1st in 1906, Papa again took the children to see the Peters family. By now, Helena knew what that would mean and looked forward to being able to go back home and find another surprise! It was a short ride to the Peters' house and even though they were bundled up with wool blankets over their coats and wore thick wool zocken on their feet, the girls felt the cold. The wind howled and the snow blew and it was hard to make little Katherina stay under the blankets.

A few hours later Papa came back with Mrs. Peters and took the five little girls back home. Little Katherina was just over a year old and a baby herself and now there was another little sister. Baby Elizabeth joined the family and the older girls had even more to do! Helena helped with the housework and the milking and Agnes gathered the eggs and set the table for meals. Anna tried to keep Susanna and Katherina happy by playing with them and helping them dress in the mornings.

The house seemed crowded that winter with five little girls playing and the oldest girls helping with chores. With all of her babies Mama had sung a soft lullaby as she put them to sleep, and now because Helena and her sisters also knew the song they could often be heard singing softly as they rocked the cradle to put their baby sister to sleep.

"Jgu jgu meen pop-ye vaut zaul eck dee zingen? Ahpple en barren vaut papa dee bringen. Ahpple en berren en ein schoena schtock, dan vaut mean kintye schlopen schmock. Ahpple en barren en ein schoena schtock, dan vaut mean kintye schlopen schmock."

Translation: "Shhhh my baby doll what shall I sing for you? Apples and berries your papa will bring for you. Apples and berries and a nice big stick, then my little baby will sleep real quick. Apples and berries and a nice big stick, then my little baby will sleep real quick."

"Helena and Agnes! The wood box is empty. Please bring in some armloads of wood," Mama often called.

"The water barrel near the stove is almost empty so please bring in some snow."

Wash tub, wash board with home-made soap squares. (Osler Museum)

"Why can't Anna help?" asked Agnes. To which Mama replied, "Yes, Anna, get your coat on and help bring in the snow and then you girls can play outside for a while." The girls bundled up in their coats, hats and mitts. Taking pails outside, they filled them with clean snow and brought them into the house, dumping them into the barrel. The snow would melt quickly and then they had water to use.

Every day there were diapers to wash. Katherina was only a year old and not yet trained and with baby Elizabeth in diapers too, there seemed to be no end to washing them.

Mama heated water on the stove and poured it into a galvanized metal tub. After putting the wash board into the tub she often called, "Helena – come wash diapers." Sometimes the girls complained about all the work they had to do and Mama would say, "Girls, we are a family and families work together to get the work done!"

Helena rubbed homemade soap onto the diapers and bent over the tub, rubbing the cloth over and over in the water and on the rough wash board. After much rubbing, rinsing and wringing, the girls and Mama hung the diapers outside on the clothes line to freeze. The other clothes were washed in this way too.

When the diapers and other clothes were frozen solid, Helena and Agnes bundled up in their coats and brought the stiff clothes into the house. The frozen clothes brought a wonderful fresh smell into the house as they thawed. Mama helped them hang the clothes on chairs near the stove. Sometimes she was too tired to keep up with the washing and hung the wet diapers outside to freeze without washing them and reused them after drying them indoors.

One of the daily chores for the girls was to take the ashes from the stove outside so that there was more room for burning wood. Some of the ashes were collected in a pail and Mama poured boiling water over them. After a few days, she strained the ash water through a piece of cloth into another pail. The water from the ashes turned into lye which is a very strong acid.

Taking two gallons of soft snow water, she added five pounds of lard (pig fat) and several cups of the lye. After heating that on the stove and carefully boiling it for a while, she poured it into wooden moulds for it to harden. This turned into home made bars of soap which worked very well for washing clothes.

The round metal tub was also used as a bathtub for their Saturday evening baths. Only a few inches of water were used in the tub so that it wasn't wasted.

Work never seemed to end for Mama these days. There were dresses and aprons to sew by hand for Helena and Agnes; the worn holes in the zocken needed to be darned (patched); sweaters needed to be knit and quilts made from left over pieces of cloth.

"Helena and Agnes, you need to learn how to darn socks and sew patches over holes in your dresses," Mama told them.

The girls often sat by the window in the afternoon learning how to sew. The younger girls had to wear the dresses the older girls had outgrown. They often needed to be patched to keep them wearable and they usually had only one dress each.

The girls' dresses were washed on Saturday so they would be clean for church. The rest of the week they wore the same dress. The clothes the girls wore were usually made of dark fabric, sometimes with a flowered pattern on it. The skirts and sleeves were long, and over the skirt they wore pleated aprons. Underneath their dresses they wore warm cotton petticoats.

In the summer and fall, whenever they butchered a chicken, duck or goose for a meal, they saved the feathers for making warm quilts and pillows. The village women shared the feathers if they had enough and often they got together to stitch quilts with each other. It was a good way to visit.

Spinning wheel for wool (Rosthern Museum)

Some of the village farmers had sheep on their land and in the spring they cut the wool off of the animals. Then the women took the wool which was very dirty and washed it many times in cold soapy water until it was clean. It was dried in the sun and then combed for quilts, or twisted into yarn on a spinning wheel for knitting and crocheting.

Mama spent many evenings by the dim light of a coal oil lamp or candle, crocheting or knitting warm woollen zocken to keep the girls' feet warm and sweaters to wear over their dresses when the weather was cold.

Grandma Klassen sometimes sent over sweaters and zocken for the children. The girls loved to watch Mama comb the wool with the big square combs that looked like paddles. She twisted some of the wool into thicker yarn for zocken. The square pieces of combed wool were used to make warm quilts for their beds. The oldest three girls were kept busy helping with the many chores and going to school.

Paddle combs to fluff up the wool. The Combs have many tiny 'teeth'. (Osler Museum)

A Christmas They Would Never Forget

CHAPTER 10

In the winter of 1906, the Banman family went back to Kleefeld to spend Christmas with Grandma and Grandpa Klassen. The girls were so excited! Papa arranged with a neighbour to milk their cow for that evening as they would not return until the next day. Mama and Papa put lots of wood into the brick stove so that it would burn slowly and nothing in the house would freeze before they returned. It was a long drive again and very cold, but they bundled up as much as they could for the trip. They could hardly wait to get there and see their grandparents and cousins!

It was Christmas Eve and as they arrived at the Klassen farm they were greeted at the door by their grandparents with, "Froehliche Weinachten (Merry Christmas)!!"

"Oh my!" exclaimed grandma Klassen as she hugged the girls, "How big you have grown since I saw you last! After faspa you can each put a plate on the table so that Santa can leave you a gift."

The girls could hardly wait until faspa was done so they could put a plate on grandmother's table. They got ready for bed and Grandma led them into the living room where she had laid out lots of thick wool and feather quilts in the schlope-benk for them. The girls were so excited they found it hard to fall asleep and lay listening to the adults talking in the kitchen, until their eyelids slowly drooped down and closed.

The next morning the girls excitedly ran to the table before breakfast and found an orange, nuts and some candy on each plate! This was their Christmas gift and they ate slowly, enjoying these treats. The children played until dinner time. Grandma had made roast goose, bubbat dressing(a sweet biscuit-like dough with raisins and prunes baked inside), potatoes, canned peas, and custard pie.

After the dinner dishes were cleared away, they all gathered in the big room where they sang some of their slow church Christmas hymns. One of their favourite songs was 'Ihr Kinderlein komet, O komet doch heut' (O Come little children, O come one and all).

Grandpa read the story about the first Christmas when Jesus was born, from the big German Bible. Then he said, "Now children, it's time to hear your verses." It was the custom for grandchildren to recite scripture verses or short poems or prayers for their grandparents at Christmas time. Shyly the girls lined up in front of their grandparents and softly recited the verses Mama had taught them at bedtime every evening for the last few weeks.

That was followed by faspa with buns, coffee and soft cream cookies covered with icing, and after a wonderful time of re-acquainting with their cousins, they started for home again in their horse-drawn sleigh. The girls were bundled up and huddled together, covered with blankets to keep out the cold.

As they neared the village of Neuendorf, they could see smoke and flames of fire rising up into the cold air. Soon they could see where their house was supposed to be, but there was nothing but smouldering black wood on the ground. Mama's hands flew to her face in disbelief.

"Oba nay!" she cried out. "Ons hoose!" (Oh no! Our house!)

Papa snapped the horses' reins on their backs and made them gallop the rest of the way down the snowy village street. When they arrived home, all that was left standing of their home was the chimney of their brick stove. Because the house and barn were connected, everything had been destroyed by a raging fire. They had nothing but the clothes on their backs and the blankets with which they were covered in the sleigh. The neighbours had managed to save the animals.

Helena's parents were devastated. They didn't have much to begin with and now it was all gone. The neighbours, Mr.& Mrs. Henry Giesbrecht, came over and told them they could stay with them until they found another place to live.

Near the Giesbrechts' kitchen stove Mama sat rocking and weeping quietly, holding the baby, Elizabeth. Papa paced the floor, his face white and fearful. The little girls watched their parents and huddled together, wondering what would happen to them.

"Come." Mrs. Giesbrecht said softly as she knelt down in front of the girls. "I have a bed ready for you."

They allowed her to help them undress and followed her into the big room where she had spread thick blankets and quilts on the floor. Helena, Agnes, Anna, Susanna, and Katherina snuggled close together. Helena put her arm over the sister next to her, and as they fell asleep, she lay sobbing quietly until finally her eyes closed as well.

Starting Over

CHAPTER 11

Three days later Papa said, “I’ve found a place for us to live for a while but we have to share it with another couple. It is the old house Mr. & Mrs. Heiden used to live in.” Helena remembered that house, but it was very old and only had two rooms. A Russian couple lived in the smaller room with their small child and the two families would have to share the large brick stove which stood in the centre of the building, taking turns baking and cooking.

When the Banman family arrived, they found a large chest standing in the middle of the floor of the larger room. When they opened it, they found it full of gifts of clothing and blankets which the neighbours had collected for them. Besides these gifts, neighbours had also collected a schlopebenk for the children, a bed for Helena’s parents, a table and 2 chairs.

There were tears in Mama’s eyes as she bowed her head and quietly said, “Danke, Leibe Gott! (Thank you, dear God)."

The rest of the winter of 1907 was very hard for the Banman family. With their house and barn destroyed by fire, the meat and garden vegetables they had stored for the winter and also the grain to feed the cattle were all gone. They could still milk the cow for a while but she would soon be out of milk because she would be having a calf in the spring.

"We need some flour so that I can bake bread," Mama said

to Papa. "Can we buy some grain and get Mr. Neufeld to grind it for us?"

"I'll see if I can borrow some grain. I don't have much money left," Papa said gruffly.

Neighbours sometimes brought over sausage, potatoes and other food because they felt sorry for this family with so many little ones to look after. Grandma and Grandpa Klassen travelled from Kleefeld to Neuendorf, bringing more clothing and food.

"I also brought you some vegetable and flower seeds," Grandma told Mama. "You will need them in the spring for your garden."

"Dankeschoen, Mutter (thank you mother)," said Mama. She was already looking forward to spring with the chance to get outside in the fresh air.

Gradually life returned to a more normal state and in the spring, the Russian couple moved out. Helena's family had the house all to themselves. Now they wouldn't be quite so crowded for sleeping and the girls didn't have to be reminded to be quiet so they wouldn't disturb the other family living with them. Happily the girls played outside with new kittens and puppies.

Papa was able to borrow grain for seeding the land and they also planted a garden. The usual summer work was again in full swing. This summer Helena spent a lot of time in the garden, pulling weeds. It was hot work and some days she was very tired.

"Helena," Mama said one day. "I'm going to get the cows from the field for milking. I want you to watch the children. Be careful with the baby."

The six little girls were home alone, with nine year old Helena in charge. Suddenly the door opened and in came two Indian women. The girls had heard many stories of Indian raids and were terribly frightened!

"Mama? Mama?" the women said as they tried to ask the girls where their mother was. That was the only word the girls understood as the women spoke in their own language. Thinking that the women had come to kidnap them, the children crowded close together, while Helena held the baby tightly on her lap and Agnes held little Katherina. After looking around the house for a while, the women took an old kettle and left. The girls didn't move and froze in fear as they saw the door open again – but it was Mama that walked into the house. Then they flew towards her, all chattering at once.

"Wait!" Mama said,"One at a time. What happened? Why are you so frightened?" After hearing their story, Mama reassured them and they settled down again. But their parents were concerned and didn't want to leave the children alone again.

Soon the fall harvesting and pig butchering season was upon them and they were very busy getting the vegetables out of the garden and into storage. The piglets had grown and gained weight so they had meat for the winter and lard for frying potatoes and for baking bread, pies and cookies.

Christmas at Home

CHAPTER 12

That winter they did not travel to Kleefeld to see their grandparents. The memories of the last Christmas reminded them of the tragedy of losing their home and everything they owned. The girls still memorized special Christmas poems and on Christmas Eve they each put a plate on Mama's table for their gifts.

Helena thought about the past year as she lay in bed waiting for sleep to close her eyes, and then smiled in anticipation of the next morning. What would they find in their plates this time?

"Wake up!" whispered Anna as she shook her sisters. The room was still dark because the sun wouldn't be up until several hours later. Helena groaned as she rolled over.

"It's Christmas morning!" Anna whispered again as she shook the girls harder. Agnes and Helena sat up. Now their eyes were wide open.

"Light the lamp, Helena," Susanna yawned as she woke up as well. Quietly and cautiously Helena tip-toed shivering in the cold to where the lamp stood and reached for matches. After the light shone around them they put on their zocken, pulled blankets around themselves and went to the table. On each plate they found some candies and nuts.

Hearing the girls, Papa got up and put wood on the glowing

embers in the stove. Once it was burning, he sat down near the table and watched the girls with a smile on his face. It was good to see their happiness in spite of the hard year they had. He reached for the nut-cracker to shell nuts the girls couldn't break open by themselves.

Soon Mama was up to feed the baby and then made porridge for the family. After chores were done, Papa went out and killed a chicken for their Christmas dinner. Mama boiled water, poured it into the wash tub and dipped the chicken into the hot water until all the feathers were soaked.

"Here, girls," she said to Helena and Agnes. "You can pull the feathers off." The feathers came out easily and soon the chicken was naked and ready for mama to take out the insides. The girls held their noses as the smell of wet feathers and stinky intestines filled the room. After cutting the chicken into pieces, she washed them thoroughly in cold water.

"Get dressed and dump the chicken insides in the back yard for the dogs and cats." Mama told Helena. Helena put on her clothes and bundled up to go outside and dump the garbage as she had been told.

"Girls!" Helena said as she stuck her head back into the house, "Get dressed and come outside! It isn't very cold and the sun is shining on the snow. Come play!"

Soon there were four little girls bundled in coats, scarves and mittens, laughing and rolling around in the snow and throwing snow balls at each other. Chasing each other in the snow as the sun rose higher in the sky left the girls with bright red cheeks and sparkling eyes. It was a beautiful day. They were happy for the gifts they had received and happy to celebrate Christmas together. Back in the house they stomped off the snow and brushed it off of their coats as they gathered near the brick stove to warm up.

At noon they enjoyed their dinner of chicken, potatoes, bubbat, and cream cookies. Then Papa said, "All right – I want to hear your verses!" The girls were not shy with Mama and Papa like they had been with their grandparents and recited their poems, sometimes giggling and laughing at their mistakes. Papa grinned and teased them.

Tucked into the schlopebenk that night, Mama knelt beside them as they said their prayers together.

"Did you have a good Christmas?" Mama asked.

"Yes!" they all replied.

"I liked the pink candies the best!" added Anna.

January and February passed slowly with the long dark nights and short days of sunshine. March began to lighten with longer days, but brought a few snowy blizzards. They looked forward to spring.

A Sore Foot

CHAPTER 13

In the spring of 1908, Helena, Agnes and Anna had to help more with planting the garden. Mama was moving slowly and was soon to have another baby.

June 21, 1908 brought another little sister, Maria, into the family. Now there were seven little mouths to feed and Papa wasn't quite the same anymore. Losing the house and barn had been a big shock. They didn't have a very good barn now and the house they rented was small and not close to their land. It was hard to grow enough food in the garden and hard to feed the animals when they were such a poor family. They still had very little to live on.

Papa Julius was thirteen years old when he came from Russia with his family. Now he remembered and longed for the life they had before the persecution they faced in that country. His papa had his own business, making men's suits; they had nice clothing to wear; most families had Russian servants and they had land that produced good crops. Now they were struggling to make a living and wondering how they would be able to live a better life again.

As Papa worried he became harder to get along with. He had been so much fun to be with but because he was so worried he turned to drinking liquor and was often very angry. The girls learned to stay out of his way when he had too much to drink.

One day Mama roasted a chicken for supper. Papa stumbled

into the house after coming home from a friend's home. The girls shrank back because they could see he had been drinking too much.

Mama and Papa sat down and began to eat. Since the fire had destroyed their home, they only had two chairs so the girls stood at the other side of the table waiting for some chicken. They were so hungry. But Papa just looked at them and tossed the chicken bones to them after he had eaten the meat off of them. After a while gentle Mama put her hand firmly on his shoulder and he felt badly for how he had acted. Mama could usually calm him and comfort him when he was feeling down. She got up and gave each of the children something to eat.

After supper he stumbled over to the bed and Mama told the girls to be very quiet because their Papa had a bad headache. She took the girls outside to finish doing the chores.

Summer was warm and the children enjoyed being outdoors and with the beautiful weather their father seemed to be feeling a bit better about things. He worked at cutting hay for the cattle to try to get ready for the next fall and winter. In the meantime the children of the village enjoyed the sunny weather and spent lots of time playing after doing their chores. Since they seldom wore shoes in the summer they ran around barefoot, enjoying the feel of the grass and warm dirt in the gardens and village streets.

One day Helena was running in the garden and stepped onto a plum tree thorn. "Ow vei!!(it hurts)" she cried, as she rocked back and forth on the ground, holding her foot. Agnes ran to get Mama who hurried to the garden as she heard the crying.

Helena cried out in pain when Mama pulled out the thorn. Her foot was still very painful, even after the thorn was removed. After several days it was very swollen, and she could not walk or put any weight on her foot.

"It hurts so badly!" she cried as Mama helped her back on to the bed. Mama felt the swollen foot and found it was very hot and red in colour. It was very infected and Helena had a raging fever for days. Her parents were afraid and didn't know what to do. There was no doctor around. Many people suggested their home remedies, but nothing helped.

"Here, Helena," Mama said. "Mrs. Harms suggested you drink this." Her mother had cooked some sort of weed and made her drink the water.

"No – it smells bad," Helena said, but tried it. It did not stay down.

She had to soak her foot in thick sour milk and someone even suggested putting fresh cow manure on the wound! Of course none of that helped and probably even made it worse. She was sick for many weeks. Finally, after spending a long time in bed, her fever left. She started feeling hungry again and the wound started to heal on its own. Helena was very weak for a long time and couldn't help with the chores.

A Big Decision and a Very Long Train Ride

CHAPTER 14

In the fall of 1908 when Helena was 10 years old, her father Julius Banman decided to sell his land in Manitoba, have an auction sale and move out west. Trying to farm on his little plot of land was not working out well. They did not have their own house and were paying rent. He heard about a homestead that was for sale near the town of Aberdeen, Saskatchewan. Mama had a cousin there and so they decided to settle in that area.

Papa Julius had another reason for wanting to move. In Neuendorf it was easy for him to get liquor and drink and he felt very bad about this habit. He hoped that when they lived on the new farm which was farther away from a town, he could be free of this. He often prayed that God would help him to stop drinking.

He was able to sell the small bit of land they had in Neuendorf and set the date for the sale of their possessions. All the neighbours gathered around the auctioneer on the day of the auction sale. Their horses, cow, ox, pigs and chickens were sold and one by one most of the things they had were bought by the neighbours. They packed up what was left.

A few days after the sale they said their goodbyes and after a long wagon ride, the little girls found themselves on the wooden platform of the train station in Winkler, Manitoba. Grandma and some Aunts had given them food to help them for the long train ride.

Mama had toasted lots of bread. The girls were excited, but also shrank back in fear. Never in all their lives had they experienced anything like this!

The big black train pulled into the station, blowing smoke and making a very loud chug-chug noise while fiery sparks flew from the metal wheels on the train tracks. The whistle blew loudly. They crowded close to the wall of the station and the smallest girls clung to their Mama and each other. Papa went to buy their tickets.

Soon they heard the conductor call, "All aboard!" The conductor showed them where to sit and took the tickets. He stood for a moment and stared at this family with seven little girls and then walked away, shaking his head.

Coal/steam train – the kind used in 1908. (photo permission courtesy of Cecil A. Barrett of Langham, Sask,)

For the first part of the trip, they pressed their faces against the windows, watching in excitement as the fields sped by so much faster than when they travelled with horses. The girls looked around at the inside of the train and at the people who sat near them. They chattered quietly, but excitedly about what they could see, both outside and inside.

There was enough food packed to keep them fed all the way to Aberdeen, Saskatchewan, where they would be met by relatives. The conductor often walked to the back of the train where the family sat and stared at this large family – all girls and all from the same family. After a while the wooden benches were hard to sit on and the trip began to be very uncomfortable for the little girls as they realized they needed to use a bathroom.

"Mama," the girls whispered. "We have to go to the outhouse."

The train swayed and jerked as it moved onward and it was hard to keep their balance as they walked. Mama took the children to the train bathroom but they were terrified. There were the toilet holes, very much like the ones in the outhouse they were used to, but as they looked down into them they saw the ground underneath as the train moved rapidly over the tracks. The clickety-clack sound of the train wheels was so much louder in the bathroom than where they had been sitting. They were too afraid to sit down and now Mama really had problems! She had most of their few clothes packed and was not prepared to have to change underwear. Helena, Agnes and Anna managed to be persuaded, but clung to Mama in fear. They were afraid of falling through the toilet holes and under the train.

Finally, after several days of travelling they arrived in the small town of Aberdeen, Saskatchewan. Mother's cousin Anna Buhler and her husband, Jacob, came to meet them. The family stayed with the Buhlers for a few days, and then moved into the school house in the village of Olgafeld.

This was a very small village, with people by the name of the Peter Boschmans living at one end and the John Peters and Peter Wiebes living at the other end. School lessons were taught in this school house and the teacher was Mr. Peter Fehr. He boarded with the Banman family so the girls also began attending classes with him. Classes were held at one end of the school house and the Banman family lived at the other end. The family lived in the school house for almost a year.

The Banmans had brought a small table, two chairs, a schlopebenk, a bed for Mama and Papa, and a cradle for little Maria who was only six months old. Their cousin Anna Buhler also gave them some furniture but they still didn't have much and what they were given was old and almost worn out. One morning when Mama was pouring coffee, the handle on the old coffee pot broke, the pot landed on the dishes and coffee poured out all over. She had to heat the water all over again and make more coffee in the handle-less coffee pot.

While living at the Olgafeld school house, Papa spent a lot of time at the homestead they had bought, ploughing some hard ground with a neighbours' horse and plough and then shaping the grassy dirt chunks into even blocks to build a sod house.

He placed rocks on a large beam of wood and had the horse drag the beam over the ground where he had cut the dirt chunks out to even it out for a floor. This is where he would build the house.

Winter soon arrived and it was too cold and too hard to get to the house site so Papa had to stay in Olgafeld and wait until spring to finish the house. He got some work at a farmers place and was able to earn a little money.

A Place of Their Own

CHAPTER 15

In the spring Papa spent several months working at their homestead and soon the house began to take shape. He framed the walls with wooden beams and boards and then laid the sod pieces along the outside walls to the top. He filled any spaces between the sod with more grassy dirt. The floor inside was hard-packed dirt. The roof and ceiling was made of wooden beams. In the middle of the room he built a clay-brick stove for Mama to cook and bake on. A small cellar was dug down into the floor and covered with a trap-door. The walls had several small glass windows.

The next July he bought a pair of oxen and a big wagon and after packing up all that they owned, they moved to their new home 10 miles south of Aberdeen. It was a very hot day. The children tired of the bumpy, slow ride and often walked behind the wagon.

"I'm too tired to walk any more," one of the girls complained. "I need some water to drink!" complained another. "My head hurts!" a third child said.

Mama was concerned about the sunburns the girls were getting and she tried keeping the smallest children covered up with blankets part of the way, shading them from the sun. She was glad they had brought a pail of water with them so that they could have a drink. As they got nearer to their new home they drove past a lake. It seemed very big to the girls and they wanted to run down to cool off in it.

"No, girls," Papa said, "That is salt water – you won't get clean and it doesn't smell very good."

They arrived at their new home in the evening. Mama got down from the wagon and walked into the little house, looked around and checked her new stove. The children, glad to be free of the wagon and so much walking, also explored the new place.

"Papa," Helena called "What is this trap door on the floor inside the house?"

"That's the cellar for vegetables and canned goods," he answered. There were steps going down into the cellar.

Their parents carried the furniture and other belongings into the house and the girls helped to carry the small things. Mama and Papa's bed was moved to one end of the house with the schlopebenk on the opposite wall. At the other end of the house they put their table and chairs. Wooden boxes would have to do for shelves for dishes and food. Papa set up the stove pipes for the brick stove in the middle of the room.

The girls' faces were badly sun-burned from the hot sun and wind and their skin blistered and peeled for several days. There were many tears when they got their faces washed. Some of them felt sick with headaches and vomited because of sun stroke.

After a few days, the girls felt better and went exploring in the hills and found many wild strawberries. They had never seen so many strawberries at one time before.

"Mama may we have a bowl to put strawberries in?" they asked.

"Here, take this syrup pail," she answered. The girls ran back out to the place they had found the berries and had a great time picking and eating them. Mama laughed when she saw the girls coming in the door with their pail.

"Look at you!" she exclaimed. "Your mouths and hands are red! Did any of the berries get into the pail?"

That evening and for several weeks while the strawberries lasted, they enjoyed the special treat. It helped to make their simple meals more interesting. They were a very poor family and sometimes didn't even have bread to eat. If Mama didn't have the ingredients to bake bread, they ate boiled potatoes with salt. Often they didn't have butter for their bread and used salt or lard as a spread. The girls thought this tasted very good!

One day the oldest three girls climbed a hill and looked down at the big lake of water. They walked down the hill and waded at the edge of the lake. The homestead had many water ponds.

"Papa, we went to see the big lake!" Helena told him. "We walked in the water at the edge of it."

Papa looked up quickly from sharpening his scythe and said, "Girls, do not walk into the lake any further than that! There is quick sand at the bottom of the lake and the neighbours here have told me that we need to watch our animals because some people's cattle have wandered into the lake and sunk to the bottom in the mud." The girls promised to be careful.

They loved to run up and down the small hills and their peals of laughter could be heard at the house. Living way out in the country, the girls had no school they could attend so Mama became their teacher. In spite of the work raising such a large family, she managed to give her daughters a good education. She taught them arithmetic, how to read the German Bible and prayers.

Mama knew it was important to teach her girls that God loved them and that they needed to know right from wrong. She also taught them that Jesus died on the cross for our sins – the wrong things we have done. Jesus did not stay in the grave, but rose again from the dead.

One of the prayers Mama taught the girls was this;
"Kristie blute und gerechtichkeit, das ist mein schmuk und ehrenkleit. Da mit vill ich vor Gott beschtehen, ven ich tsum Himmel verd ein gehen."
(Translation: Christ's blood and his righteousness – that is my robe of salvation. With that I will stand before God when I enter heaven.)

On some summer evenings they sat outside as their house cooled and Mama patiently taught Helena and her sisters how to knit. Other summer evenings the family would travel to another farm for a visit or neighbours would visit them. That was always a highlight for the girls. They loved visiting.

Helena's First Job as a Maid

CHAPTER 16

One day in 1908 when Helena was almost eleven years old, her much older cousin, Mr. Henry Dyck, arrived from a nearby village in his buggy. Mama and Papa welcomed him into the house.

"My wife needs a kyaekshi (maid) to help out with our baby Jacob for the rest of the summer," he said. “Would you allow Helena to come and baby-sit?”

Helena heard her parents talking to Mr. Dyck and was afraid of what they would say. Papa talked to Mr. Dyck about what he would pay for Helena’s help and then he said, "Yes, I think Helena can go and help you for a while."

"Helena," Papa called. "Get your things and go with Mr. Dyck. You will be helping Mrs. Dyck with the baby this summer."

Helena didn’t have much to take with her and quietly went to the buggy. She fought back the tears as she looked back at her sisters and parents. She was very shy and didn’t talk on the way to the Dycks’ farm. It seemed like a long drive and it was a hot day. She was very thirsty. When they arrived, Mr. Dyck said, "Go into the house. My wife will tell you what to do." She climbed out of the buggy and watched him lead the horse to the barn.

Opening the house door quietly, Helena could hear a baby crying and Mrs. Dyck trying to comfort him. She waited by the door until Mrs. Dyck turned around and saw her.

"Well, here you are, Helena. Take Jacob, will you? I need to make supper and he's quite cranky today."

As Helena reached for the baby, he screamed louder. He didn't know this girl and was afraid. She carried the struggling, heavy, screaming child for what seemed like hours. Her arms ached but he finally fell asleep. She sat down on a chair, not knowing what to do next. Mrs. Dyck glanced over at her from the stove.

"Well," she said. "Put him in the cradle in the corner. And do it gently so he won't wake up again!" Helena was used to putting babies in cradles, so she carefully lowered him into the cradle.

"Tomorrow morning I will show you how to milk the cows." Mrs. Dyck said as she put the food on the table.

"Milk the cows! I know how to milk!" thought Helena, but she didn't dare say it out loud. She reached for a cup of water and drank the cool liquid. The next morning dawned early for Helena as Mrs Dyck awakened her.

"Come, its milking time." Walking out to the cow pen, Mrs. Dyck commented, "I am very fussy about how the cows are to be milked. You need to make sure you get all the milk out."

She led one of the cows to a post and tied her to it with a rope. Then she picked up a milking stool and a pail and sat down beside the cow. As she milked rhythmically, the liquid streamed into the pail. Mrs. Dyck's arms were strong and soon there was quite a bit of milk.

"Now you try," she told Helena. Helena picked up the pail and sat down. She was small for her age and not very strong. She couldn't hold the big pail between her knees and had to put it on the ground under the cow. She grabbed hold of the teats and began to milk. The streams of milk were not as big as the ones Mrs. Dyck had milked.

"No, no!" the lady snapped. "Not like that. Here! Let me show you again." Sitting down again, Mrs. Dyck milked hard and fast. "This is the way you must milk!"

By now, Helena was feeling very uncomfortable and embarrassed. She was really trying, but it just wasn't good enough. Finally, the cows were milked and they went back to the house.

Helena often cried herself to sleep. There was so much to do and it seemed that no matter how hard she tried, she still seemed to upset Mrs. Dyck. If only the summer would end soon so she could go home again. She was getting so tired of working from morning to evening.

For the next few weeks she struggled with her aching back and arms as she helped with chores and was expected to keep the cranky baby happy while Mrs. Dyck worked in her garden and canned. It wasn't a happy place to be and Helena was so lonely for her parents and dear sisters.

Finally the summer was over and Papa came with the ox and wagon to take her home. Mr. Dyck paid him for Helena's help and they went home. As they drove onto the yard, her sisters came streaming out of the house, excitedly welcoming their oldest sister home. She was so happy to be back. The next day was August 22nd and Helena turned 11 years old.

Home Again

CHAPTER 17

After washing the supper dishes that evening the sisters walked around outside. Helena went to see the animals in the barn and the two pigs her father bought while she was away. They were in a pen that Agnes helped their father build.

"Look, while you were away Papa brought home a goose and a gander," Anna told Helena, pointing to the geese in a pen. "But watch out for the gander – he tries to chase us!" After seeing the animals the girls wandered down to the salt lake.

"How did you like working for Mrs. Dyck?" Agnes asked.
"What did you have to do there?" Anna added.

The girls waded in the shallow part of the lake throwing rocks and sticks as far as they could and then watched the ripples grow wider and wider.

"I didn't like working there! I had to try and keep little Jacob happy, but he's such a fussy baby and it was so hard to get him to stop crying and go to sleep." Helena told them. "And Mrs. Dyck got angry if I didn't do things quite right. I never could milk the cows the way she expected me to. I hope I never have to go there again!"

For a while Helena was home and she and her sisters worked together doing chores around the farm and helping in the garden.

Helena was busy feeding the chickens and gathering eggs one day when she heard her sisters calling from the pig pen.

"Helena!" Agnes called. "Help me feed the pigs." Agnes was trying to carry the slop pail full of scraps from their meals and leaves from their vegetables.

Helena left the hen house with a pail of eggs and after setting it down carefully at the door to the house she went to help Agnes carry the heavy slop pail for the pigs. As they dumped the food into the pig's trough, the grunting animals stuck their noses into the trough right under the slop pail, getting food all over their heads. The girls laughed at how silly the pigs looked with potato peelings hanging off their ears!

They enjoyed herding the cows on the hillsides and found many things to talk and laugh about. Mama often heard their giggles even from a distance. They loved to have fun!

One day Papa gave them an old rope. As they tried to skip over it, Mama came out and said, "Girls, I know some skipping songs. Would you like to learn them?"

"Yo (yes)!" they all said and listened carefully as mama chanted the songs.

"Ote boah, ote boah, lahnk naze.
Zetten opp de yreine vaze.
Kempt de bock en schtelpt dem ohm.
Kempt de pole en hayfed dem opp.
"Bringt se no de Koinich's dayha,
freicht de koinich, 'Es doah veah?'
"Yo, en zak von kringle.'
"Vaneya voahscht du vada komen?"
"Opp yoah van de roggen reepen,
van de poggen peepen,
van the cyalva bloren,
van the kinga roren,

van de mumkyis met the mest koah foren,
van et zit no fahryoah voren."

(Translation: "Stork, stork with the long nose, sitting on the green meadow.
Here comes the billy goat and knocks her over.
Here comes a post that lifts her up.
Brings her to the kings door, the king asks, "Is anyone there?"
"Yes, a bag full of kringle buns."
"When will you come again?"
"Next year when the rye is ripe,
when the frogs are croaking, when the calves are bawling,
when the children are crying,
when the women are pushing the manure cart
when it looks like spring")

The girls laughed at the silly song and it wasn't long before they learned how to skip and sing the songs their mother taught them.

Over the next year Helena was kept busy at home and at different farms in the area as she baby-sat and helped with other work.

Fall Harvesting and Pig Butchering

CHAPTER 18

In the months of August and September in 1909, Papa was busy cutting the long grass with his scythe while the girls helped to carry big armloads of the hay to the stone boat hitched to the ox. When it was piled high with hay the girls led the ox to the small barn. Papa had put up a temporary shed for the animals for the winter. Helena picked up the big pitch fork and stacked the hay near the barn. Carrying the long grass scratched the girls' arms and made them itchy.

Photo of Meea gropen, Rosthern Museum.

At the end of October and in the month of November, the farmers in the area got together to butcher pigs so they would have meat for the winter.

When it was time for their family to butcher their pig, all the neighbours came to their farm to help. The girls watched the men trying to catch the squealing pig. They didn't like to watch when the animal was killed. While the men caught the pigs, the women heated water in the 'meea-gropen' (a big cast-iron kettle). (Some outside meea-gropens had a brick base under which a fire was built. Others had a metal base like the one shown.)

"Miyalles! (Girls!)" their mother called. "Get more wood and straw for the fire." They carried many armloads of wood and straw and watched as a fire was built in the stove under the meea-gropen. The hot water that was heated in it was carried to the barn in pails and used to clean the animal after it was butchered.

Later, all the fatty parts were placed into the big kettle and cooked until all the fat had melted out of the meat. The fat was dipped out and put into pails to harden. That was lard. It would be used to bake bread, pies and cookies and to fry meat. The little roasted pieces of meat that were left were called cracklings and often served at breakfast with fried potatoes. The really fine brown pieces found in the last bit of lard left in the meea-gropen, was called crackling spread or 'griva schmalt'. It was spread on bread and sprinkled with salt. It was a real treat!

Inside the house the women made meals while they also worked at making sausage. Helena didn't like the smell caused by cleaning the pig intestines. The intestines were emptied and scraped, then washed over and over in heavily salted boiled water. The intestines were turned inside out, scraped again and soaked in more salted water. After many cleanings, turnings and soakings they were ready to be used to make sausage. They were slipped onto the sausage machine and as the spicy sausage meat was ground up, it entered the intestines, making long rings of sausage. The hams were rubbed with salt and hung in the smoke house along with the sausage for several days of curing.

The Banman family enjoyed the spare ribs, fried ham, fried sausage, head cheese, cracklings and griva schmalt that winter.

Farming New Land

CHAPTER 19

The snow began to melt, running down the hills and filling the ponds with lots of water. The ground around the little house became very muddy. The girls could hardly wait until it was warm enough to run outside barefoot and wade in the shallow edge of the ponds!

One morning as they wandered on the hillsides, looking for the first signs of grass and hoping the strawberries would hurry up and grow, Helena spied a couple of robins sitting on one of the bushes.

"Look!" she said. "The birds are coming back!" Overhead they heard geese honking as they flew toward the salt lakes to swim. Soon there were hundreds of wild geese that settled on the lakes; white geese and Canada geese, all honking loudly as they settled for a rest on their way to northern Saskatchewan.

With the spring came much work for everyone. Now the cow and ox could be outside, but there was no fence so the girls had to take turns herding them so they wouldn't wander away. Papa told the girls to find the best grassy areas and let the animals graze there. While the cattle filled their stomachs with grass, the girls picked flowers, explored and played.

Papa began to work the land the next year, but it was too hard to break the sod. He bought a larger ox, which made it a bit easier, but it still wasn't going well. Helena and Agnes had to help work the land. Oxen are very stubborn animals so Papa tied a rope around their horns and Helena led them, while Agnes followed with a whip to keep them going. Papa held the plough.

"Lead them straight!" he called out to Helena. "Agnes. Use the whip to make them go faster!" Helena pulled the rope that was tied to the oxen horns with all her strength to help make the stubborn animals move. When the animals stopped, Agnes whipped their backs with a rope and they started out with a jerk. Since the ground was so hard it was very difficult for Papa to hold the plough and make straight furrows. There were too many stones in the ground and the plough kept running into rocks and tipping over.

Sometimes Papa became very angry and impatient with the animals and the girls. Many hot days were spent helping him pick up stones from the land and carry them to a pile. They could only carry the small ones while Papa carried bigger ones. It was a very tiring job, but as the pile of stones got higher, the land became a bit easier to plough.

Papa also broke enough ground to make a garden not too far from the house. While Helena helped her father with some of the farm work, her Mama, with the help of Agnes and Anna worked hard to plant the seeds in the spring and weed the garden in the summer.

Once the planting was done neighbours came to see if Helena or Agnes could help them out and so the girls were again away from home for the summer. While the older girls were working for other farmers, eight year old Anna had to help a lot with the chores and the care of her little sisters. Seven year old Susanna was also called on to help with daily chores, but for both girls there was lots of playing time with Katherina, Elizabeth and little Maria.

At the end of August the older girls returned home just in time for a special event! Mama had another baby – but this time it was a boy! They named him Julius, after his father. The little boy was born on August 30, 1910. Papa was happy to finally have a son! The seven sisters were delighted with this little brother and the older three took turns carrying him when he was fussy and rocking him to sleep in the cradle.

In the fall, Papa built a sod barn for the animals because it would be warmer than the small wooden shack he had built for them. He built it next to the house. First he sliced the top and side of a small hill and dug down about three feet. Then he hauled the sod home where they were allowed to freeze in the fall.

Once they were frozen, he shaped the sod into even pieces with an axe. It took a long time, but once he had enough pieces cut, Helena helped him build a barn for the animals for the winter. Papa built a wood frame for the barn next to the house so they would be connected. They laid out the first row of sod in the shape of a square against the frame. After they built it high enough, they put wooden poles over the top for a roof and covered them with more sod and grass. Now they had a warmer barn for the animals. Helena was tired but proud to have helped with the building!

Now that they had more room and a warmer barn, they bought two more milk cows and a heifer. One of the cows kicked a lot when they wanted to milk her. One evening Mama tried to sit down and milk, but the cow kicked so much it was dangerous for Mama. Papa became very angry with the animal and he grabbed a whip to beat it. The cow was very frightened and tried to get away. She slipped and fell with her head underneath her body. Mama and the girls felt very sorry for the animal.

"Well," Papa said as the animal lay still. "She's broken her neck. I'll get the axe and cut off her head. We'll have to butcher her for meat." Papa went to get the axe, but as he returned he heard the girls and Mama talking excitedly.

"She's getting up!"
"Look, she's all right!"

Papa sized up the situation and decided to keep the animal. They really needed her for milk. Now they just needed to tame her somehow so it wouldn't be so dangerous. In the winter, the cows did not give them much milk because they were going to have calves in the spring, so the family was often without butter for long periods of time.

That winter brought a lot of snow – so much that there was a big hard snow drift as high as the barn roof. One warm winter day Papa decided to let the animals out for some fresh air so the barn could be cleaned out. As the cattle wandered in the bright sunlight, one of the heifers walked up the hard snow drift onto the barn roof. Since the roof was only made of poles and sod the heifer broke through the roof, breaking her leg. Papa went to get Mr. Abram Derksen to help him set the leg but it was too badly broken. They had to butcher that heifer but it did give them lots of meat for the rest of the winter.

A Scary Time

CHAPTER 20

"Girls," Papa said one evening. "You need to go to school again and our neighbours, the Abraham Derksens, will be having the school in their living room. Mama's cousin, Jacob Buhler, will be the teacher."

"May we have new dresses to go to school with?" the girls asked. Their mother asked Papa to pick up some cloth the next time he went to Aberdeen. She wanted plaid for the girls' skirts, white for their blouses and also some red yarn so they could knit stockings.

Mama got busy measuring the girls for their new school clothes. After measuring Helena, she turned to Agnes who said, "I can't wear the same size as Helena anymore. She's shorter than I am."

Mama measured her and looked up laughing as she said, "You are right, Agnes. You've grown a lot this past year and you're becoming a "himmel schtenda!(a pillar holding up the sky)." Agnes didn't like to be called that and got tired of hearing it every time some visitor or neighbour would comment on how tall she was getting.

Their grandpa Klassen sent the children wooden Klompen (shoes) that he had made and so the girls were ready to go to school.

Mama was a good, patient teacher, but now they could be with a few other neighbour children. Sitting still so long was hard though and they were always happy when classes ended and they could walk home.

The weather soon changed and with the cold came the snow. It was often hard to see where they were going when the wind blew the snow around the hills.

One evening Mama called the girls to her and said, "Papa and I will be going away to Aberdeen for a few days to visit your teacher's aunt. We're taking Maria and Julius with us. Agnes, you'll take Anna and Susanna to school with you, and Helena, you stay home with Katherina and Elizabeth. The Derksens will be checking in with you to make sure everything is all right. You'll need to feed and water the animals and milk the cows both morning and evening."

Helena's Coal oil lamp, now at her daughter Nettie's home.

Preparations were made and very early next morning Mama and Papa left. The bottom of the sleigh was filled with straw and they were dressed warmly with woollen coats and quilts to cover them. The girls watched them leave the yard. They were on their own. As it grew dark later in the afternoon, Helena lit the coal-oil lamp and they had supper. Then she and Agnes got the little ones ready for bed. It took a while for her to fall asleep, because she heard every noise.

The next morning, Helena made a fire in the brick stove and cooked porridge. The girls all had breakfast and Agnes made sure the other school girls were dressed warmly as they left for school. Helena felt quite grown up to be in charge but also a bit afraid. She cleaned up the porridge bowls and then after dressing Katherina and Elizabeth in their coats, they went to the barn where she milked the cows, fed the animals and gathered eggs from the few chickens they now had.

Back in the house again, she looked out of the window and saw it was snowing hard. Soon the wind began to howl around the house. They stood close to the stove to try to warm up. Helena put more and more wood on the fire. Soon it would be dinner time and she wanted to make something for the girls when they came home from school for their noon meal.

She fried up some potatoes in lard and waited for the girls to come, but they didn't arrive. Helena fed the little girls and while they were eating, Katherina pointed toward the ceiling.

"Helena, is it supposed to burn up there?" Helena looked up to where her little sister was pointing and found the ceiling around the stove pipe was smoking, beginning to burn.

"Girls, quickly get your coats!" she urged. Hurrying them into their coats, she rushed them outside and into the barn. "Stay here until I come and get you!" she said.

She ran outside looking up at the roof, but there was no fire showing through. Shaking with fear, she ran back inside, grabbed a pail and dipped water from the snow-water barrel standing near the stove. Over and over she threw pails of water at the ceiling until all the fire was out and the wood was not smouldering any more.

When she was sure it was over, she ran back to the barn and brought the little girls into the house. She hugged her little sisters, crying and still shaking, but so glad she had been able to put out the fire. The house was connected to the barn and if she hadn't been able to put it out, everything would have burned including the animals. It would have been a quarter of a mile walk in a blizzard to get to the Derksens.

After school, the Derksens brought the older girls home and came to see if everything was all right. When they walked into the house, they smelled the smoke and Helena showed them the blackened, burned ceiling and told them how she had put the fire out. Mrs. Derksen said, "Helena, God was with you this afternoon!"

Mama and Papa came home a few days later. They were shocked at the blackened ceiling and listened to the story the girls told them.

"Helena, I am so proud of you," Mama said. "Mrs. Derksen was right – God really was with you!" That evening, Mama and Papa sat quietly talking while she put little Julius to sleep. How close they had come, again, to losing everything!

"We should have cleaned the stove pipes before we left," Mama said.

"Yes," Papa replied. "It's been cold and we've been burning a lot of wood. The pipes were probably full of soot." Helena was a very responsible girl but she was still only 12 years old - a bit young to be left in charge of so much in the winter.

The winter was hard for them and food was scarce, but Mama was thankful for the small amount of milk they got from the cows and the few eggs the chickens laid. They also had some canned beef and smoked pork but they didn't have enough money to buy sugar or fruit. When they had flour, she was able make bread and they still had some vegetables in the cellar.

Baking bread was a lot more work for them than it is now. People made their own yeast and ground their own flour. Baking the bread was different too. They heated the brick stove with straw and wood and when the inside of the stove was really hot, they removed the glowing ashes and put the loaves of bread inside. The bricks stayed hot long enough to bake the bread.

A Surprise Parcel

CHAPTER 21

Papa went to Aberdeen early in the spring before the snow melted for some seed to plant for grain and for the garden. While he was in town, he checked at the post office to see if there was any mail. The postman said, "Yes, come out to the shed. There is also a big parcel for you from Manitoba, and two letters."

"My wife and children will be very excited," said Papa. "I will leave the parcel here until the morning. It will be too late to go home tonight."

Papa stopped at the bar for a drink and some company with the other men who had come to town. After staying with the Buhlers for the night, he prepared to make the long trip home again. He put the few things he had bought and the parcel on the sleigh and urged the ox on its' way. It was a long trip with such a slow animal, and Papa had to walk most of the 10 miles, leading him when he refused to move or went the wrong direction.

Finally he arrived back at the homestead and untied the ox, leading it to the barn. When he walked into the house, Mama and the girls met him at the door. "Did you go to the post office?" she asked. "Were there any letters from Manitoba?"

"Did you bring us something?" the girls asked. Papa handed Mama the letters and then put the heavy parcel on the table.

"This also came from Manitoba," he said with a smile.

The children gathered around and watched in excitement as Papa tore off the many layers of paper. Inside they found clothes, zocken, mittens, and best of all - a large smoked ham!

The girls jumped up and down with glee and chattered excitedly as they tried on the new clothes. Their aunt had sent the parcel and the whole family felt like it was Christmas! What a blessing the smoked ham was for their meals! Now they had more meat with their potatoes and bread! Papa also had some more news.

Second Banman family home.

"I have bought an old house from a farmer nearby and we are going to have it moved on to our yard. It has more rooms and we need a bigger place."

"When, Papa?" asked the girls excitedly while Mama smiled at the idea of a bigger house.

"It will be moved as soon as I build a foundation for it to sit on," he said. "The house will be put closer to the lake and to the spring where we get water."

For the next months the girls followed Papa around, sometimes being in the way and at other times helping him. The big day finally arrived when a team of six horses made its way to the new site, hauling the house to the foundation. With many farmers from the area helping, the house was soon in place and the weary horses were fed and given water while Mama fed the working men.

"Girls, you can go look inside the house now," Papa said as he turned toward his daughters.

They ran eagerly to the house, opened the door and ran from room to room. There were only two large rooms and one bedroom, but the place looked huge compared to their little sod and beam house. There was a trap-door on the floor with a new large cellar to explore.

The family moved into the house at the end of September and Papa decided to use the old sod house for more barn space until he could afford to build a better one.

Sad News

CHAPTER 22

At the end of November of 1911 when Helena was 13 years old, Cousin Jacob Buhler drove out to the Banman homestead. Papa was out in the barn and heard the team drive up.

"Ho!" ordered Mr. Buhler as he reined in the horses.

"Welcome," Papa said as they shook hands. "What brings you out here this cold day?"

"I have some sad news for your wife. I received news yesterday that her mother died," he replied. "I came out as soon as I could this morning."

"Come in to the house," Papa said.

The men walked into the house. Mama turned from making dumplings for the milk soup, and saw her cousin. Surprised she said, "Welcome! Did your wife Anna come with you? Can you stay for dinner?"

Jacob looked at Papa, and clearing his throat, he said, "No, my wife did not come with me. I have come with some sad news." Mama stood silently, her face sober, waiting for him to speak.

"I received news yesterday that your mother died on November 24th. The town office received a telephone call from your brother in Manitoba. The funeral will be held on Sunday, the 27th." Mama gasped in shock and sat down on a chair. There were tears in her eyes.

"Helena," she said quietly. "Please stir the soup. Agnes, set another place at the table for Mr. Buhler."

Helena and her sisters looked at each other sadly, as their mother got up, turned, and walked to the window, looking out. As Helena stood at the stove, stirring the soup, she saw her mother's shoulders shake as she cried. Her own eyes filled with tears as she remembered how she had loved to visit this grandmother who was now gone.

The meal was eaten in silence, except for the little ones asking for more soup. After dinner, Jacob Buhler pushed back his chair and clearing his throat, thanked them for the meal.

After he left, Mama and Papa talked quietly as the girls cleared the table and washed the dishes. "Maybe we could borrow the money for you to go for the funeral on the train," Papa said. But Mama reminded him that it would take several days to get there by train, and then several days to get back. She wished she could go, but how could she leave all the little ones at home?

The next few days were especially hard for her as she mourned the loss of her dear mother. How she would miss her! The girls helped as much as they could to make life easier for their mother.

Water Barrels and Old Shoes

CHAPTER 23

The next spring and summer Helena and her sisters were kept busy every day. Helena along with Agnes and Anna often had to lead the oxen as they pulled a stone-boat with two wooden barrels on it. The girls had to go to a spring some distance away that had good water in it. The ponds around their house were salt lakes and not good for drinking or washing clothes.

Wooden water barrel drawing by NB

"Look," Agnes said one morning when they were leading the oxen to get water. "There is an old pair of shoes here in the grass."

"Let's put them on the road when we go back," Anna said "The Derksen children come here to get water too and they'll have to drive over the shoes to get to the spring!" The girls giggled about this idea and carried the shoes with them.

After carrying many pails of water and filling the barrels, the girls were ready to lead the oxen back home. They started out, but the oxen were very stubborn. The barrels of water were heavy and they didn't like pulling them.

"HO!" yelled Helena when she saw the oxen wandering off the road and on to the slant of a hill. Before the girls could stop them, they had managed to tip the barrels enough to spill most of the water.

"Oh no!" groaned Agnes. "Now we have to fill them all over again, because of these dumb oxen!"

Turning the animals around, they started back to the spring and filled the barrels again. This time, Helena led the oxen with ropes tied around their horns. Agnes followed, hitting the backs of the animals with a branch whenever they tried to stop pulling. Anna carried the old shoes, and set them on the road, pointing them toward the spring behind them."There!" she said. "I wonder if the Derksens will notice and drive over them?"

As they neared home, they saw the other girls herding the cows near the strawberry patch. They stopped to check for strawberry plants, but there were very few left. After the cows had grazed there last summer and now again, there weren't many left. They continued on their way and brought the stone-boat near the house and untied the oxen, leading them to the garden where Papa waited to use the oxen to do some ploughing.

Papa ploughed the garden plot while one of the girls led the oxen and another followed with a whip. This spring the girls had to work hard in the garden because their mother was going to have another baby. After the potatoes and other seeds had been planted, it was a never ending chore to keep the weeds and quack grass from crowding out the small plants that tried to come up. Mama spent as much time as she could in the garden, but there was so much to do with making baby clothes, mending the other children's clothes, making sure the meals were made and the chores done.

On another warm spring day Agnes, Helena and Anna went to get another load of water. As they neared the spring Anna ran ahead and called back, laughing, "Look at this! The Derksen children came to get water and found the old shoes! They've turned them in the other direction!" The girls giggled about this and talked about where they would put the shoes this time!

Eight Dollars a Month – and No Clothes

CHAPTER 24

One day early in the summer of 1912, Helena saw Mr. Dyck's horse and buggy drive onto their yard.

"Oh no!" she thought. "I hope he doesn't want me to work there again!" She watched from the garden as Papa and Mr. Dyck talked. Papa turned to look toward Helena, and beckoned for her to come. She walked over soberly, knowing what he was going to say.

"Helena, Mrs. Dyck needs your help again," he said. "I will take you over there tomorrow but you need to help your sisters finish weeding our garden first."

Mr. Dyck left, and at the supper table that night, Papa said it would be good for Helena to bring in a little money. It would help them all. Agnes was going to work for another neighbour, Anna was to baby sit at another farm. Susanna helped at home and in the garden and Katherina and Elizabeth had to herd the cows.

So it was decided and as Helena washed her only dress so it would be dry by morning, she felt sad and worried. Mrs. Dyck was not easy to work for. She complained a lot and Helena was afraid, wondering how long she would have to be there.

"I wish you didn't have to go and I don't want to go the Schellenbergs either," said Agnes quietly while they undressed for bed. They lay on their bed whispering for a while before they fell asleep.

The next morning Papa told Agnes that it was time for her to walk over to the Schellenbergs. Elizabeth walked with her as far as the fence at the edge of Schellenbergs farm while Agnes cried about having to go.

Papa got the oxen hitched to the wagon and Helena said goodbye to the others. It seemed like a long trip and it was a quiet one, except for her father talking about how the money she would be paid was going to help them out. He said that Mrs. Dyck was also going to give her clothing over and above what she would be paid.

Mrs. Dyck was out in the garden when Papa and Helena arrived. Little Jacob was running around now and Helena saw Mrs. Dyck pick up a little bundle from a blanket before walking over to meet them.

"Gouden moryen (Good morning)," she said when she got to the wagon. "I'm glad you've come, Helena. You see Jacob is a busy little boy, and this little one is Mary." Mrs. Dyck unwrapped the bundle and there was a little baby girl.

"Come into the house, Helena. Mr. Banman, Henry is out in the barn." With that she turned and walked to the house, calling Jacob to come.

"You can wash those dishes that are on the cupboard first and then peel potatoes for supper," Mrs. Dyck ordered.

Helena went to the stove where a kettle of water was standing. It was still warm so she filled a basin, put it on the table and washed the dirty dishes. After finding a good knife, she looked for the potatoes. Mrs. Dyck was sitting in the living room, nursing her baby.

Timidly, Helena approached her, "Taunte Dyckshi," she

said, "Where are the potatoes?"

"In the cellar, of course!" spoke Mrs. Dyck. "You should have remembered that from the last time you were here." She pointed to a trap door on the kitchen floor. Helena picked up the dish pan and walked quickly over to the heavy trap door. It was hard to pull it up and lean it against the wall without falling into the cellar, but she managed and walked down the steps. It was very dark down there. She heard Mrs. Dyck calling, and went back up the steps.

"You can't see anything down there without a lantern. There is one over there by the outside door. The matches are on the shelf above the stove," Mrs. Dyck said.

Helena lit the lantern and went down the steps again. She found the potatoes in a bin and wondered how many she should bring up. For her family she would need a lot, but there would only be four of them at the Dycks, counting Jacob. The baby wouldn't be eating solid food yet.

Coming back up to the kitchen, Helena quickly peeled the potatoes and found a cooking pot. She added cold water and then thought, "It's too early to cook these. It's not supper time yet." Just then Mrs. Dyck came into the kitchen.

"I see you have the potatoes peeled. Leave them in the water in the pot and we'll go back to the garden."

Then seeing the potato peel still lying on the table she said, "Helena, I'll have to teach you how to peel thinly. You're peeling too much off the potato! If the marriage match-maker comes around and sees this, she will never find you a husband!" She chuckled at her own joke and smiled at Helena as she picked up the peelings and put them in the slop pail by the door. "The pigs will enjoy these," she said.

After weeding in the garden they went back to the house for some dinner and then Helena was asked to wash the kitchen floor boards with soapy water and a big scrub brush. The afternoon went by quickly with many things to do. Mrs. Dyck put the potatoes on the stove to boil and while they simmered she said, "Now it's time to do the milking."

Back in the milking pen, Mrs. Dyck continued to complain that Helena was not doing it right, just like she did the first time Helena worked there. Over the weeks that followed Mrs. Dyck managed to find something wrong with nearly everything Helena did and the complaining about her milking the cows was getting frustrating. She had heard that complaint so many times! Helena got angry one day and slammed down the milk stool!

"Helena!" Mrs. Dyck spoke sharply. "This won't do, for the $8.00 a month plus the clothing that we pay you!!"

That evening, as Helena lay on her bed she fumed, "$8.00 a month! Ha! I never get to see that! Papa comes every few weeks and takes the money home for the family. And clothes? She has never given me any clothes!" She punched her pillow and turned over to face the wall. At the end of August Papa came to bring Helena home and collected the money she had earned.

"Welcome home!" Mama said as she hugged her. The sisters and Julius all crowded around, wanting to hear all about the summer. Agnes was also home after working for the Schellenbergs. The girls talked and laughed as they caught up on the summer's events, both at the Dycks and Schellenbergs, and also at home. Helping with chores at home was different from working at the Dycks.

Home-schooling

CHAPTER 25

On September 3, 1912, Agnes took her sisters and Julius over to the Derksens and told Mrs. Derksen that it was time for Mama to have another baby. Helena stayed home to heat lots of water on the stove. Papa waited in the big room until Mrs. Derksen arrived. Then Helena also walked over to the Derksens to wait until they were told to come back home.

In a few hours Papa brought Mrs. Derksen home on the wagon and all the girls and Julius ran out to meet them. As the children climbed on to the wagon, Papa smiled broadly and announced "We have another boy!" After thanking Mrs. Derksen, the family left to go home.

"Oh, he's so small!" the girls commented. Over the last few weeks they had wondered what Mama and Papa would name the next baby. Now when they asked, Papa said, "His name is Peter."

For the next few weeks all the girls were kept busy canning vegetables and harvesting the rest of the garden produce. Mama couldn't do much for a while.

Winter came early that year and that fall there was no school at the Derksens, so in spite of all she had to do with a new baby, Mama taught the girls at home. After many long hours of sitting at the table doing their lessons, the girls often asked to go to the outhouse. When Mama gave them permission to go out, they quickly ran to the outhouse, but they really had something else in mind!

"Let's quickly go sliding down the hill before we go back to the house!" one of the girls said as they waited their turn to use the outhouse.

"Yes! Let's go!" they all chimed in, and grabbing some pieces of cardboard, off they ran to have some winter fun.

In the fall and winter, the lake around the homestead froze and the children loved to slide on the ice. Since the pond was at the bottom of a little hill, they loved sitting on pieces of cardboard, sliding down the snow and on to the ice.

The girls' laughter echoed on the snowy hills as they slid and tumbled down the hill nearest the house. Then the girls heard Mama knocking hard on the window pane to make them come in. As they stamped off the snow before they entered the house they heard little two year old Julius, screaming and crying.

"So you didn't just go to the outhouse," their mother said. Sheepishly the girls admitted they had done some sliding.

"What's wrong with Julius?" Helena asked.

"When Julius climbed up on the bench at the window he saw you girls sliding on the ice and he was afraid and started crying. Then I realized where you were. You've had some fresh air, now come and sit down for more lessons!" their Mama said.

New Shoes

CHAPTER 26

One day Mr. and Mrs. Henry Dyck came for a visit and spent some time talking to Papa and Mama. After they left Papa called Helena over to where he was sitting.

"What did they want?" she asked him.

"They said that since there won't be any school at the Derksens this year, there will be a school at their neighbour's place. They also want you to come back in a few weeks and work through the winter, to help them out." Papa said.

Inwardly Helena groaned in despair. She did not want to go back to the Dycks, but if Papa and Mama decided, she knew she would have to do as they said.

"I'll ask the Dycks tomorrow if it would be possible to board your sisters with them so they can go to school." Papa said. Turning to the other girls he said "Agnes, you, Susanna, Anna and Katherina should be in school."

"Papa," Helena said softly while she looked down at her feet. "Look at my shoes; they are worn out and too short for my feet. How can I work through the winter without proper shoes?"

"Let me see." Papa reached for one of her shoes and turned it over. "You're right. You do need new shoes. I'm going to Aberdeen tomorrow and will try to find some. Find a piece of paper, put your foot on it and draw around it so that I can find the right size." Helena happily drew around her foot and gave the paper to Papa.

The next morning he went to Aberdeen and Helena waited anxiously for him to return with new shoes. However, it was past supper time when he returned and it was obvious he had been to the bar.

"Papa! Where are my new shoes? Couldn't you find any?" Helena asked.

Papa angrily moved a chair to the table and sat down. As Helena continued to pester him about how she couldn't go to work without shoes, he suddenly reached out to hit her. Shocked, she tried to get out of his way but tripped and fell over the cradle. The impact hurt her ribs and Papa's fist connected with her arm. She cried out in pain and ran from the room and outside. Sobbing, she ran out to the nearest bush and sank down to the ground. Her ribs hurt and her arm stung where Papa had hit her, but that was not nearly as painful as the hurt in her heart.

Eventually Helena returned to the house. By this time Papa was asleep and everyone was as quiet as possible as they also prepared for bed.

The next morning when Helena got up her father was sitting by the table. She avoided eye contact and went to the stove to help with breakfast even though it hurt to move.

"Helena," Papa said softly. "Will God forgive me for what I did to you?"

"I don't know," she said, and looked up to see tears running down his face. Then she turned back to the stove to fill bowls of porridge for the table. Her younger siblings were awake and gathered around for their breakfast. After Papa finished eating, he took his hat off the hook by the door and went out.

"Helena," Mama said, "He is going back to Aberdeen this morning to get your shoes."

A few days later the school aged girls and Helena were taken to the Dycks and the year of working and studying began.

It was probably easier for Mama not to have to teach the girls, but having five of her daughters leaving for the rest of the winter left her with less help with the little ones.

At the Dycks, Helena was kept very busy as she had to do the usual baby sitting, all the house work, milk the cows and help cook for so many people. After school was over for the day, the rest of the sisters also helped with evening chores and dishes. That made it a bit easier.

Often Helena had to go down to the cellar to get potatoes and other vegetables. Sometimes she took a bowl and knife down with her, peeling the potatoes there. The Dycks had two barrels of apples in the cellar and one kind of apple tasted delicious. Helena often ate an apple while she peeled potatoes. She knew she should have asked for them, but was afraid to. She felt guilty about it because it was really stealing.

Helena worked out in the fields stooking oat sheaves, weeded in the garden, fed pigs and chickens, and gathered eggs, as well as doing the house work. She became very tired and also very tired of working there so they finally took her back home. By now, Anna and Susanna, as well as Helena and Agnes had to work for other people. The little bit of money they all earned helped Mama and Papa a lot.

Baby Slippers and Dirty Dishwater

CHAPTER 27

When Helena was 14 years old she worked at the David Martens' place in the village of Rosengart. Mrs. Martens was Helena's mother's cousin. Although she had to work hard, she did not mind working for these people. The worst job she had was to untie the cows after milking. They were tied to the bottom of a sleigh while they were milked. When they heard the cow bells of the neighbour's cattle, they became wildly excited and she could hardly untie them.

She also had to let the sheep out of the barn and lead them to the pasture. This was very different from the cows that had to be herded and prodded to get them out to the pasture. Sheep are different. Helena soon learned that sheep need to follow someone; otherwise they became confused and ran in any direction. So she would call to them and walk towards the pasture with the sheep baa-ing and following her.

In the evenings after the chores were done, Helena cleaned the kitchen and swept the floor while Mrs. Martens sat beside the window, crocheting little baby slippers.

"This is my own pattern," she told Helena, "I don't let anyone see how I make these because they are different from any that the other women around here make. It's my secret pattern."

Helena smiled to herself and decided that she would begin

to watch how the lady made her stitches! Each evening she looked over Mrs. Martens' shoulder while sweeping or cleaning up the kitchen. Since she had already learned how to crochet at home, it did not take long for her to understand and when she got to her bedroom she lit the lamp and brought out her own crochet cotton and hook. She only had dark blue and black cotton thread but soon she had a pair of little slippers. She hid them among her things. Mrs. Martens never knew that the young girl who worked for her had caught on to how she made her little slippers!

The Martens had a small building they used as a summer kitchen. They cooked their meals there during the summer in order to keep the house cooler. Most summer kitchens had only a hard packed dirt floor.

Helena was small for her age and after washing dishes she put the edge of the dish pan on the edge of the table, balancing it with her stomach so she could wipe the crumbs off the table into the dirty dish water.

"One of these days you are going to spill that water," Mrs. Martens stated as she watched her clean the table.

After supper one evening Mrs. Martens said, "Helena, you can go out and get the wash from the line before it rains. I'll clean the table."

Helena came back to the summer kitchen just as the lady began to wipe the table. She was holding the dish pan just like Helena did. However, the pan slipped from her grasp and dish water poured all over the dirt floor, making it muddy.

"Well! That is a foolish way to clean the crumbs off the table! I will never do it your way again!" the lady said angrily.

Helena hid her face behind the load of clothes she was carrying trying hard not to laugh, but when she went to get the cows from the pasture that evening, she laughed out loud until the tears came, remembering the shocked look on Mrs. Marten's face when the water spilled all over the floor.

For two years during summer and fall, Helena worked at the Martens' farm and while she was there, the tenth child was born into the Banman family. Little Eva was born on September 8th, 1914. Helena looked forward to going home and seeing this newest member of their large family. At the end of the month she was able to go home. She loved carrying her tiny little sister around the house. Two year old Peter and four year old Julius got lots of attention too as the family visited and worked together.

Quick Sand and Berries

CHAPTER 28

One morning back at the Banman farm, sisters Katie and Elizabeth went off to herd the cattle as they usually did each day and were soon heard chattering and laughing as they urged the mooing cows on to greener grass on the other side of the hill. The two sisters were only a year apart and did everything together.

As the day wore on Mama wondered if the girls were all right. Usually one of them came home to get food to take back to where the cows were grazing so the girls could eat.

"Helena and Agnes, could you please go and find out where Katie and Elizabeth are with the cows? It's nearly milking time." Off went the oldest sisters to see what problems or mischief their little sisters might have gotten into. Anna and Susanna followed to see where the girls were.

Soon they could hear the tinkling sounds of cow bells and knew they were close to where the little sisters were. As they rounded the curve of a hill they saw two little girls without their dresses on! Startled by the sound of footsteps and voices, Katie and Elizabeth ran behind a small bush.

"Girls!" Helena called. "What are you doing? Where are your clothes?" They came out from behind the bush, shaking their dresses hard. A cloud of dust blew around them.

"It's Katie's fault!" Elizabeth said. "She made me go into the lake to see how deep I could go into the water. My feet got stuck and I was sinking in the mud. I was really scared!"

"I thought she was just joking when she started yelling for me to help," said Katie. "But then I saw how scared she was so I went into the lake too and we got out, but I nearly got stuck too."

Shocked, Agnes asked them, "Don't you realize that mud is quick sand and that animals have died by going deep into the water? They have sunk right down into the mud! Girls, why didn't you think about that?"

Katie and Elizabeth hung there heads while Helena continued with another question. "Why didn't you come home to get some lunch at noon?"

"Our dresses were wet and full of mud and salt from the lake so we couldn't let mama see us like that. We took them off and dried them by hanging them on the bushes. We found some berries and ate them," Katie said.

"She made me try them first in case they were poisonous." Elizabeth put in.

Helena and Agnes looked at each other, rolled their eyes, stifled a giggle and began rounding up the cattle to take them home for chores.
As they neared the barn, Katie said, "Please don't tell Mama!"

Mama came out with a milk pail, looked at the girls and said, "Girls! How could you get your dresses so dusty? Were you rolling in the dirt? Go wash your hands and have some supper. Susanna, take the girls' dresses, wash them and hang them on the line to dry."

While Susanna, Katherina, Elizabeth and Maria helped with the house and farm work at home, the three older sisters again went to work for other farmers for the next few months. They returned home for Christmas. They carried on the tradition of putting plates on the table on Christmas Eve and waking up Christmas morning to find a few candies, some cookies and maybe an orange on each plate.

The Christmas break was over too soon and the older girls went back to work for the many farm families that needed maids. Helena went back to the Martens' farm and by now was very familiar with the housework, babysitting and farm chores. Because this family treated her well, the weeks and months flew by and soon it was spring.

The Dolls that Couldn't Keep a Secret

CHAPTER 29

Helena returned home in spring to help with the seeding and gardening. One day as she helped her father bring seed grain out of the barn to be planted she heard him say, "What's this?!" and he came out of the barn looking angry. "Katherina! Elizabeth!"

The girls came running to the barn and saw their father carrying some very strange looking rag dolls. They had sprouts of wheat growing out all over their bodies. Katherina and Elizabeth's faces fell and they looked very guilty.

"I told you girls not to get into the seed grain! These seeds are ruined and I can't plant them!" Papa said. He dropped the dolls, grabbed the girls by their arms and spanked their bottoms. They walked away crying as Papa told them to get busy and do their chores.

That evening when they went with their older sisters to haul water from the spring Helena asked them, "Where did you get those dolls?"

"We wanted to play with dolls," Katie said...

"..and we didn't have any," continued Elizabeth, "So we found some old sacks, some string and small sticks and made some dolls."

Katie added, "but the dolls looked silly being so flat and we wanted to fill them with something."

"We snuck into the grain bin when Papa was out in the field

and filled the dolls heads and tummies," Elizabeth finished.

"After playing with the dolls for a while we heard Papa coming home and decided to hide them in a corner of the barn so that he wouldn't see what we did." Katie said.

When winter came, Katie and Elizabeth forgot all about those dolls. In spring, when the weather got warmer and the grain in the dolls got wet, the grain sprouted.

As Helena grabbed a full pail of water from Agnes and handed her an empty one, she glanced at Anna who had a big grin and twinkling eyes.

"Green hair! Imagine that!" Anna giggled.

"And not just on their heads – all over their bodies!" Helena laughed. It became the topic of conversation with teasing, joking and laughter. The more they talked about it the funnier it seemed. The guilty little girls were not quite ready to laugh at first, but after a while the peals of laughter from their big sisters got them smiling too – thinking about those dolls with green sprouts growing out of their tummies!

Naughty Johnny... and Other Places of Work

CHAPTER 30

In the years of 1915 and 1916, Helena worked for Mr. & Mrs. Jacob Peters in the spring and summer. Mrs. Peters was another of her mother's cousins and she treated Helena well. There was a lot of work to do both in the house and with the animals, but it was a pleasant place to be.

Helena was able to go home for a little while and then she worked for the Wienses in the fall. The Wiens children were not well behaved, especially the boys, and life was difficult as Helena tried to do her work. She would no sooner have the cows herded toward the barn when the boys would sic the dog after them. This would send the cattle all running in different directions. The boys kept playing tricks on her and interfering with her work. Helena never knew what to expect from those mischievous boys.

The harvesting was in full swing and she had to work in the fields stooking oat sheaves, then hurry back to the house to help Mrs. Wiens make meals to take to the field and bring water and cold coffee to the men. There were cows to be milked, pigs to be fed, chickens to feed, eggs to collect and always weeding to be done in the garden.

The garden vegetables needed to be harvested and she was busy with that as well as house work. There was a large amount of weekly laundry to do and all of it had to be washed by hand. One day she was busy bending over a wash tub, rubbing clothes on a wash board. The tub was close to the summer kitchen and suddenly one of the Wiens boys jumped off the roof and onto her back. Helena screamed in pain and lay on the ground in agony.

"What's wrong?!" Mrs Wiens called as she came running out of the house. Her boys ran away.

"What happened?" Mrs Wiens asked as she tried to help Helena get up. She could hardly move as the lady helped her into the house and had her lie down on a bed.

"Johnny jumped off the roof and onto my back," Helena gasped between groans of pain.

Mrs. Wiens found Johnny and he received a hard thrashing for what he had done. Helena spent several days in bed. She tried to get up and help with dishes but she could hardly walk and so finally Mr. Wiens took her back home. The bumpy wagon trip hurt her back but she was so glad to get home and have Mama look after her. Papa took her to see Mama's cousin, Mrs. Peters, who was a chiropractor. Mrs. Peters was well known in the area for having the ability to put peoples' bones back into place. After Mrs. Peters worked on her she got better and in a few months she was able to do some work around home.

"Helena! Anna!" called Papa one November day as they were carrying in pails of snow to melt in the barrel in the kitchen. The girls went over to where their father was talking to some men who had driven out to their farm on their sleighs.

"The Cornelius Nickols and the Jacob Peters need maids to work over the winter. I will take you to Aberdeen tomorrow and they will meet you there to take you to their farms."

The girls turned to get some more snow to melt while the men continued to visit. Both girls dreaded having to be away from home again but they knew they would have to go.

At supper that evening Papa said, "With Agnes working at the John Schellenbergs again and with you girls working at the Peters and Nickols, I will have enough money to buy some seed grain in the spring. It will help a lot."

The Banman girls knew that the money they earned also helped to make life a bit easier for Mama to look after all their little sisters and brothers. It was a way of life for most large families. The oldest children earned a living to help their parents and siblings but sometimes the girls wished they could keep a little of the money to buy things they needed or wanted.

Before the girls left home for their places of work, Mama had asked that Papa make arrangements to pick the girls up a few days before Christmas so that they could all be together. Papa agreed and it made the girls feel a bit happier.

When Helena and Anna arrived at the farms where they were to work, they realized that the two families were close neighbours!

"We can visit each other on Sundays after church!" Helena whispered to Anna. Over the next weeks before Christmas that is just what they did. It was a relief to have a break from the work and to spend time together.

Just before Christmas, the weather was very cold and the day before the girls were to be taken to Aberdeen, the Peters came to visit the Nickols. Mr. Nickol was going to take the girls to Aberdeen the next morning, however as the men discussed the bitterly cold weather, they told the girls that they did not think their father would venture out with oxen on a 10 mile drive to pick them up.

"He said he would pick us up!" Anna said.

"He will be there! We have to go to meet him!" Helena added.

Seeing how anxious the girls were to spend Christmas with their family, the men consented and the next morning they bundled up and drove the few miles to Aberdeen. When they got there, they saw Papa's team of oxen standing near the store. Excitedly the girls jumped off the sleigh and ran into the store to greet their father and to get warm near the pot-bellied stove. Mr. Nickol handed the money the girls had earned to Papa and after he had purchased a little candy, some coffee, sugar and flour, they were ready to leave for home.

As the girls got into the sleigh their father handed them each a Russian fur coat and some stones that Mama had heated for them. Covered with the big fur coats and with their feet on the stones the girls were warm the whole way home, but Papa walked most of the 10 miles, sometimes behind the sleigh and sometimes leading the oxen to make sure they went the right way. Sometimes he swung his arms, clapped his hands and stamped his feet to keep from freezing while he walked.

Don't be Angry – Just Pray

CHAPTER 31

In the spring of 1917 Agnes went home to help Papa work the land and Helena was asked to go to the Schellenbergs, and then to the Henry Wiebes who lived near the village of Olgafeld. Helena hadn't been back to this village since she was 10 years old, when her family had arrived from Manitoba and moved into the Olgafeld school house before moving to their homestead.

While Helena was busy working for the Wiebes, Mama had another baby who was born September 11, 1917. They named her Margaret. Little Eva was three years old and their mother really needed some cloth to make a little dress for the new baby.

After a few months of trying to keep the baby in dry diapers and dresses, Mama asked Papa to get some cloth for baby clothes.

"When you go to Aberdeen today to pick up supplies, I would like you to please bring back some dark coloured cloth; enough to make a little dress for baby Margaret." She told him how much to buy and what kind of cloth she would like.

Papa hitched the big ox up to the wagon and left for town. He spent some time in the bar with friends and then went to the store. Looking through the material section he found some light coloured cloth that he thought would look nice on the baby and bought enough for two dresses. Then he drove to the Wiebe farm near the village of Olgafeld to see Helena and to bring her home for a short visit so she could see the new baby. On the way home Papa would take a drink out of a bottle every once in a while. It was quite late by the time they got home.

Helena was greeted quietly by her sisters and her mother and bent over the cradle to admire the new baby. After a short visit they all went to bed.

The next morning Mama looked at the cloth Papa had bought and said, "Oh – but I wanted dark coloured material because my eyes are so sore. I cannot look at light coloured material for very long. It will be too hard on my eyes to sew two dresses!"

Papa was upset that the cloth he bought was not good enough for Mama to use and so he sat down near the table holding his head in his hands. He also had a headache from too much drink.

"Agnes," Mama said, "put the dishes on the table for breakfast."

Agnes put a cup on the table near Papa. He raised his head at the noise of the cup on the table and furiously grabbed it flinging it across the room where it broke.

There was a shocked silence as all the sisters and brothers stopped what they were doing and realized they had better be quiet because Papa was upset.

"Pick up the broken glass pieces, Agnes, and sweep the floor." Mama said. Agnes cleaned up the broken glass and tried again to set the table, but every time she put a dish on the table, Papa flung it away breaking it. Agnes stomped over to the broken pieces and angrily flung them into a metal pail where they made a loud clanking noise.

"Don't be like that, Agnes," Mama said. "Let's pray for your father instead." Everyone turned to look at Papa who sat with his head hanging because he heard what Mama said. Abruptly he got up, grabbed his cap and said, "I'm going to pick stones!" and left the house.

Looking out the window at the field where Papa had gone, they could see that he was not picking stones, but instead was looking up at the sky, raising his hands in the air and then sinking down to the ground with his head in his hands. Later he told Mama, "When I say I am going to pick stones, I am really going out there to pray."

On Monday afternoon Helena was taken back to Olgafeld and back to the Wiebes. After dropping her off, Papa went to the store and bought some new dishes. When he got home he asked Mama, "Does this make up for what I did?"

Working for the Wiebes

CHAPTER 32

When Helena began working for the Henry Wiebes, she looked around the farm house and yard and liked what she saw. Mr. Wiebe rented the land near the house and Helena had to help with the farm work. First thing in the morning she brought the cows to the barn, milked them and strained the milk through a cloth over a wire sieve. After the cows were milked she fed the pigs and chickens and gathered the eggs. Then there were dishes to do and the kitchen to clean.

The summer went by quickly with so much work to do, but the Wiebes were pleasant people to work for and Helena worked hard as usual. Soon it was harvest time and Mr. Wiebe began to cut the crop with a binder pulled by horses. The binder cut the grain stalks and tied them into bundles.

"Here, 'Lena, I want you to pack up this food and take it to the field for you and the other helpers," Mrs. Wiebe said after breakfast. Helena packed up cold chicken, buns, a bottle of cold coffee and some cold water from the well. As she walked past the barn she saw Mr. Wiebe working on the binder.

"Helena!" Mr. Wiebe called. "Come and unhitch the horses so I can grease the binder. They aren't standing still enough. Give them a drink and then hitch them to the stone-boat and haul some water from the well to the barn."

Helena was mostly used to oxen but loved horses and so she

set down the food she was carrying, bravely walked up to the big animals, unhitched them from the binder and led them to the water trough for a drink. Then she hitched them to the stone-boat that had two barrels on it. She stood on the stone-boat next to the water barrels and drove the horses over to the well.

Well with bucket to haul up water.
Drawing by NB

After tying their reins to a post near it she hauled up the water from the well with a rope tied to a bucket, filled the barrels and returned to the barn. The water trough for the animals was nearly empty so she filled it and then drove back to where Mr. Wiebe was working and unhitched the horses.

Then she picked up the food she had packed and walked out to the field where the other workers were stooking the oat sheaves. Putting the food in a shady spot, Helena grabbed two oat sheaves and started to work alongside the others.

Oat sheaves stacked up to form a 'tee-pee' stook. Drawing by Nettie Balzer

"Stooking" was picking up bundles of grain and stacking them up-right in a tee-pee formation with the grains at the top. If there was rain, it would run off the sheaves and not soak them with water.

Each evening when she returned from working in the fields most of the day she had to do the chores all over again. The wages she earned at this farm were more than at some of the other places she had worked. Here she earned $15.00 per month.

One evening while eating supper, Mr. Henry Wiebe said,

"There will be a new teacher coming to our village. He's my nephew Jacob Friesen, from the village of Blumenheim, across the river. He'll be staying with us when school starts after we have finished harvesting. Since there are people living in the old school house, he will be teaching classes in our summer kitchen."

Mr. Wiebe paused to take a bite of fried ham and after a moment he continued, "My brother Jacob and his wife at the next farm want you, Helena, to work for them when we are done with our harvest. They want a maid to help with housework and chores. I will talk to your papa when he comes to collect the money."

Helena Meets Jacob

CHAPTER 33

Every Sunday the families gathered with the other villagers at the Old Colony Mennonite Church in the village of Edenberg. Here Helena got to know other young people like herself, some of whom were also working for farmers in the area.

She met other girls and young men in the village of Olgafeld near where she worked and they became friends. Some evenings the village girls enjoyed singing and circle-dancing. The young men stood around visiting with each other and watched the girls singing, dancing and laughing with their arms around each other's shoulders.

One evening one of the girls pointed and whispered in her ear, "Helena, do you see that young man over there?" She pointed to one of the young men talking with the others. "His name is Jacob Friesen and he is the new teacher for our village. He's the nephew to Henry and Jacob Wiebe. He's staying with the Henry Wiebes."

Helena glanced toward the group of men and saw a handsome young man who looked to be about her age. He turned and saw her and she shyly looked down.

"I haven't met him yet," she said, "but when I was working for the Henry Wiebes, I was told he was coming."

Over the next few weeks, Jacob Friesen was often seen visiting with the young men after evening chores and on Sundays after church. Many young men in the villages took up the habit of smoking while they visited and Jacob also joined his friends in this habit.

One evening when Helena had finished supper with the Wiebes, Jacob Friesen knocked on the door and walked into the house.

"Vilkommen!" Mr. Wiebe said. "It's good to see you again and good to know that you're teaching school here in the village. How are your parents? Are they well?"

Jacob Friesen with his class in Olgafeld, teaching in Henry Wiebe's summer kitchen in 1917.

"My Mother is sometimes ill and father's eyesight is getting worse - but the farming is still going well," Jacob answered. "My brothers are busy helping with the farm."

He cleared his throat and asked, "I was wondering if I could ask Helena to go for a buggy ride with me." Mr. Wiebe glanced at Helena whose face had turned pink and who looked like she was about to burst into giggles of embarrassment.

"Yes – that is all right with us. You can use our buggy and horse, but remember Helena must be in the house by 9:00 o'clock. She has chores very early in the morning." Jacob and his uncle went to the barn to get the harness and then to the pasture to get the horse. After leading him to the buggy and hitching him up, Jacob helped Helena up to sit on the seat. Smartly snapping the reins onto the horses back he urged the horse forward. It was a lovely evening and they enjoyed riding around the countryside. Gradually it became easier for Helena to join in conversation instead of just answering Jacob's questions.

Jacob was busy teaching German school classes. In those days, a German school teacher did not earn very much money. It was enough for a young unmarried man to help out his parents with the family farm – or for a married man to help with his own farm. Helena kept working for the Wiebes. Both of them attended the Edenburg Village church which was several miles from the village of Olgfeld.

Helena wanted to know all about Jacob's family and sometimes they sat in the Wiebe living room talking about the Friesen and Wiebe families.

"My father David was born to David Friesen and Elizabeth Bueckert in Russia in 1870," Jacob told her one evening. "He was five years old when they left Russia and emigrated to the Winkler, Manitoba area in Canada in 1875. They farmed near the village of Blumengart. My mother Anna was born to Jacob Wiebe and Katherina Rempel in 1872. She was seven years old when they emigrated from Russia to Manitoba, also to the Blumengart area. My parents met there and that's where I was born and lived until we moved to Blumenheim, Saskatchewan in 1901 when I was five. Both of my parents came from the Chortitza Colony in Russia."

Helena looked at him in surprise. "You were born in Blumengart and I was born in Kleefeld! I was ten years old when we moved from Manitoba, but I remember those two villages are very near each other! Imagine that! We were born within a few miles of each other and both of my parents were from the Chortitza Colony as well."

Helena went for many buggy rides with Jacob while he was teaching in the village and they became very good friends. Within the year they discussed marriage.

(NOTE: The farm where the Friesens lived near Blumengart, Manitoba, is now a Hutterite Colony)

Catechism and Baptism

CHAPTER 34

In the Old Colony Mennonite Church it was very important that one took catechism classes, was baptised and became a member of the church before marriage. Helena and several other young people took catechism classes with Elder Jacob Wiens.

There was so much to learn about God and the Bible in the classes they took. Helena took the question and answer times very seriously and began to understand many things about God.

Elder Wiens taught the Holy Scriptures carefully in those sessions. The young people memorized the questions and answers from their catechism booklet which, although a small book, had 60 pages to memorize! Elder Wiens helped them to understand what they were learning, beginning in the Old Testament with Creation and God's old agreement with mankind and on through the New Testament and God's new agreement with us through Jesus Christ. Here are just a few of the many questions;
Question: Who made everything?
Answer: God the Lord. He first created heaven and earth. (Genesis 1:1)

Question: What did God create in His own image?
Answer: God created mankind in His own image (Genesis 1:27)

Question: Who is God?
Answer: God is the Father, the Son, and the Holy Spirit. (Matt: 28:19)

Question: Does that mean that there are three God's?

Answer: No: there is only one God and the three are One. (Mark:12:29)

Question: How can we know that God exists?
Answer: We know from the things that are created and from the Holy Scriptures.
(Job 12:7-10)

Question: What does the Scripture say about God?
Answer: That He is a Spirit. (John 4:24) He is One, everlasting, unchanging, all knowing, always present, all wise, almighty, holy, righteous, patient and gracious.

Question: Did God's first created people remain holy and happy?
Answer: No – they disobeyed God and were sent out of paradise.

Question: What did God do to bring people back to Himself?
Answer: He sent Jesus, His only Son to die for our sins, to be buried and to rise again from death to life after three days.

Question: What is the only way to receive God's forgiveness and everlasting life?
Answer: Believe in Jesus, God's Son.

Question: What does believing do for us?
Answer: It brings about a change of heart.

Question: What did scripture call a 'change of heart'?
Answer: It is called being 'born again' – becoming a new creation. (John 3:3, Galations 6:15)

Question: How can one be born again?
Answer: God Himself works in us through His Word and His Spirit if we are obedient to Him. (1 Peter 1:3, John 3:5).

There were many other things Helena memorized and understood as she faithfully studied in the evenings after chores.

Helena was very sure of what she believed, however, the Old Colony Church did not teach that you could know for sure that you would spend eternity with God. You could only hope to get to heaven. Sometimes this was confusing to her.

On a beautiful Sunday in June of 1917, all the young people who had studied the catechism questions sat at the front of the church for the morning service. After the singing and long sermon, Elder Jacob Wiens called them forward one by one and as they knelt before him, he asked them if they believed in Jesus as the way to God and if they were willing to follow the teachings of the church.

After they each answered, "Ya (yes)," Elder Wiens poured water on their heads and said, "I baptise you in the Name of the Father, the Son and the Holy Spirit."

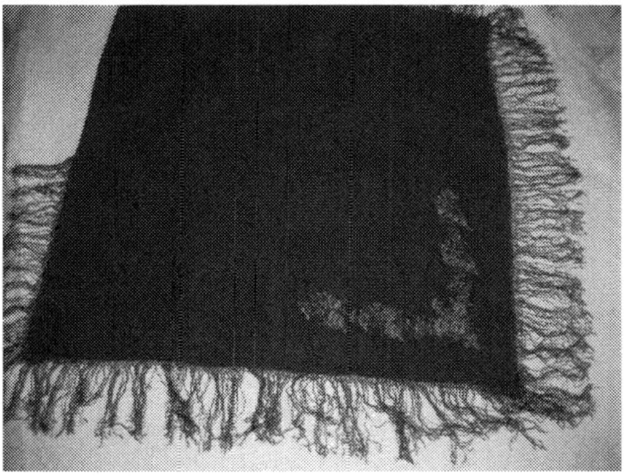

Helena's shawl – now at Nettie's home.

The baptism was followed with a communion service where the young people were allowed to take part in the bread and cup for the first time. Now they were members of the Old Colony Church.

Helena and the other girls were each presented with their first black shawl. There were fringes on three sides of it. The corner without fringes was folded over to make a triangle. The bottom corner had beautiful embroidered flowers on it. Helena put her shawl on her head and tied it under her chin. The pretty embroidered part hung down on her back.

Disappointment

CHAPTER 35

One Sunday evening after the young people had enjoyed a time together with singing and dancing, Jacob again asked Helena to go for a buggy ride. As the horse trotted down the country trail, they talked about the fun they had with the others.

"Helena," Jacob said. "I think it's good to have fun with friends but I think the dancing is too worldly and when we get married I would like you to stop dancing."

"After working so hard all week, I don't think it is worldly or wrong to dance with the other girls," Helena said. "We are just enjoying ourselves!"

"Well, I was hoping we could get married soon and I wanted to let you know what I think."

Helena sat silently for a while and then said, "Maybe we shouldn't go for buggy rides for a while. I am not yet ready to be married and I want to have some more fun."

Jacob's face turned very sober and he turned the buggy around, taking Helena back to his uncle and aunt's place. Helena quietly got off the buggy and walked into the house. Jacob drove to the barn, unhitched the buggy and opened the gate to the pasture for the horse. Then he walked back to his other uncle's place.

Mrs. Wiebe glanced at Helena as she walked into the house.

"You are back already?" Then she noticed Helena's troubled face as she walked to the bedroom.

School was out soon after that, since the boys and girls of the villages would be expected to help with the spring planting and seeding preparations. After breaking up with Helena, Jacob moved back across the river to Neuanlage where he took catechism and became a member of the church there.

He couldn't get Helena out of his mind though, so one morning he decided to make his way back to Olgafeld. Since he was done with teaching for the year, he went back to his village of Blumenheim. From there he drove about a half mile south to where there was a bend in the river, hauling a row boat and some paddles. He left his horse with a nearby farmer and found a place where the river was not too wide. He pushed the boat out into the water and carefully got in. Sitting very still to keep from tipping over, he began to paddle hard to cross the river hoping the current would not catch his boat and capsize it. After getting across he had to walk about two miles to get to the village.

On the way he wondered if Helena's mind was often on him like his was on her. Was she missing him and wishing they had not broken up?

Just before noon Helena was weeding the garden. She heard foot steps coming from behind the trees in the garden and was startled to hear "Hello 'Lena" from a familiar voice. She turned to see Jacob standing with his hat in his hand. Dropping the hoe she hurried toward him and threw her arms around his neck. Laughing, Jacob hugged her and swung her in a circle.

"What are you doing here? I didn't hear any buggy or horses coming!" Helena said.

"I came across the river on a row boat," he replied. "It was hard rowing against the current, but I got here safely."

"Jacob! That river is very dangerous! Come – it's almost

dinner time. Lets' go to the house and you can eat with us!" Helena said, and they walked toward the house where his uncle and aunt were surprised to see him.

"Vilkommen! Dinner is ready!" he was greeted by his relatives.

That afternoon the Wiebes gave Helena permission to visit with Jacob instead of finishing the weeding and as the couple talked they decided to get married the following year. Jacob wanted to earn some more money and find a place for them to live.

Since he was not teaching just then, he decided to stay for a few days, taking Helena for buggy rides in the evenings. His uncle informed him again that Helena had to be in the house by nine o'clock.

As the horse trotted down the village street, Jacob said, "Helena, when we have children and they are grown up, they will be able to stay out as long as they want!" Helena laughed at his comment.

They talked about how their separation had affected them and Helena told Jacob what she had been thinking.

"I wondered if dancing was really so important to me that I would give you up. I thought if I got another chance things might be different." They again discussed marriage and thought about a few possible dates for their wedding.

The few days were over too soon and Jacob's uncle took him back to the river with the horse and buggy. He pushed the boat back into the river and paddled across. Weary from the rowing and walking, Jacob fetched his horse and headed to his parents' house and to bed, smiling to himself as he looked forward to a future with Helena.

Wedding Plans

CHAPTER 36

In the month of May, 1919, Mrs. Wiebe approached Helena one day as they were cleaning the kitchen after supper.

"Helena – you and Jacob are getting married next month and I think you should take some of the money you have earned to buy something for your wedding before your Papa comes to collect your wages."

This is the chest of drawers Helena bought before she was married. It is now 96 years old and in use at her granddaughter's home in Calgary, Alberta, Canada.
The top middle drawer held the handkerchiefs used to blow noses before tissues were invented.
The top long drawer held great-grandpa's leather razor strap used to sharpen the razor for shaving his beard, and it was also used sometimes to spank the children when they were naughty

The wedding dress is also 96 years old and is being stored at her daughter Nettie's home in Osler, Saskatchewan, Canada.

Helena wanted so much to have something nice for her wedding so she went to the store with Mr. Wiebe. She ordered a 'kamoud' (chest of drawers) and some black fabric to make a wedding dress. All the young Old Colony Mennonite girls wore black to their weddings. It was meant to be a sign of humility.

When the material came in Helena carefully cut the pattern out of the cloth. The material had a nice sheen to it and she sewed every evening. She wanted lots of tucks on the bodice and pleats on the skirt. As she worked on her dress she was warned by Jacob's Aunt that the bishop might not approve of all the extra tucks and pleats in her dress along with the shiny look of the fabric. This might be looked on as her being too prideful.

Helena looked up from her sewing and said, "What about the bishop's wife. Have you seen her kruzchel metz?(black lace and ribbon cap worn by Mennonite women) She must have 60 yards of satin ribbon in that, plus yards of black lace!"

"Helena!" Jacob's Aunt said. "You mustn't judge her like that."

"And what about Mrs. Schellenberg's black shawl? She has the most embroidered flowers and the most fringes on the edges of the shawl than anyone else in the church," Helena added. At the look Jacob's Aunt gave her, Helena looked down for a moment and then said quietly, "Last Sunday the preacher said that people look on the outward appearance, but God looks on the heart. I don't think I'm being proud. I just want to look nice for Jacob."

Even though she knew it might result in excommunication from the church, she continued working on the dress but only took out a few pleats from the skirt, hoping to be able to wear it. She also wanted to buy some other pretty clothing but her Papa came to collect the money and took her with him back to the Banman farm. She couldn't go shopping again.

The second last week of May, Mama Banman, Helena and some of her sisters busily made bun dough for the engagement party. It would be happening at their house on May 27th. It was an exciting time and when the day rolled around, Jacob and his parents, brothers, sisters, aunts, uncles and friends arrived to celebrate their engagement.

As they gathered for the faspa, Helena bit into a bun and her heart sank with disappointment. The buns all tasted sour and she had so wanted to make a good impression on Jacob's parents! His parents were not poor like hers and she wondered what they would think.

The party guests left and Jacob went to stay with his uncle and aunt in Olgafeld. For the next week, he arrived by horse and buggy every day as he and Helena travelled from farm to farm to let people know that they would be getting married at his parents home in Blumenheim the next week, on June 3rd. This was the way they invited people to their wedding. As they travelled on the buggy, they talked about their future.

"My sister Katherina and her husband Isbrand Regier are living on a farm near Olgafeld now. Isbrand and I have bought some land there and I have a few cows. That's where we'll live after we're married," Jacob told Helena.

"Then we'll be able to go to church in Edenberg where I was baptised and where we have so many friends," Helena replied.

By now Papa had horses and so Helena, her parents and a couple of her sisters got ready for the long ride across the river by ferry to go to Blumenheim for the wedding. It wasn't possible to take all the children with them. They left the night before in order to be there next morning for the church service.

After the Sunday service that morning, the people gathered

at the Friesen farm where Preacher John Loeppky married them. Helena wore her dress and even though there was some disapproval on the face of the preacher, nothing was said. After the ceremony and fairly long message of advice the preacher gave them, it was time for their wedding faspa.

Tables were set up outside and the men were served first along with the newly married couple. Then the women and children ate. Helena noticed right away that the buns the Friesens had baked were delicious. Their wedding meal was just buns, coffee and sugar cubes. It was the regular faspa served at all weddings and funerals. After the meal the couple went into the living room to see the wedding gifts people had brought. The women gathered around to watch as they opened and looked at their gifts.

Helena's cut glass dishes, now in Nettie's home.

There were several lovely wool quilts, a few dishes, some pots & pans, bread baking pans, casserole dishes and some pretty cut-glass sugar bowls. Some of the cut-glass dishes were pink and some were blue.

Helena also received a blue glass hen which sat on a blue bowl that looked like a nest with eggs around the sides. She loved these gifts since she had never had such pretty things before.

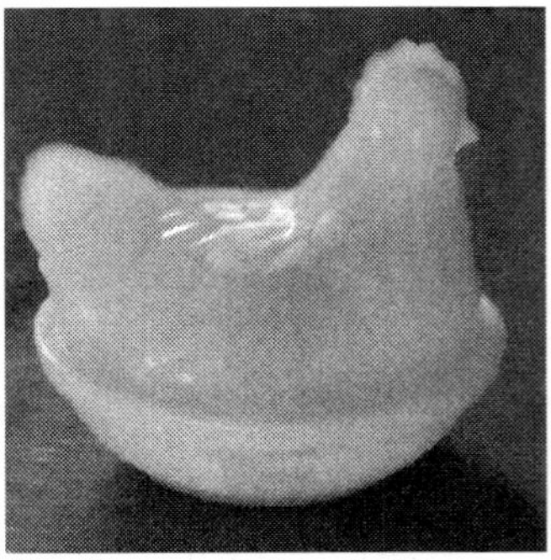

Similar to Helena's blue hen candy dish.

Helena's mama walked up to her and gave her a lacy black kruzshel metz. She was now a married woman and that was how they dressed. Helena smiled and put it on.

Jacob's Aunt – Mrs. Henry Wiebe for whom Helena worked. She is wearing the kruzshel metz. Picture taken by Helena's son Julius in 1965.

After packing up their gifts Helena reached for her black embroidered shawl and wore it over her lace and ribbon metz, tying it beneath her chin. They climbed up into their buggy, driving off to their new home across the river while the many relatives and friends waved and called goodbye.

Jacob reached for Helena's hand and they smiled at each other. They were beginning a new life together!

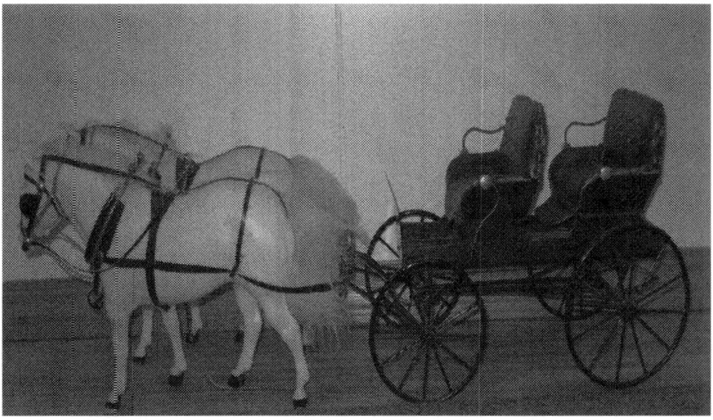

Model of buggy - photo from Osler Museum.

Just Married

CHAPTER 37

After their wedding, the young married couple drove down the hill to the Clarkborough Ferry, urging the horse on to the wooden floor. Once across the river they continued on to Olgafeld and the farm that the brothers-in-law had bought. Isbrand and Katherina Regier lived in the house on that land and there was another small building that had been used as a summer kitchen. That was where Jacob and Helena would live.

Clarkborough Ferry – still in operation today

On the way to their new home they stopped at Jacob's uncle's place to pick up the lovely brand new kamoud (chest of drawers) Helena had bought. After moving it into the little house, she carefully folded all their clothes and gifts of linens and put them into the drawers.

The brothers-in-law farmed the land, however, after a few months they realized there was not enough work to go around for them. The farm would not support four people.

One day as the men milked the cows and fed them, Isbrand said, "I've been asked to teach at the German school in the village of Reinland. I've decided to take the job because it will bring in a little money. We would like you and Helena to move into the house and take care of the cattle for the winter."

Jacob agreed and he and Helena worked on the farm for a month when Jacob was also asked to teach school - in Edenburg.

"We have very little money left," he told Helena, "So I welcome the chance to earn some, but we need to find someone to look after our place while we are gone for the winter."

"There's a young couple who are living with their parents right now," she told him. "They would probably like to be on their own. You can talk to them. They're at the Schellenberg farm."

Jacob visited the couple. They were very glad to move into the farm house as soon as Jacob and Helena left for Edenburg.

Helena was happy to be back in Edenburg where she had friends. She wrote a letter to her mother telling her of their move. Her mother soon sent a letter in reply. There was sad news. Helena's grandpa Klassen from Manitoba had died on October 1, 1919.

Just a few months after their wedding Helena found it hard to eat in the morning.

"What's wrong?" asked Jacob. "Are you sick?"

"Just for a while first thing in the morning," said Helena. "I feel good the rest of the day."

One evening as they visited the Henry Wiebes in Olgafeld, Helena was alone with Mrs. Wiebe in the kitchen and mentioned that she felt sick most mornings.

"I do feel better by the afternoon though," she said. Mrs.

Wiebe turned to look at her and smiled.

"So you are going to have a baby!" she said. "That's how most women feel when they are expecting a baby! How long have you felt this way?" Surprised by this comment, Helena said, "Well, only a few weeks now."

"Then you will probably have the baby in March or April! This is exciting news."

As the couple was bundled up warm in the buggy for their ride home, Helena said, "I think I know now why I've been feeling sick. Your aunt thinks I'm going to have a baby."

Jacob turned to her with a grin. "That's wonderful! When do you think it'll be born?"

"Your aunt thinks it will be March or April," she answered.

"That's good because it will be before seeding time and we'll have time to enjoy the baby before we get busy with farm work again."

Soon winter was upon them and it was hard to get around. They had horses that Jacob was very proud of. Their names were 'Babe' and 'Topsy'. They were a light dapple grey colour and they were young and strong enough to pull the sleigh easily, but the snow drifts were high and when school was done at the end of the day the couple often just stayed home instead of going visiting. Jacob prepared school lessons in the evening while Helena knitted or crocheted.

"Jacob," she said one evening. "Do you think we could go to my parents' farm for Christmas?"

"Well, it'll depend on the weather. It's a long trip to make and harder for the horses in the winter."

When December rolled around they began to make plans for

Christmas. At school the students learned recitations that they would be saying at their grandparents' homes. Helena baked schmaunt kuken (cream cookies) to take with her to her family. She filled a metal cookie box with them and put it on the porch to freeze. That would keep them fresh until Christmas.

Christmas at the Banmans

CHAPTER 38

Finally December 23rd came and the weather was cold but sunny. "I'll ask my uncle Henry if I can use their caboose (closed in sleigh) for the trip to your parents," Jacob said. He drove his team over to his uncle's place and soon returned with the caboose.

Early next morning, while it was still very dark, they set out for Helena's parents' home. Jacob hung a lantern from the front of the whiffletree (the wooden crossbar the horses are hitched to) between the horses, which shed a bit of light on the snowy trail.

Helena was excited. She snuggled close to Jacob to keep warm, listening to the familiar sound of jingling harnesses and horses snorting as they trotted down the trail.

As the sky began to lighten, the snow banks and shadows turned a blue-grey colour. It was beautiful – but very cold. A light wind made the soft snow swirl around in front of the horses and the sleigh. Jacob listened to the horses and suddenly he called, "Ho!" as he pulled the reins tighter, stopping the sleigh.

"What's wrong?' asked Helena.

"I think they're having trouble breathing," Jacob said. "I want to make sure their nostrils are not plugged with ice crystals. Hang on to the reins," he said as he handed them to Helena.

Walking slowing to the front, talking quietly to the horses, Jacob felt the horses noses and found he was right. Their sides were heaving and so he held tightly to the bridle while he cleared the ice and frost from each of the horses' nostrils. Once they could breathe more easily Jacob went back inside the caboose.

"Their noses were full of frost so they couldn't breathe very well," Jacob said. "We'll let them rest for just a few minutes before we start out again. We're nearly at Aberdeen now. They can rest there for a while and I'll give them water and food before we continue."

By the time they started out again the sun was shining brightly and the snow sparkled like diamonds. The heavy hoar frost on the bushes near the road swayed in the slight wind that was blowing and made the sunshine on the frosty branches look like blinking lights.

Soon they reached the town of Aberdeen and stopped at the livery stable to let the horses rest. After tying the reins to the hitching post, Jacob reached into the back of the sleigh where he had put some hay and went to feed them.

Helena got off the sleigh and caught up with her husband as he turned toward the nearby store. They warmed themselves by the big potbellied stove. She walked over to the candy counter and looked at the pretty red and white striped candy canes and the round white peppermints. Turning to Jacob she said, "Can we buy some of these for my little sisters and brothers?"

They bought half a pound of each kind. They saw some oranges as well and bought a few of those. The children would have to share oranges slices.

After their feet were warm again, they climbed back into the sleigh for the final 10 miles of travel. Now the sun was higher in the sky and as it shone on the bright white snow it made them squint until their eyes got used to it. The last 10 miles seemed to go slowly for Helena. She could hardly wait to see her family! Soon they rounded a bend and saw the Banman farm house. Jacob drove to the barn and stopped. The door of the house opened and Papa and some of her sisters poured out.

"Vilkommen!!" called Papa as he threw on his winter coat. "I'll help you get those horses into the barn."

Helena picked up her box of schmaunt kuken and the bags of candies and hurried to the house where she was greeted by a chorus of excited sisters and brothers!

"Ye zent toos fe Wienachten (You are home for Christmas)!" Mama said as she hugged her oldest daughter. The sisters crowded around and everyone talked at once. The little ones tugged at her coat as she removed it and then she knelt down and pulled the little girls into her arms. Eva and Margaret, aged five and two put their little arms around Helena's neck.

Soon Papa and Jacob came in, stomping the snow off of their boots. Agnes and Anna attended the noon meal at the stove while the other sisters washed dishes, set the table and prepared the house for Christmas. All the while, the family kept up a constant chatter and soon the girls were bantering back and forth with their quick wit and humorous comments which sent them into fits of laughter. It was good to be home!!

Papa sat back with a grin, joining in the conversation every once in a while, as Jacob tried to take it all in. His family was much more serious about everything but even he could not keep the smile off of his face as he listened to his in-law family. It was good to see Helena having such a good time.

On Christmas Eve the family sat visiting while the little ones prepared for bed. Helena remembered their blankets in the sleigh.

"I need to get our quilts and pillows from the cotta," Helena said.

"I'll get them," Jacob said. "I have to check on the horses anyway." He put on his heavy winter coat and went outside, breathing deeply of the fresh air. Papa followed him in order to check on his animals as well.

Meanwhile the schlope-benk was opened up – it would sleep three people. Mama and Papa had their own bedroom where they made room on the floor for a straw tick mattress and quilts for the youngest two girls. The rest of the family would sleep on couches and straw tick mattresses on the living room floor.

When the men returned to the living room, Mama turned to the younger children and said, "Now you can each put a plate on the kitchen table to see what Santa will bring you in the morning."

Soon the family was tucked into bed except for Mama, Papa, Jacob, Helena and her next oldest sisters. They visited until late into the evening. The younger children lay on their mattresses quietly listening until they drifted off to sleep.

As Helena's mama went to the kitchen to bank up the fire for the night, Helena followed her and quietly said, "Mama – I have something to tell you." Her mother turned to look at her.

"I'm going to have a baby." Mama's face registered joy and sympathy because she knew what it was like to have babies. Now the emotion of it all hit Helena and she began to cry softly. Mama led her to a corner of the room where they could talk privately.

"Do you know when it is to be born?" asked Mama.

"Jacob's aunt thinks it will be in early spring," Helena replied.

"It is good news, Helena! I will be praying for you. Your own little baby! This is wonderful!"

That night Helena sighed as she lay staring around the dark

room. It took a while to fall asleep. Life would never be the same again and she wondered about being a mother and how her own children would turn out. What kind of Christmases would they celebrate?

It seemed she had just fallen asleep when she heard the patter of little feet and excited voices as the children ran to see what 'Santa' had brought them. Helena brought out the oranges, peeled them, and gave each one two slices. It was a real treat for them all. Fruit was hard to find in the winter.

After breakfast they visited and the little ones played with the cloth dolls and wooden toys their parents had made. Julius and Peter liked their new brother-in-law and soon had him involved with the wooden horses and wagons they had received for Christmas. The women and girls prepared their dinner of roast goose. Once they had finished their special Christmas meal, Helena brought out the schmaunt kuchen, another treat for her siblings.

The girls finished the dishes quickly and they all sat in the living room. The younger ones stood one at a time, and recited the Christmas verses they had learned at school and at home. Then it was time for Jacob and Helena to return to their home in Edenberg. This time they took hot stones to keep their feet warm. Papa gave them more hay for the horses.

First Baby – First Angel

CHAPTER 39

It was dark when they arrived home and it was good to be back in their own quiet little place. Helena had happy memories but Jacob was especially happy to be home. He had enjoyed himself but was not yet used to the Banman family. As the fire in the stove began to warm up the house, they sat close to each other and to the fire, contentedly talking about Christmas and how they would celebrate with their own children in the future.

The second week of March, 1920, Helena received a letter from her mama saying that step-grandpa Peter Hamm had died in Mexico at the beginning of February at the age of 90. Helena really did not remember him at all, but thought about her Grandma Banman/Hamm.

It was becoming harder for Helena to walk and do her work now that it was nearly time for her to have the baby. One evening she voiced her concern to Jacob, "How will this baby be born… I mean… how will it happen?"

Jacob was a bit surprised but cleared his throat and explained about birth. He had grown up working with animals that had babies but in the culture Helena had grown up in, children - girls especially - were not allowed to be near the barn when animals gave birth. They were sent to neighbours during the births of their siblings. Even though Helena had worked for many farmers, she was always told to leave the barn if an animal was about to give birth.

"It will be painful when you have this baby. Have you ever been in pain?" Jacob asked.

"Yes. Once I had a very sore foot and once I had some cracked ribs," she replied. Jacob stared at her for a moment but said nothing.

The morning of March 15th, Helena really did not feel well. She was sick to her stomach and had a fair bit of pain. The pain left in a little while and then came back again. She made breakfast and cleaned up after the meal while Jacob went to teach the children in the room at the other end of the school house. She heard the children coming. Their chatter stopped when Jacob called them to sit down and recite their lessons.

In the little living area, Helena lay down on the bed for a while to see if the pain would go away, but it kept coming back and getting worse. She did not want to disturb Jacob and could hardly wait for classes to be over.

When the children stopped for their lunches at noon, Jacob came back for his lunch. There was nothing on the table and he found Helena curled up on the bed, crying and in obvious pain.

"Are you going to have the baby?" he asked.

"I don't know…" gasped Helena.

Taking another look at her, Jacob hurried back to the classroom and talked to the children saying that his wife was not well and that classes were over for the day. The older children helped the younger ones get dressed and they left the school.

After they were gone, Jacob hurried to the barn, brought out the horses and hitched them to the sleigh snapping the reins as he drove down the snowy village street to get Mrs. Schellenberg to be the midwife. Soon they were back at the school house and hurried in to see Helena.

Jacob was excited and concerned. However, it was three days before the baby was finally born. It was a beautiful little girl but the baby had taken too long to be born and Mrs. Schellenberg could not get her to breathe.

Jacob held her and was heartbroken. The baby had died. He sat down on a chair gazing at her and weeping. Meanwhile the midwife hurried back to the bedroom. Helena's face was very white and she seemed to be sleeping. It was then that Mrs. Schellenberg realized something was very wrong.

Jacob!" she called out suddenly. "Stop looking at the baby and get me some help or you will lose your wife too!!" The panic in her voice startled Jacob into action.

"Get Mrs. Dyck! Hurry!" she said.

He didn't need any further urging. He ran out the door and to the barn, hitching the horses to the sleigh. At the snap of the reins they galloped down the village street and beyond to the Dycks' farm.

Jumping off the sleigh, he ran into the house, "Our baby was born and it's dead. There is something wrong with Helena!" he gasped out.

Mrs. Dyck threw down her tea towel and hurried into her coat. They both climbed into the sleigh and Jacob urged the horse to run quickly back to the school house.

When Mrs. Dyck walked into the bedroom and saw Helena's condition she said, "Tie a string or belt around her thigh and tighten it!" The women found a cloth belt and tying it around Helena's thigh, they tightened the tourniquet.

"Leave it for a while and then loosen it. She is bleeding inside and we have to stop the bleeding," Mrs. Dyck said.

The women worked hard through the night with Helena,

tightening and loosening the belt. They shook her once in a while to wake her up and coax her to drink.

The next morning Helena was awake and thirsty. She looked at them and asked, "Where is my baby?"

"I'm so sorry," the midwife said. "You had a little girl but she did not live." Helena stared quietly for a moment and then turned over and cried into her pillow.

She was too weak to get out of bed so Jacob and a few others held a funeral for the baby and buried her little body. Before they left, Helena said to Jacob, "Her name is Helena".

Someone sent word to Helena's parents and a week later they arrived to visit. As her mother walked into the bedroom Helena's tears flowed and Mama cried with her.

"Papa will be going home this evening, but I will stay for this week," her mother said. Helena was relieved to hear that but although her Mama and Jacob tried to get her to eat so she could get well, she did not have an appetite. One day her mother asked her, "Is there anything you are hungry for?"

"I think I would like some 'heina zup met noodlen' (chicken noodle soup)," Helena replied.

"If you want noodle soup, we will have noodle soup!" Mama said, relieved that her daughter actually wanted to eat something! At the end of classes that day she asked Jacob for a chicken so she could make soup. Jacob drove the few miles over to his relative's home and asked if he could buy a chicken.

"You can have the chicken – just so that Helena will get better," they said. Uncle Henry and Jacob went to the chicken barn, found a plump chicken and cut off its' head. They dipped the bird into some boiling water so the feathers could be stripped off easily. Inside the house Mrs. Wiebe carefully held the bird over the fire to singe off the hair and the rest of the feathers. Jacob took the fresh meat home.

Mama Banman washed the chicken and took out the insides. After cutting the chicken up into pieces and washing them again, she put the meat into boiling water on the stove and cooked it for over an hour to make sure the meat was done. She added the bay leaves, star-aniseed, salt, pepper and a small piece of cinnamon bark to give it the right flavour.

While the chicken was cooking she made noodle dough and rolled it flat and thin. Then she rolled the dough up in a long roll and cut very fine noodles with a sharp knife. Supper was late that night, but the soup smelled so good. Finally Helena felt like eating. Over the next week she became stronger. Having her mother with her at this hard time was a big help.

After Mama left, Helena slowly began doing her own chores and tried to get over her loss, but when a mother loses her baby it takes a very long time to get over that sadness.

A Letter from Mexico

CHAPTER 40

In spring, after school was out, Jacob worked for a local farmer and then in the summer they moved to Kronstahl on the other side of the river for another teaching job. There were many wild strawberries in the fields that July, so Jacob and Helena got up early and picked strawberries before the children arrived for school.

One day a neighbour brought over a letter from Helena's mother. Her mother had included a letter from Grandma Banman/Hamm which was written in Mexico. Helena sat down to read:

(translation of actual letter written in German, from her grandmother in Mexico)

"Blumengart, the 21st of March, 1920.

"Dear children Julius Banmans. A heartfelt greeting to you from your loving mother with wishes that this letter finds you in good health and in good condition both spiritually and physically.

"Thank you, first of all, for the news you sent in your letter dated February 10th. So I will also let you know how things are with me; and I can say that in my old age I am still doing fairly well. The Lord be praised for that, and being with the children is also good.

"On the other hand, I hope that my days on earth will soon be counted out so that I can go to be with my Heavenly Father and for that I hope that the Lord will make me completely ready and if there is anything that does not please Him, that He will forgive it so that I can have a safe passage into eternity.

"I feel like I have been on this earth long enough and even though I have nothing to complain about I do admit that it is very lonely without your step-father. That is why I long for him and say with the poet;

"World, I am tired of you. I want to go to Heaven where there is righteousness, freedom, happiness and peace.

"World, with you there is war and quarrelling; nothing but loud vanity;

"In Heaven there is always freedom, peace and bliss."

"Yes, dear children, in this time of Grace we need to let go of the cares and troubles we still have in our hands so that we can prepare for the coming eternity. As also our confession in the catechism reads;

"How shall a man conduct himself in this life?

Answer; To live in godly community and grace and to long for our eternal salvation."

"We can long for this salvation because our dear Lord Jesus went through so much agony, of which we will again be reminded to reflect on this coming Easter. The Lord wants to extend His grace to us so that we will be blessed. Amen.

"You wanted to know how old your step-father was when he died. He was 90 years, 5 months and 9 days. And we were married 17 years, 1 month and 9 days.

"And here is my register from the first marriage, except for those children that were born in Russia;

Father John Banman born July 28th, 1828, baptised in 1851 and died December 13, 1901. He married me, Agenetha Driedger on September 7, 1855. I was born May 18, 1832 and baptised in 1853.

"Children;

Peter Banman, born October 5, 1866, baptised 1889.

Jacob Banman born September 1, 1868, baptised 1889.

Solomon Banman born August 31, 1872, baptised 1893. His death date was not recorded.

Julius Banman born September 18, 1876, baptised June 3, 1906.

Grandchild Johan Banman born February 16, 1886, baptised June 3, 1906.

That much is written in the church register book.

Once again I wish you heartfelt greetings with love from

your mother, and in view of your souls standing the Lord Jesus said to his disciples; "Seek first the kingdom of God and His righteousness and all of these things will be added to you."

"Now goodbye and I remain your loving mother, Agenetha Hamm. Write often to let me know how you are."

Helena put the letter down and thoughtfully went about her chores. These grandparents were a distant memory for her now, but it was good to hear about them again. She thought about the verse that her grandma had written about and went to find her catechism booklet and her Bible to see if she could find it.

When she found Matthew chapter six verse thirty-three, she read it carefully; "Seek first the kingdom of God and His righteousness." She definitely wanted to know more about God. "All these things will be added to you." What things would be added? Right now she was quite sure she was expecting another baby and she wanted this one to live. The next verse in chapter six said, "Therefore do not worry….." Helena bowed her head and silently prayed that God would keep this little one safe.

'Lena Joins the Family

CHAPTER 41

Jacob taught in Kronstahl until harvest time in the fall and then he was called on to teach school in the village of Rosenfeld. This village was only a few miles northwest of Blumenheim and they lived there for a year. It was a good year, because on March 19, 1921 they had another baby girl. This time the birth was much easier.

"Look at her!" Helena said as she lovingly examined each little finger and each little toe. "She has such tiny hands and feet and look, a little dimple in her chin!"

"She has your dark hair," Jacob said. He loved holding this precious little bundle and they decided to call her 'Helena', even though their first baby had the same name.

The next months were busy with Jacob teaching and Helena tending to the new baby and planting a little garden in the spring.

One day in the beginning of July one of Jacob's brothers arrived saying that their mother was very sick and might not live very long. After school was over for the day and Helena had packed up a few diapers, they travelled the few miles to Blumenheim.

They walked into the bedroom to see his mother and she smiled and reached out for the baby. Helena held her baby up for her mother-in-law to see.

"I am so happy this baby lived," said Jacob's mother, "But I may not live much longer." She had tuberculosis and was becoming weaker.

They returned to Rosenfeld, but were called back a week later when they received word that his mother died on July 15, 1921. The funeral was held in his parents' home and it was a very hard time.

"Your little sisters and brother are still so young," Helena said as they travelled back to Blumeheim for the funeral. "Justina is only three and needs her mother. Maria and the twins, Henry and Anna, do too."

"I don't know what my father will do. He is blind and has to rely on Wilhem, Herman and Isbrand for the farming," Jacob replied.

A few months later they learned that Jacob's father was going to marry a widow. Her name was Maria (Wiens) Janzen and her husband had died the year before. She had eight children. Her oldest daughter was already married.

On November 6th, just four months after Jacob's mother died, his father married Mrs. Janzen. Once again Jacob and Helena travelled to Blumenheim.

On the return trip Helena said, "Your parents' house is going to be very crowded with seven of your step-mother's children and seven of your own brothers and sisters still at home."

"Well, if all of the older children from both families work hard, it should make the farming and gardening easier," Jacob replied.

Weddings for Two Sisters

CHAPTER 42

The summer of 1922 they moved to Blumenheim with their one year old baby and stayed there for two years. They found a little house to rent and Jacob again taught school.

A few months after they arrived, Helena received a letter telling her that her sister Susanna was going to be married to Cornelius Peters on November 26.

"Do you think we could go?" Helena asked Jacob.

"I don't think it would be safe. The ferry won't be running anymore and the river ice might not be thick enough to travel on with the horses and sleigh," Jacob replied. They decided not to risk it, but Helena was disappointed. It would be so nice to see her family again.

They were often at the Friesen grandparents' family home, helping out with things on the farm and with the younger children. Baby Helena was a favourite with her young aunts, Anna, Maria and Justina. Everyone called her 'Lena.

Just before Christmas they travelled the six miles to the town of Osler to buy a few things for Christmas and for some material for Helena to sew something new for her little girl. It was good to be able to wander around the little store and look at all the things for sale and also good to get away from Blumenheim for a while.

The winter months passed slowly and they looked forward to spring and some warmer weather. Helena and her sisters-in-law did some quilting and the family visited relatives in the area.

Warm spring weather arrived and changed the dirty white landscape into a dark muddy place. Fortunately, the soil in the village was sandy and the water soon soaked into the ground. Helena looked forward to seeing the plum and cherry trees bloom at Jacob's father's farm. When gardening time arrived in May, Helena was able to plant a bit of a garden. She enjoyed weeding and looking after it.

After a hot summer with lots of rain, the gardens were looking lovely and Helena began to pick the peas, beans and beets she had planted. Some days were very tiring. She was expecting another baby in December.

Harvesting days arrived soon and the young Friesen and Janzen men cut hay and oats for the cattle for the winter. Helena and her sisters-in-law canned vegetables and fruit, and made big meals for the large family. It was a loud, noisy place with arguing and laughing during meal times. It was good to be able to go back to the quiet house they were living in and have some space and peace.

In November of 1923, Helena and Jacob received a letter from her sister Anna, telling them that she was going to be married to David Buhler on December 4th.

"Why do my sisters have to get married in winter?" Helena asked. Her baby was due at the end of December and she wasn't sure she could travel.

"I'll see if anyone knows if the winter road across the river is safe. The last few weeks have been very cold," Jacob said. In a few days he had an answer and told her that several people had already travelled that road. They could go!

The day before the wedding they hitched up the horses to the cotta and after putting warm quilts and some food in the sleigh, they bundled up little Lena and began the trip. They were concerned about travelling over the ice on the river and drove slowly. It would be terrible if the horses slipped and were injured. However the ride went well and they stopped in Aberdeen to rest the horses before going on to Helena's parents' home south of the town.

The next day they went to the Buhler's home for the wedding and Helena enjoyed spending time with her parents and siblings. Her sister Anna was now married as well and that made three of the sisters married women. They had a lot to talk about.

Baby Jake Arrives

CHAPTER 43

After returning from the wedding, they busily prepared for Christmas. Jacob's school children were ready to recite all the poems they had learned and Helena baked cookies. On December 22nd, she realized their baby was coming and called Jacob to get a midwife to help her.

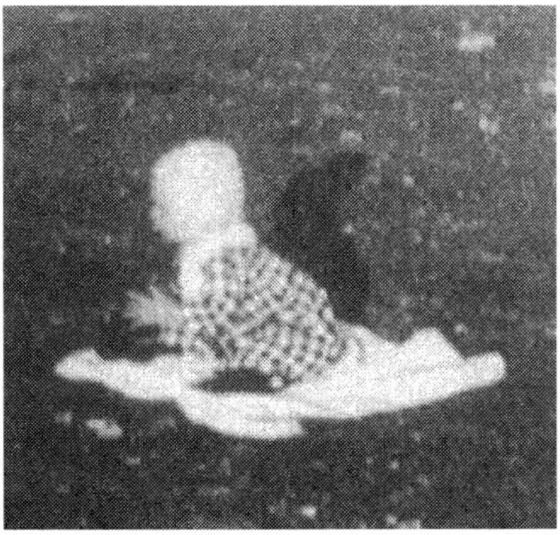

Baby Jake at about seven months

It didn't take long and Helena was holding her first baby boy. After the midwife washed the baby and wrapped him in a new blanket, she walked into the living room and held him out to Jacob.

The new father beamed with pride as he looked into the tiny face looking up at him. Sitting down beside Helena on the bed with the little one in his arms, he said, "Our first boy. He has dark hair just like little Lena does and he will have my name, 'Jacob'. We can call him Jake."

Lena was two years old and was able to talk and understand what was said to her. Life was happy for her. She had loving parents and aunts to play with her.

One summer day some friends came over for a visit and brought a camera. Not many people in the village owned a camera so it was exciting to have your picture taken. People had to sit or stand perfectly still so that the pictures would turn out.

As Jacob and Helena watched their friend take pictures, Jacob said, "Take a picture of little Lena!" and he stood his daughter in the yard as the camera man said, "Lena! Eck voa de auf namen!" at which Lena looked terrified and began to cry because she thought she would die. Direct translation of his words was 'I am going to take you off'.

Helena comforted her little girl and explained that she would not die, but Lena was still very afraid when her picture was taken.

Two year old Lena

A Confession

CHAPTER 44

In the spring of 1924 they moved back to Olgafeld. The Regiers moved off of their farm and Jacob & Helena tried again to work their land and look after their cows.

Soon after their arrival, they were invited to a wedding. While visiting with a family a few days before the event, Helena heard something interesting.

"There are some families getting ready to move to Mexico because they don't want their children educated in the English schools," one of their friends said. "One of the families leaving is the Henry Dycks. They'll be at the wedding too."

Helena sat up a little straighter. "Really? The Henry Dycks?" she asked. She had not seen that family for many years. It had been the first place she worked when she was almost eleven years old.

Her mind was working hard as they travelled back to their farm. She had an anxious feeling in the pit of her stomach and when the children were tucked into bed and Jacob was out making sure the horses and cattle had enough feed for the night, she knelt down beside the rocking chair.

"Liebe Vater im Himmel (Dear Father in Heaven)," she prayed, "I have always wished I could make things right with Mrs.

Dyck. I have felt guilty for so long because I took apples from her cellar when I was peeling potatoes down there. I know it was stealing because I didn't ask for them. Now we'll be at the same wedding. Please help me make it right."

The day of the wedding arrived. When the ceremony at the groom's home was over and people were eating their faspa, Helena saw Mrs. Dyck walk over to the garden area. With a prayer in her heart, she followed and greeted the lady.

"Helena! It's good to see you again. Now you're grown up and married with a family of your own."

"It's good to see you too, Mrs. Dyck," Helena answered. "I've wanted to make something right with you for a long time now. Do you remember when my sisters boarded with you for school and I was working for you?"

"Yes I remember."

Helena took a deep breath. "When I went to peel potatoes down in your cellar I sometimes ate an apple from the barrel without asking you first. I just wanted to tell you that I am sorry."

Mrs. Dyck looked at her for a moment and then said, "Well I have something to make right with you, too. I was very hard on you because you couldn't milk as well as I could. When my daughter Mary was old enough to milk, she couldn't do it either. I was much too hard on you and I am sorry for that too."

Helena was relieved and surprised. Suddenly she was wrapped in a tight hug as Mrs. Dyck said, "Now we'll be better friends than before!"

As Helena and her husband returned home from the wedding, she felt so free, forgiven and happy. Many times as she went about her chores over the next few days she softly thanked God for giving her the opportunity to make things right with Mrs. Dyck.

Selling the Farm and Welcoming a New Baby

CHAPTER 45

The farm work kept the couple busy, but in his spare time Jacob was able to build a little table and chair set for Lena. It would be her Christmas present. He made a little wooden horse for Jake.

Every day the cows had to be milked, fed and given water. There were chickens and pigs to look after but there was no way to really make money to pay bills unless they sold some of their animals.

One day in November of the next year, 1925, they received notice that the mortgage payment was due. Helena saw the worry on her husband's face as he sat staring at the letter from the bank.

"We'll have to sell the farm," Jacob told Helena. "We don't have the money for the payment."

"But this is the house your Wiebe grandparents built in 1902." Helena said. "Isn't there some way we can keep it in the family?"

"No. Isbrand and Katherina can't afford the payment either and they wanted us to take it over. We just don't have enough."

So even though they were both disappointed, they found a buyer. Mr. Isaac Schellenberg was able to take over the mortgage payments and give them a little money which they divided between themselves and the Regiers. Jacob and Helena moved into a house in the nearby village of Edenburg.

As they brought their things into the house they had rented, Helena saw a lovely, dark red corner cabinet with glass doors, in the living room.

"Look, Jacob! This is such a nice cupboard. It's almost like the one in your parents' home. I really like this house."

"You can put your good dishes in it. My mother kept her best things in her corner cabinet," Jacob told her as he wrestled the heavy kamoud (chest of drawers) over to where she wanted it.

She felt like she was in a very special house and wasted no time unpacking her things. She placed her pretty cut glass wedding gifts on the shelves and her blue glass hen bowl on the top shelf.

Jacob went back to teaching school. Helena enjoyed just being a wife and a mother to her two little ones. Lena was now four years old. Jake was nearly two and another baby was on the way. Helena was busy sewing little blankets, diapers and nightgowns.

A visit from her parents, brothers and sisters near the end of that month was exciting! Papa Banman enjoyed jiggling little Jake on his knee while the young aunties and uncles played with little Lena. Her auntie Margaret was only four years older and they had fun playing together.

"I really like your corner china cabinet," Mama said as she looked at the pretty dishes displayed there. Turning to Helena she asked, "How are you feeling these days with another baby on the way?"

"I'm all right, except that I'm so very tired most of the time," Helena answered.

"That is understandable since you look like you could have

this baby any day now. Are you ready? Do you have enough baby clothes?"

"I think I have enough, although I wish I had more diapers. I've washed and folded all the little clothes from the last two babies along with some new ones that I sewed. I've put them in the top dresser drawer," Helena said as she walked over to the kamoud to show her mother the baby clothes and blankets.

After faspa and a good visit, the Banmans left. Helena waved goodbye from the doorway of the house.

On the evening of December 1, 1925, a little baby girl was born.
When the midwife left and Lena and Jake were brought home, Helena asked, "You have a little baby sister. What would you like to name her, Annie or Tena?"

Lena looked down at the new baby and said, "I want to call her Annie!" She was delighted to have a real baby to play with. Two year old Jake found his new sister interesting but had to be watched so that he didn't touch her too roughly.

Moving to Osler

CHAPTER 46

A few days after the new baby was born, Jacob told Helena, "My brother David Friesen is living on a farm near Osler and I heard they want move off of it. He's going to be working for the Railroad. I'm interested in renting it."

"Moving again?" Helena said in a tired voice. "I really don't want to leave this house and you have a teaching job here."

"Yes, I know, but for how long? I am often asked to teach in other villages and we've moved several times to teach on both sides of the river. But if I could farm, have some cows, I could earn enough to buy some land and we would have our own place again. And you know there's a train running through the town to the city of Saskatoon and Osler has some stores as well. I'm going to write a letter and tell them I'm interested."

Osler farm house before renovations

A week later, Jacob took his horse drawn sleigh down to the river, crossed the ice road and drove to the farm. His brother David met him and they walked around the yard in the snow and looked at the house.

"The land belongs to the Trust Company Bank," David told

him. "You'll have to rent it from them. I'll give you the address to write to." Jacob saw that the house was old, but it had three rooms on the main floor and two upstairs. There was a veranda on the outside of the west wall.

"We'll take it," Jacob told his brother. He mailed a letter to the bank and returned to Edenberg to tell Helena what he had decided.

"We'll move as soon as I hear from the bank," he told her. Helena's heart sank at the prospect of moving in the cold winter with three little ones and at the thought of leaving the house that she loved. On top of that she had just had a new baby and was feeling very weak.

Little Annie was barely three weeks old when they packed their belongings on an open sleigh, bundled up the children, put heated stones at their feet and began the journey to Osler. Helena sat beside Jacob holding the baby wrapped in extra blankets while little Lena and Jake were covered with blankets on the floor of the sleigh.

The sun shone brightly on the snowy road and as long as there were no clouds covering the sun, it was not that cold. After nearly an hour of travel they arrived at the river and began the descent down to the river road. Jacob hung on to the reins and pulled back to keep the horses from running too fast down the hill. It was hard on the horses because the sleigh was heavily loaded with all of their things.

About the time they were nearly across the river, the baby began to cry. She was tightly wrapped up to keep out the cold, but needed more space to breathe. Besides, she was hungry and needed to nurse.

"Can't you get her settled down?" asked Jacob.

"She's hungry and probably wet. We need to stop at a farm so that I can feed her," Helena replied.

"That will slow us down and we might not get to Osler until dark".

"I can't feed her outside - it's far too cold for her!" Helena answered.

Annie's cries decided it for them and when they got to the nearest farm, they stopped and asked if they could go in to warm up and feed the baby. The family living there gladly welcomed them in and Helena sat quietly in a bedroom feeding the fussy baby.

The lady of the house made some faspa and they had a light lunch before they continued on. They finally arrived at the farm only to find out that David and his family had not yet moved out. They turned around and drove six miles to Blumenheim and stayed with Jacob's parents for a few days.

It was good to get off the sleigh, out of the cold and into a warm place but the next few days were almost a nightmare for Helena. With such a full house of children and teenagers, there was not much privacy and they didn't have their own room to sleep in. Helena found it stifling and worried about the baby keeping everyone awake at night. Besides, she was still so very weak and not getting much sleep with the new baby needing to eat every few hours.

A few days later they again set out for the farm near Osler. It was a bitterly cold day and the six miles seemed very long. When they got there, they found the old coal and wood burning cook-stove was not set up and there was straw on the floor.

Jacob connected all the stove pipes and got a fire going and then they cleaned up the straw.

Cook stove photo –Osler Museum

Before Helena could wash herself and the children she had to bring in snow to melt so that they could have water. Then she wondered what she would feed her family. All they had was some buns that her in-laws had sent with them. Their other food was still packed.

After they set up the beds and lit the kerosene lamps, she got the children ready for bed. Jacob went outside with a lantern and took the horses into the barn. He fed them hay and gave them pails of well water to drink. The barn was old and not very big but it would keep some of the cold out for the animals.

First Impressions

CHAPTER 47

The next morning, after building a fire in the old cook stove, Helena found her pots and pans and the oatmeal and made porridge. She ground up the coffee beans while heating the water in the kettle and then poured the coffee grounds into it. She pulled the table as close to the stove as she could so they would all feel warmer.

Four year old Lena and two year old Jake climbed out of their bed and shivering in the cold came running into the kitchen.

"Here," Helena said as she helped them on to the bench at the table. "I'll wrap this blanket around you two and then we'll have breakfast."

Jacob reached for the coffee kettle and brought it to the table, filling his cup and Helena's. Setting the kettle back on the stove, he came to the table, sat down and bowing his head prayed, "Come Lord Jesus, be our guest and bless the food you have given us. Amen."

"Do you want some sugar Lena?" Jacob asked as he leaned over to put some on her porridge. The little girl nodded and little Jake pointed to his bowl. Papa sprinkled it onto their cereal and they picked up their spoons.

"Mama, I want milk on my porridge," Lena said.

"There is no milk yet. We have to buy some," Helena replied. "Just eat it – your Papa will get some from the neighbour today."

So the porridge was eaten without milk and after the two oldest were fed and occupied with a few toys, Helena pushed the table out of the way and pulled the rocking chair close to the stove. She went to the cradle where Annie was beginning to cry and brought her to the kitchen. Sitting down in the rocking chair, Helena nursed her tiny baby.

Jacob filled another cup with coffee and sat down in a chair for a while, looking around at the old house they had moved into.

"With some cleaning and fixing, I think this will be a good place some day," he observed.

Helena gazed at the bare wooden floor boards and at the shelves that served as cupboards. She saw the thick frost on the inside of the window panes and the boxes of their things still unpacked and said nothing.

Instead she looked down at the little fair haired baby gazing up into her face and at the tiny little fist resting on her breast and thought, "Somehow I have to make this place nice for my little ones. One of the first things I want to do is to paint the floor boards." Annie paused in her nursing. Her little mouth curved briefly into a smile before she began to nurse again.

"She smiled!" she said. Jacob grinned and leaned over the baby.

After breakfast Jacob went to Osler to buy flour, sugar, eggs and sausage and then drove to the nearest neighbour, the Nickoli Dycks, to ask if he could buy some milk.

"Komm inen (Come in)!" Mrs. Dyck said as she opened the door for Jacob. "You must be our new neighbour. Welcome!"

"Gouden moryen (Good morning)," Jacob said. "I'm Jacob W. Friesen. My family and I moved here from the village of Edenburg. I was wondering if we could buy milk from you until we can buy our own cows, if you have some to spare."

"Oh yes, we usually have more than we can use," she said. "Could you use some butter and cream too? I made the butter yesterday."

"Yes we could. Dankeschoen (Thank you). It would help a lot," Jacob replied.

Soon he was home again and brought the groceries in as the children ran to meet him at the door. Jacob chuckled as they looked at him expectantly.

"Here you are – I brought you each a candy," he said as he handed them each a peppermint. Lena sucked her candy, enjoying it slowly, while little Jake quickly crunched his. Meanwhile Helena took the food out of the bags.

"Butter and cream! Did you get it from the store too?" she asked her husband.

"Our neighbours, the Nickoli Dycks live just over there." he said as he pointed south of their home. "I stopped in and asked them if they had any milk to spare and Mrs. Dyck offered the butter and cream as well."

As dinner time neared, Helena decided to make miylk zup (milk soup). She heated some milk slowly on the stove and made tiny dumplings out of flour, egg, cream and butter and then crumbled them into the milk, cooking them until they were done. She added salt and pepper for seasoning.

After dinner she put both Annie and Jake down for naps and

gave Lena a pencil and a piece of the wrapping paper that the sausage had been wrapped in. The paper was waxed on one side, so she wiped it off with the dish cloth and then turned it over for Lena to draw on the paper side. She needed a nap herself and lay down on the bed for a rest. It wasn't long before Lena appeared at the bed, waking her and asking for a drink.

Helena got up, glad that the other two children were still sleeping and gave Lena her drink. Then she started cleaning. First she swept the kitchen floor and then unpacked the rest of the dishes and food.

Jacob walked back into the house and saw her cleaning. As she began to sweep the living room floor, he moved the kamoud out of the middle of the room and over to one side for her. Looking down, he saw a trap door in the floor.

"There's a cellar here!" He said to his wife. Moving the kamoud out of the way again, he picked up the trap door by the latch, swung it up and leaned it against the wall. Helena went to the kitchen, lit a lamp and went back to the living room. On the way down the steps of the cellar to join Jacob, she saw Lena getting down from her bench to follow her.

"No, Lena, stay back. You might fall in and get hurt," she warned her.

Shining the lamp light around the dark cellar, she spied the potato bin and was happy to find a few potatoes and carrots had been left there. Seeing an old pail under a shelf, she handed the lamp to her husband and put some of the vegetables into the pail. She brought it up the stairs. After looking around the cellar some more, Jacob brought up the lamp and closed the trap door.

"What did you find?" Lena asked.

"I found a few potatoes and carrots. They will taste good with the farmer sausage for our supper tonight," Helena answered.

Over the next weeks she worked hard at scrubbing the floor boards with a big brush. She also spent many hours carrying in pails of snow and melting them on the stove so she could wash the diapers over and over again. Since it was so cold outside, she hung them on chairs close to the stove. Her hands became rough, cracked and sore. Sometimes she rubbed lard on them at night just to soften them up.

Helena was exhausted with the work of looking after two busy children, a crying baby, washing diapers, making meals and cleaning the house. Some days she felt overwhelmed with a sadness she couldn't understand and thought back to Edenburg. She wished she hadn't had to leave her nice house.

Gardens and a Dog named Pup

CHAPTER 48

As winter turned to spring and the sun shone longer in a day, Helena began to feel stronger both in body and in spirit. Now that the baby was sleeping through the night, she was getting more rest. She eagerly looked forward to decorating the house and wondered what kind of a garden patch lay under that last bit of snow.

"Seeds!" she thought. "That's what I need – I need to write to Mama for some garden seeds!"

As the bright sun melted the snow and the air turned warmer, Lena and Jake could run outside in the fresh air. Helena wandered around the yard while they played and Annie slept inside.

"Look," she told Jacob, "there's a lot of space for a garden and there are a few trees too. I would like to plant some fruit trees like your parents' garden has."

"Maybe you can get some tree-shoots from my step mother and plant them here," he answered.

Helena smiled in anticipation of what her garden would look like. When the children needed to go inside to warm up she fed them a snack. Then she went to find some writing paper.

After feeding the little ones, she sat down at the table with her paper and pencil. She wrote to Mama, telling her how excited she was to plant a garden and could Mama please send her some garden seeds.

Jacob worked hard to make this farm work for them. He bought three cows so they had milk to drink and cream to make butter. He bought a second hand plough and used one of his horses to pull it so he could plough a garden patch for Helena.

It wasn't long before Jacob brought home a little package from the Post Office after going to Osler for some supplies. It was from Mama! Helena now had her garden seeds. She got busy making rows and planting vegetables.

One day they drove over to Jacob's parents in Blumenheim to dig up some fruit tree shoots for Helena's garden. She wanted red plums, yellow plums, cherries and gooseberries. The plants needed lots of water and Helena hauled up many buckets of water from the old well near the house, and carried them to her garden plants.

Jacob thought he needed a good dog for the farm and got a black and white female collie from some neighbours. It was a puppy but it was nearly full grown.

"I want to train this dog to fetch the cows for milking," he told Helena at supper one day.

"She also needs to be good with children," she said. "I don't want her biting them when they try to play with her. What should we call the dog?"

Little Lena answered for her, "Her name should be 'Pup'! Her parents laughed and agreed, and 'Pup' it was.

So the training of the dog began. Jacob would call her to come with him to the pasture to get the cows.

"Sic'em!" Jacob said as he pointed to a cow wandering off. The dog learned quickly and ran for the cow, but kept nipping at its' heels. After a stern punishment whenever the dog bit the cows, she learned to obey. Now she only barked at them, running around them and herding them toward the barn.

After each successful round-up of the cattle, Pup was praised and petted. She obeyed when told to 'stay', 'sit' or 'lie down'.

Lena and little Jake loved playing outside, running around the big yard with the dog following them.

One day when Helena was busy weeding in the garden and Lena and Jake were playing nearby, she decided to see if she could trust the dog to take care of little Annie. Placing the baby on a blanket near the garden, she called "Pup!" and the dog came running.
Helena pointed to the baby and said, "Stay. Watch the baby."

Pup walked over to Annie, sniffed her and lay down beside her. After a while little Annie decided to roll over. She crawled on her tummy to the edge of the blanket. Pup watched her for a while and then got up, walked over to her and picked her up by her clothing! Helena gasped in alarm, but Pup merely pulled Annie back to the middle of the blanket. Helena relaxed. A smile spread over her face.

That evening Helena told Jacob about the dog. "I watched her pick Annie up and pull her back to the blanket! Now I know we can trust this dog with the children and Lena and Jake love playing with her."

"She is getting better with the cows all the time. I'm glad we got her," Jacob said. "It will also be good to have her around to let us know if coyotes or foxes come near the farm."

At the end of July they received word that Helena's Grandma Banman/Hamm who lived in Mexico had died on July 15th, 1926. She had lived to be 94 years old.

The sun was warm. The rain was just enough to help the hay crop and, along with buckets of water from the well, Helena's garden was doing well, too. Her little fruit trees were growing new leaves! Jacob's relatives brought over rhubarb and currant bushes to plant.

Soon Lena and Jake were helping to pull up new carrots. Helena showed them how to rub off the dirt with the carrot top and then they munched the crisp sweet vegetables. Then there were fresh young green pea pods and they loved to chew on these too.

Early in the mornings after feeding and changing Annie and before the other children awoke, Helena spent time in her garden while Jacob milked the three cows. She listened for sounds of the children from the house, but it was her quiet, restful time, pulling weeds and thanking God for His good gifts. She had not wanted to come to this poor house and farm, but now she loved this place; the feel of the ground, the perfume of the flowers, the soft cool morning breeze and the songs of the birds in the old trees that stood in the middle of the garden.

She imagined the caragana hedge she would plant one day along one side of the garden and the rows of fruit trees she would one day be picking from. And flowers... she would grow so many more kinds of flowers!

"Mama!" she heard Lena calling from the house, and her quiet space was interrupted by the needs of her little ones. Walking back to the house she pulled one more Russian thistle plant from her flower patch and then went into the house to make porridge for her family.

Jacob brought in two pails of milk and poured them through the cloth strainer into clean pails. They sat down for their breakfast and talked about their work for the day.

"I still have a lot of milk left from two days ago," Helena said. "By tomorrow it may be sour and thick enough to make 'glums'(cottage cheese)."

"Good!" Jacob said. "It's been a while since we had vereneki (perogies)."

Two days later Helena checked the sour milk. It was thick enough but first she made a summer treat for the noon meal. She dipped out some of it and poured it into a big bowl, whipping it up smoothly. Walking to the garden with the children chattering and following her, she broke off some onion greens and checked to see if there were any cucumbers ready for eating. Finding several, she returned to the house. She washed the greens and cucumbers and sliced them into the thick sour milk.

Lena and Jake watched, begging for cucumber slices which they ate with a little sprinkle of salt. Then it was time to run outside and play again.

Meanwhile, Helena put more wood on the fire and set the rest of the sour milk to heat on the stove. At noon she called Jacob and the children who were all at the barn. Setting the table, she put a bowl of thick sour milk in each place, along with slices of bread and butter. It was a hot day, so the cool sour milk with the vegetables in it tasted creamy and good to them all.

Taking some cream, egg white, salt and flour, Helena made vereneki dough while the sour milk on the stove slowly turned into cottage cheese. When it was ready the cheese curds remained at the top of the cooking pot and the whey stayed at the bottom. She strained the cheese curds in a colander and then crumbled them into little pieces in a bowl. Adding egg yolk, salt and pepper to the cheese curds, she set that aside while she roll out the dough.

After cutting round pieces of dough with a big cup pressed on the dough, she put several spoonfuls of the cottage cheese mixture in the middle of each round. She folded the dough circles over, pressing the edges to seal the vereneki and then dropped them into boiling water to cook for several minutes.

Supper that night was wonderful! Jacob and the children loved the meal. They poured cream gravy over the vereneki and enjoyed every bite.

"Tomorrow we'll have summa borscht!" Helena told them. She set the pot of whey at the back of the stove. It would be used for the borscht the next day.

On Sundays, Jacob hitched the horses to the wagon and they travelled to Blumenheim for church. It was a day of visiting with family and old friends and faspa at Lena and Jake's Friesen grandparents. Their uncle Henry and Aunt Anna (twins), loved to play with them. Henry gave them many wagon rides, one day being careless and tipping it over. Then he tried to comfort the children. Aunt Justina, only a few years older than Lena enjoyed carrying baby Annie around.

One Sunday Jacob looked over at Helena and said, "Helena, you haven't worn your kruzshel metz for a long time. Why don't you wear it?"

"It just doesn't feel right. I feel like it's for old women. I think I look old when I wear that so I'd rather just wear the shawl." Jacob raised his eyebrows a bit and shrugged. "You don't look old, but if you don't want to wear the metz, that's fine with me."

In August, Jacob began to cut the hay with a scythe and pile it on to a stack near the barn. It was hard work but rewarding because he knew he would have almost enough hay for his animals for the winter. Meanwhile, Helena picked peas and beans, canning them for the winter. They enjoyed corn on the cob meals, fresh cabbage and carrot salads, and the fresh potatoes.

At the end of August the family drove to the ferry and crossed the river to go and see Helena's family. The whole Banman family tried to get together once a year in the summer and everyone looked forward to seeing each other again. By now her sisters, Anna and Susanna, both had children and the little cousins got to know one another.

Smelly Foundations

CHAPTER 49

In October there were pig butchering days. Even though at that time they didn't have their own pigs, Jacob and Helena helped the farmers and relatives in the area and were able to bring home some meat from each place.

One day a wagon loaded with firewood drove onto the yard. The drivers were First Nations people from northern Saskatchewan. Jacob went out to meet them. Between their broken English and his broken English it was hard to make a sale, but Jacob understood they wanted to sell the wood so he bought it.

Both Jacob and Helena were relieved that they now had firewood and hoped it would last all winter.

Through the winter, the family spent a lot of time inside the house, trying to keep warm.

Each day when Jacob shovelled the manure out of the barn before it froze in the gutters, he hauled it to the house in a wheel barrow and dumped it against the foundation of the house for extra insulation.

"It smells so bad!" Helena complained.

"It will freeze," Jacob replied. "Along with the snow I

shovel against the house it will be a little extra insulation."

"And when it melts in the spring?" Helena asked.

Jacob frowned at his wife and said, "I'm doing the best I can to make the house a little warmer!" Helena decided not to comment.

They found someone who wanted to sell their small pot-bellied stove and bought it for the living room. That room and the bedroom were both too cold so now they would have heat in them as well as in the kitchen.

Now Annie was a year old and had learned to walk, toddling after Lena and Jake wherever they went. There was so much to get into: the curtains covering the cupboard shelves; the wood box and the coal scoop. Lena was constantly pulling her away from things, but determined Annie screamed her protest. Jake telling her "No!" and taking away the pot lids, the black coal pieces and small blocks of wood only helped make her more upset.

Sighing, Helena calmed the chaos by giving Lena and Jake a box of buttons play with and occupying Annie with a rag doll.

She looked forward to the day they could be outside again and she could be in her garden. Jacob brought small toys home from the Osler store and whittled wooden horses for the children while he sat near the warm stove. Helena sewed and mended clothes and knitted zocken and stockings for them all. When the children were down for the night, she crocheted pretty doilies and baby slippers remembering the patterns she had learned while she watched one of the women she worked for so long ago.

Some days Jacob walked to Osler to sit near the big pot-bellied stove in the store and visit with other men who did the same. He came home one day, walking fast to keep warm and as he stepped into the door and took off his cap he looked at Helena with a pleased "Wait 'til you hear this!" look on his face.

Drawing out a piece of paper from his pocket, he handed it

to Helena who looked at it blankly. "What's this? You know I can't read much English," she said.

"This is a form to order baby chicks! They come from the hatchery in Saskatoon and are shipped on the train. On the day they arrive in the spring, everyone has to pick up his order and take them home. Helena! We can order chicks and you can raise them and have your own eggs and chickens!"

She beamed at him. "I have been wishing we could get chickens! I didn't know where to get them." Sitting down at the table, they carefully filled out the order for one hundred baby chicks.

Helena was filled with excitement. Her mind moved ahead to the future. This year would be good. By fall, the chicks would be fully grown into hens and roosters. She would keep some of the hens and one rooster. She could butcher some for food and she would have eggs to sell in exchange for flour and other things at the store.

Baby Chicks

CHAPTER 50

The spring of 1927 came early and Helena welcomed the melting snow, warm air and the sound of birds returning. One day Jacob returned from Osler with the horses and wagon and drove near the house. He got down and pulled a big square blanket covered box from the wagon.

Helena was stirring soup at the stove and she turned to see him walk into the kitchen with the box. He grinned at her surprised face as she realized what he was carrying. From the box came tiny little "cheep, cheep" noises! The baby chicks had arrived! Helena frowned suddenly. It was still too cold to put them in a shed outside. "But we'll figure something out," she thought and smiled.

"Look, kingya (children)!" Helena said as Jacob put the box on the floor near the stove.

Lena, Jake and Annie gathered round while their papa took the lid off of the box. Tiny little balls of fluffy yellow milled around each other in the box, cheeping loudly and looking at the people above them.

"May we hold them?" asked Lena. Her mama picked up a little chick and put one in each of their cupped hands. "Hold them very carefully. Don't squeeze them." she told them.

Jacob watched the delighted faces of his little ones with a big smile on his own. "I brought some 'Chick Starter' food for them," he said. He turned to look at Helena, "I know they'll make a mess but we'll have to keep them in the house until the little shed on the yard is warm enough for them."

Helena nodded. She didn't like the idea of her house smelling like a chicken barn, but it would only be for a short time.

It didn't take long for the baby chicks to grow feathers and hop out of the box. The children were kept busy putting them back many times a day. Finally Helena was tired of the mess the chicks made all over the floor, and the smell, so she and Jacob prepared the little shed for them. Now she could wash the floor and try to keep it cleaner.

At the beginning of May she was thinking about her garden. She had harvested as many seeds as she could from last year but wanted more, so picking up a pencil and paper, she wrote to her mother to tell her about how their second winter at their farm had turned out.

She asked for more seeds if her mother could spare them and added, "And could you also send some watermelon and flower seeds?" The middle of May would be a good time to plant her garden.

She led the horse as Jacob held the plough and worked up the garden soil for her. It was tiring but exciting to see the black ground loosened up and ready for planting. Ah! New life in spring! She couldn't wait to plant and put in potatoes and all the seeds she had harvested the year before.

Near the middle of the month of May a letter arrived from Mama; *(this is a translation of an actual letter)*
Aberdeen – May 18, 1927

Dear Children,

Since we have received another letter from you, I must answer it. Yes, dear daughter, you ask about watermelon seeds – I will send them to you, but the flower seeds you mentioned completely slipped my mind and I had them all planted by the time we received your letter.

You asked about the Cornie Peters. They have a little baby boy whom they named David. He was quite chubby when we were there. Since then we haven't heard from them, but if things were not going well, I'm sure we would hear from them. Susanna did not have to endure as much this time as she did for her first child. Maybe they will be able to come here at Pentecost. If only you could all come home – that would make me happy.

The seeding time around here is not nearly finished. We have 40 acres seeded to wheat and 5 to oats. Right now Julius is seeding and Father is harrowing.

The Jacob Martens were very glad to get some potatoes from us. They didn't have many.

I must stop writing. I've given you lots of news. We are all well, which is what we wish for all of you from our hearts.

Goodbye from your parents, J. and H. Banman.

Plans for a Dairy Farm

CHAPTER 51

One warm day in June, while Jacob framed a new chicken coop and Helena worked in her garden, Mr. Abram Driedger drove on to the yard. He was an elevator agent in the town of Osler.

"Ho!" Abram told his horse as he pulled on the reins. He climbed off the buggy as Jacob welcomed him. They led the horse to the water trough and tied the reins to a fence pole.

"What brings you out here today?" asked Jacob.

"Well, I wanted to tell you that I've bought the land you're living on from the trust company. I'm making payments on it, so now your rent will be paid to me instead. I also know that it is nearly impossible for you to make a proper living on these 160 acres unless you have the farming equipment you need." He paused in speaking and Jacob wondered what was coming next.

"I wonder, what do you think of making this a dairy farm and shipping milk or cream to Saskatoon?"

"I would like that very much," replied Jacob, "but so far I can only afford the three cows we have. They give enough milk so that I can bring some to town and trade it for other things, but last winter when there wasn't much milk, it was hard to make ends meet."

Abram took a deep breath and continued, "Well, I would

like to move an old barn onto this property. It would be much more suitable for your cows and it would be warmer in winter than the old one you use now. If you do the work of re-modelling it for a cow barn, I will bring you four more cows. You can pay me for the cows when you earn enough from the milk they will bring."

Jacob thought for a moment and said, "Let me think about it and I will let you know, but come inside for some faspa first."

Abram nodded and they both walked into the house. When Helena saw the men walk toward the house, she hurried from the garden, calling the children to come with her.

She found Jacob putting wood on the fire in the kitchen stove. Helena filled the kettle with water and set it on to heat.

The men visited while the table was set with buns, sugar lumps, and the butter that Helena had made that morning. As she listened to the men's conversation she began to get an idea of what they were planning. She couldn't wait until Abram left so she could ask Jacob about all the details!

After Abram left, Jacob saw her questioning look and explained what Abram had offered.

"It sounds like a good idea," he said. Helena agreed. After some more discussion, they decided that Jacob would go to Osler in a few days and talk to Abram again.

A week later Abram Driedger returned and he and Jacob walked over to where they had decided to put the barn. They measured the ground for the foundation and cement floor that would have to be poured.

They figured out how much cement and gravel would be needed for the floor and how much wood they needed for the stanchions (a stanchion held the cow's head while it was being milked). They went to the local lumber yard to check the prices.

A few days later a truck arrived with a load of gravel. Jacob and Abram went to Osler to load up bags of cement. The Lumber Yard had a cement mixer they could rent. They brought that back as a second load because the cement was heavy for the horses to haul.

The next morning began early with some of Jacob's brothers arriving to help. They built wooden forms for the floor and manure gutters and then filled barrels with water from the well near the house. They also dug a deep hole in front of the barn and made forms for a cistern that would hold water.

The men poured gravel, cement and water into the mixer and took turns turning the handle until it was mixed. They dumped it into a wheel barrow and then poured it into the floor forms.

After many loads of cement and several days of very hard work the foundation was ready. A week later, a large truck arrived pulling the barn which sat on heavy beams and with much shouting of orders and moving around, it was settled on the foundation. Jacob breathed a sigh of relief. Now it was time for him to get started building a lean-to at the south end of the barn which would also cover the cistern.

Helena had a lot of days of uninterrupted work in the garden and the house, as the three little ones followed their papa around the new barn as he built the stanchions. She could hear their laughter as they ran in and out of the barn, their voices echoing inside the empty building.

She took the opportunity to paint the wood floors in the house. While the paint was drying in the kitchen the family used the back door in the living room.

After the paint dried, Helena moved the furniture back into place. It looked so fresh and clean in the house. It took about a week to finish painting all the floors.

She and Jacob wandered through the barn and admired the new stanchions and the new cement floor. Helena looked up into the beams of the barn ceiling and felt her heart begin to swell with pride. Quickly she took a deep breath and squelched those feelings. She had been taught that pride was a sin. She mustn't be proud.

Lena Goes to School

CHAPTER 52

The summer was hot and windy and they checked the oat crop in the field often as they waited for rain. The garden needed rain too, but Helena carried lots of pails of water from the well to keep things growing.

Finally there was a big downpour of rain with a bit of hail. It didn't do much damage and the farmers in the area were thankful for the moisture.

In the fall Mr. Abram Driedger arrived with four more cows and the men unloaded them into the pasture to get acquainted with the other three.

"I guess you won't get too much milk during the winter," Mr. Driedger said. "All four cows will have calves in the spring, so maybe you can ship cream until next spring. Then all seven cows will start producing a lot of milk. You'll also need to build a cooling house for the milk before the inspector allows you to ship it."

That evening as Helena helped Jacob with the milking they discussed the building of a cooling house while the children played with Pup the dog.

"I'll build a little house with a cement trough in it. We'll have to haul water from the well to fill it. The cooling house will also have to have insulated walls so that the water stays cold. It's a good thing we built that cistern in the barn. We can hang the pails of milk down in there until the new trough is finished," Jacob said.

They applied to the Dairy Pool in Saskatoon for a permit so they could ship cream. It was a lot of hard work to get the little house built and then they needed to buy a milk and cream separator.

"It seems like everything we need so that we can make some money costs more money to buy!" Helena commented.

"We should be able to start shipping by September," Jacob replied. "After that it will be good to get those cream checks in the mail."

So the days were filled with work – hard work, and Helena was often called on to help with holding up walls and bringing Jacob the things he needed. Then there were the seven cows to milk every morning and evening.

After the milk had sat in the pails for a few hours, all the cream rose to the top, so Helena collected as many empty jars as she could find and filled them with cream. Then she stirred the cream and milk that was left and put it in syrup pails with lids. Everyday Jacob took the cream and milk to Osler to sell it or exchange it for groceries.

That fall the family had a visitor from the school district. He told them that all children in the area who were six years old and older must now go to the English school in Osler. After he left, Jacob and Helena discussed the situation. Jacob had always taught in German schools, but now things were changing. The government had decided that children must learn English.

"I know that many of the Mennonite families don't want their children learning English," Jacob said, "but I think it would be good for our children to learn it. I would also like to learn the language properly so that I can understand and speak it better when I go to town and to the bank."

They decided to take Lena to the school when it started at the beginning of September. Helena washed and ironed her little dress, combed and braided her hair and packed a little lunch. Jacob hitched the horses to the wagon and drove Lena to Osler.

When Lena returned home after school, her parents wanted to know what she thought of it.

"I can't understand what they say," Lena said, "but the girls played with me on the swing! The teacher calls me 'Helen'."

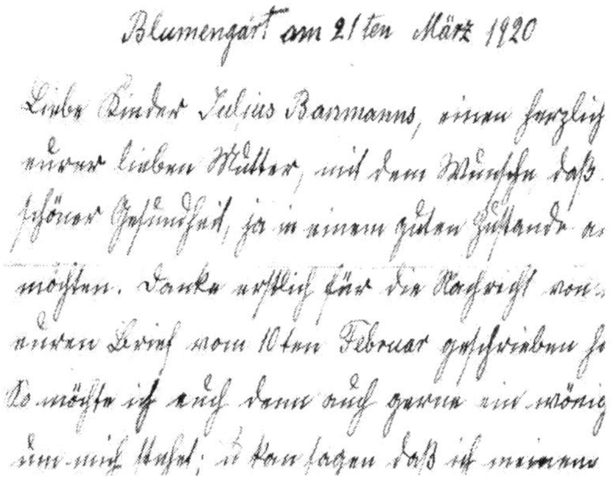
Blumengart am 21ten März 1920

Liebe Kinder Julius Barmanns, einen herzlich

euren lieben Mutter, mit dem Wunsche daß

schöner Gesundheit, sie in einem guten Zustande

möchten. Danke erstlich für die Nachricht von

euren Brief vom 10ten Februar geschrieben

So möchte ich euch denn auch gerne ein wenig

[illegible] ich kann sagen daß ich meinen

As the weeks went by, Lena was learning more and more words and reciting the alphabet. Not wanting her to forget the German language, her papa began teaching her the German alphabet and taught her how to write the script letters.

Jacob began cutting hay and harvesting the oat crop. It was disappointing to see that there might not be quite enough to feed the animals through the winter. With a hot summer and not enough rain, the farmers in the area were worried.

Jacob also decided that in order to keep the house warmer for winter, he needed to close off the door to the back yard and the door leading to the veranda. So he was very busy with that as well as harvesting.

During that fall season, Helena was not feeling very well. She was expecting another baby in winter. She hadn't heard from her parents for a while and decided to write a letter to ask about how their family was doing and to tell them they would become grandparents again. She received a reply early in December.

*Aberdeen – December 5, 1927 (*translation of actual unfinished letter*)*

Dear Children,

Since we recently received a letter from you in which you state that you have not been well, I hope that you are feeling better by now.

Our going to see you will probably not happen very soon, because your father is not well at all. Last week he lay around most of the time. Today he slept some but still isn't able to eat.

We are not nearly ready for winter, but it has arrived anyway. Today they went to haul some straw and if it is nice out tomorrow and your father feels well enough to go with them, they want to start out early in the morning. Julius and Peter are doing most of the work around the farm. The weather is getting colder and they are trying to get more straw so that the animals will have enough to rest on in the barn through the winter.

Your parents, Julius and Helena Banman

Helena was very concerned after receiving the letter. Kneeling beside her rocking chair she prayed for her father and for her family. She soon wrote another letter and asked if it was possible for her parents to visit them in Osler. Annie and Jacob both had bad colds and Helena told her parents about them in her letter, asking for prayer for their health and hoped that her father would soon be well. Another letter arrived the day before Christmas Eve.

Aberdeen – December 19, 1927

Dear Children,

I want to write a little bit about visiting you. It is just not possible now; however, I would like to come on my own.

You asked about Father. If he stays in a warm room he's not too bad, but yesterday we drove out to the Henry Peters and then on the way back we stopped at Martens and visited until evening. On the way back we were travelling against the wind and that was far too cold for him. So last night he could hardly lie down. He had to sit at the stove, or walk until the pain would recede enough for him to lie down again.

We received a letter from the Jacob Klassens on Saturday. They write that Uncle Jacob is not doing well. He has rheumatism in his legs so bad that he sometimes moans in pain.

With our neighbour, Mr. Martens, it seems his life is slowly coming to an end. He is very swollen. Last week they had the doctor come out, who said that he will most likely not live until New Years. But he doesn't know that for sure.

Now about what we're working at here; we want to haul flax straw from Jacob Schellenberg near Aberdeen. We can take as much as we want. We butchered our pigs awhile ago. They were not very fat so we only got approximately one pail of lard per pig.

Now we don't have much to do – at least not in the house. The men are puttering around, but I don't have anything to do.

Now – will you be able to come for Christmas? Please write soon and let me know if your children are well again or not, but we probably won't be able to go to see you before Christmas.
We give you our heartfelt greetings,

From your Parents, J. and H. Banman

Lena's First Christmas Concert

CHAPTER 53

At the farm the Friesen family felt snug and warm as long as their kitchen and living room stoves were kept filled with wood or coal. The children were getting excited about Christmas and learned special poems and scripture to recite at grandma and grandpa Friesen's place on Christmas Day.

Lena excitedly told her family about the school concert that was coming up and sang some of the songs she was learning. Some of the songs had nothing to do with the real meaning of Christmas – Jesus being born in Bethlehem – and Helena and Jacob weren't sure they approved.

The Christmas concert was held on December 23rd and the little school room was crowded with children and parents. There was a decorated tree at the front of the room. Jacob wasn't sure about that either. It seemed a worldly thing to do in light of the true meaning of Christmas but the tree was pretty and sparkling and added to the children's excitement.

Seeing Lena on the stage with the other children singing carols and songs, eased their minds as they saw her shining eyes and heard her voice singing right on key above the other voices! They met many neighbours and parents of Lena's classmates.

After the concert was over the teacher and a school board member went to the decorated tree, picking up brightly wrapped packages. The teacher called out the name on a package and a child came forward to accept the gift. Lena waited for her name to be called.

"Helen Friesen!" the teacher called. Lena eagerly walked forward and took the big box and ran to her parents. Jacob and Helena smiled in anticipation while she tore off the wrapping.

"Oh!" Lena gasped as she took a lovely big doll out of the box. She clutched the doll to her chest and ran back to show her friends.

"Children!" the teacher Mr. Siemens called to get their attention. "Please sit down while we pass out your candy bags!" As the bags were handed out, the parents sat visiting with those sitting nearest them.

"There is another concert tomorrow evening here in the school. It's our church program. We meet here for church until our new building is finished," one new friend commented. "You should come. It's all in the German language".

As Lena, Jake and Annie snuggled under the blankets on the sleigh clutching their candy bags, Helena and Jacob discussed the idea of going to the church program the next evening.

When they got home they allowed the little ones to dig into their bags. There were peanuts, hazel nuts and walnuts, an orange and candy. Soon they were all sitting beside the pot-bellied stove in the living room, warming up. Helena and Jacob cracked the nuts and helped to shell the peanuts.

As Helena tucked them into their schlope-benk and prayed with them she couldn't help but smile at their excitement of this evening. She had enjoyed it too and hoped they could all go to that Osler church program the next evening. As she turned to walk back to the kitchen, she glanced back at Lena. Lena held her new doll close. Her eyes were closed and a smile was on her lips. Helena smiled too – there was always something special about praying with her children and tucking them safely into their beds.

Christmas Eve found the family sitting in the back row of the school for the church program. All of the singing was in the High German language which was what they sang in their own Old Colony Church. The Christmas hymns were familiar and beautiful, although the singing was much faster than they were used to. They enjoyed the evening very much and then returned home with more bags of candy. Tomorrow was Christmas day. Before going to sleep, Jacob and Helena pulled out little home-made gifts and laid them in the plates the children put on the table before they went to bed.

Helena and Jacob woke early on Christmas morning, got the fires going in the stoves and then bundled up to go to the barn to do the chores. Helena gathered the few eggs the chickens had laid.

Back in the house she prepared breakfast and soon heard the voices of the children as they woke each other and ran to the kitchen to see what gifts they had received. Jacob walked in just as they found their plates of gifts and enjoyed their excitement with them.

In the afternoon the family travelled to Blumenheim in their sleigh for the big Friesen family Christmas celebration. It was loud and busy at the grandparents' home and after everyone was gathered in the living room the children's recitations began along with singing.

After their family Christmas program, the adults visited, cracked nuts and ate knackzoat (roasted sunflower seeds). Sawdust had been spread evenly on the floor so everyone could spit their sunflower seed shells on the floor. *(After everyone left, Jacob's step mother and his sisters swept up the sawdust along with the shells. Then they washed the floors. That was what many Mennonite families did.)* As they visited everyone helped themselves to the paepanate (peppernut cookies) in the bowl on the table. Those were a favourite treat at this time of year.

"Last evening we went to the Osler school for the church Christmas service," Jacob said when there was a lull in the conversation. There was a shocked silence.

"You went to the English church?" his blind father asked.

"It wasn't English – it was all in High German," answered Jacob. "They are Mennonite too."

"They still have English worldly ways!" his father said. "It is better to stay away from there."

There was an uncomfortable silence and Jacob glanced at Helena. They both decided not to talk of it any more. However, they soon began to quietly attend the Osler church which was so much closer to their home.

Jacob's sisters; Anna, Katherina, Maria, and Elizabeth. Missing is Justina.

A Brother for Lena, Jake and Annie

CHAPTER 54

January and February were cold, blustery months and near the end of February 1928, on the 22nd day, Helena awoke early and knew this would be a special day. Shaking Jacob she said "Jacob! Please wake up and go get that Mrs. Dyck from the Osler Post Office. I heard she is a midwife."

Jacob sat up quickly. "The baby?" As Helena nodded he hurried out of bed and got dressed. He ran through deep snow to the cold barn to harness the horses. Helena climbed out of bed slowly and went to get both stoves heated up. She put several large pots of water on to heat and then woke the children and got them dressed. After feeding them she told them they would be going to the neighbours' house for a while.

Jacob soon arrived with Mrs. Dyck. He and Helena bundled up the little ones to take them to the neighbour's house. Coming back he busied himself with milking, feeding the animals and shovelling manure out of the barn. He worked very fast that morning, thinking all the while about what might be happening in the house.

"Oh Lord Jesus – please help Helena and let the baby live," he prayed. It seemed each time they had a baby he would remember that awful time when their first baby died.

As Jacob entered the house after finishing the chores, he heard a baby crying loudly. A huge sense of relief and joy flooded his heart. Hurriedly pulling off his barn coveralls and boots, he quickly grabbed the hot water kettle, poured water into the wash bowl and washed his hands.

He walked into the bedroom to see his wife lying on the bed holding the crying baby. She looked up at Jacob with a smile and said, "You have another son!" She held him out to her husband who held the little fair-haired boy close and grinned from ear to ear. Mrs. Dyck smiled as she cleaned up the room and then asked for a ride back to Osler.

On his way home from Osler, he drove to the neighbour's house and picked up the children. As they gathered around their new little brother, their parents decided on a name.

"Let's call him Julius, after my father," Helena said. After a week of rest and having a sister-in-law helping her, Helena was again kept busy with washing diapers over and over again and not getting much sleep for the first few months of Julius' life. He was a very contented baby and could be put in the cradle between feedings where he looked at his surroundings until he fell asleep. His mama was thankful for this because she could get work done without worrying about a crying baby.

It would soon be spring and gardening time. The sun shone longer and longer in the coming days and melted the snow. Soon the geese could be heard honking as they flew above them, heading north to their nesting grounds.

In April the family received a letter from sister Katherina telling them about her coming marriage to Jacob Klassen. The wedding was planned for July 29 of 1928 and would be held at the Klassen home near Aberdeen. This time Helena knew she would be able to go. It would be summer and the ferry would be running.

After planting their garden and seeding the oat crop, Helena and Jacob waited for rain. Instead, a hot wind began to blow like it had the year before. The black soil on the land blew off many of the planted seeds and left them to dry under the hot sun. Helena trudged back and forth with pails of water and tried to put the seeds further down in the ground hoping for a good garden.

At the end of July the Friesen family travelled across the river on the ferry to take part in the celebrations at Katherina's wedding and enjoyed reconnecting with Helena's sisters and brothers and nieces and nephews. Helena's sister Elizabeth came to her privately and told her, "I'm getting married too! William Braun and I will be married on November 29 – this fall."

"I hope the river ice is thick enough by then for us to come," Helena said.

The ear receiver is on the left, The mouth piece is in the centre and the crank to turn is on the right. The round 'eyes' at the top are the Bells that rang when someone called.
(Osler Museum)

That summer the new Osler Telephone Company installed long poles all the way from the highway to the Friesen farm, with the telephone wires connected to the top of the poles. Once that was done, a new telephone was put on the kitchen wall. Now they would be able to call other people on their own phone!

The crops were not good that fall. Jacob harvested what he could. Helena's garden produced well because she had worked hard to water it.

When November 29, 1928 came around they found the ice on the river was not yet strong enough to support vehicles. Helena was disappointed that she couldn't attend Elizabeth's wedding, but there was no help for it.

Snowy Days and Cozy Stoves

CHAPTER 55

Lena was back in school and learning how to read her second grade reader. When she brought it home and read it to her parents, they beamed with pride! Lena loved school and had many friends. Helena was also learning English just from hearing Lena read and from Jacob talking with Lena with the English he knew. They were all improving.

Pot-bellied coal and wood Stove – Osler Museum

As the snow swirled around them at the end of November and for several days in December, the farm yard was transformed into a wonderland of beauty: trees and fence wires covered with white frost in the early morning; bright sparkling snow during the sunny daylight hours and pink and orange colours when the sun when down in the west. Then the snow drifts turned a light shade of grey until darkness fell.

Inside, the smell of wood smoke from the kitchen and living room stoves, the light of the coal oil lamps and the soft chatter of little voices in the evening brought a cozy warm feeling.

Helena tucked her little ones into their schlopebenk and then sat down to feed baby Julius in the rocking chair close to the stove. She was thinking about Christmas. It would soon be here again and she looked forward to the school and church concerts. She had made each of the children a new pair of zocken for their Christmas gifts. Jacob planned to buy some candy.

Christmas was fun. Lena's voice rang clear and high again as the children sang their songs.

A new church had been built in Osler. Jacob and Helena enjoyed the concert in these new surroundings. The ceiling of the church was high and as the people sang the wonderful Christmas songs, the music seemed to reach the ceiling. They enjoyed hearing the beautiful harmony with people singing soprano, alto, tenor and bass. The sound of the piano and pump organ added to the joyful sounds of the people's singing.

Osler church built in 1928.

Christmas morning the children gathered around the kitchen table for the gifts on their plates. Their eyes shone as they each pulled on their new zocken and sucked on peppermint sticks. There was still some candy and nuts in their bags from the two concerts, so the day passed with playing with the toys from the school concert and eating the treats.

Inside of the church. The pews at the top left were the Choir benches.

Helena made sure the children also ate some of the chicken and bubbat she made for dinner. Baby Julius was crawling now and burbling away at his sisters and brother. January was a cold month and it was hard to keep the house warm enough. They used more coal and wood than they had planned and Jacob had to go to Osler to buy more.

During the months of February and March of 1929 Annie and Julius became sick with colds. For Annie, it progressed to a bad chest infection. Helena made many hot mustard plasters to place on Annie's chest to loosen her cough but it took a long time for her to become healthy again. As the snow melted and the weather warmed up, Annie and Julius were well again. The older children ran around the farm yard in their boots to test the puddles left from the melting snow. Julius stood at the window. He bounced and squealed as he watched his siblings run outside.

Helena often wrote to her mother to let her know how things were on the farm at Osler and received letters back from her parents.

Aberdeen – April 21, 1929 (translation of actual letter with parts added for missing paragraph)

Dear Children,

Since we received your letter yesterday and my thoughts are presently with you, I must write a few words. Yes, if we could cross the river we wouldn't hesitate to come and see you. Then we would be able to see how it is with your little one. However, I have to be completely patient, since it is not possible to come.

Well, Agnes has been working at the Schellenbergs again and wanted to come home for a while. We try to go to church when the weather is nice enough. Julius and Peter drive the horses and our small buggy because Papa is not feeling well.

This past Sunday Agnes really wanted to go home with them, but now they can't find a large buggy and with the big wagon it is too hard and rough for Papa. I don't know when she will come home.

We haven't started with Abram yet. We have built a chicken barn and surely we will be able to start working on the land soon. Father started to harrow yesterday, but said it is much too soon. Now I must stop writing and I hope your children will soon be well again, and so I give you my heartfelt greeting.

From your Parents.

Blasting a Well at Osler

CHAPTER 56

In the spring of 1929, Mr. Abram Driedger again visited the Friesen farm. Jacob welcomed him. Together they walked around the farm, talking.

"How are things going?" asked Abram.

"We're getting quite a bit of milk now that the cows have had their calves, but the hardest thing we have is the hauling of water. As you know, we have two wells: one near the house, and the other out in the field. It takes a lot of time and many barrels of water to keep the barn cistern filled as well as the cattle and cooling house troughs. If the summer is as hot and dry as last year, we'll be hauling a lot of water again."

"That's the reason I came this morning," Abram said. "I'd like to blast a deep well and put up a windmill to bring up the water. If you are in agreement, we could start in summer as soon as I can get the men who do that kind of work."

"That would be very good!" Jacob replied. After Abram left, he hurried into the house to tell Helena. How handy it would be to have a windmill that pumped up the water all on its own!

Summer arrived, along with a crew of men who found that the best place to dig for water was near the barn. They prepared to do some digging. They cleared away the area for the well and dug down as far as they could with shovels and removed many big and small stones. Jacob worked hard alongside the other men. They spent June and July digging and removing stones until it was plain that the ground was getting too hard and there were too many stones. They had dug down about eight feet into the earth.

"We'll have to use dynamite for the rest of the hole," Abram said. "With August and September coming, we will all be busy with cutting hay and harvesting our other crops. We'll continue when the harvesting is over."

As the month of August came, Jacob walked through his oat fields, discouraged. There had not been any rain since they planted the crop. The oat plants were not very high. Jacob dug down in the ground to see if it was damp, but all he came up with was dry crumbling dirt falling through his fingers. As he returned to the farm yard he saw Helena out in her garden and joined her where she was weeding.

"The garden looks better than my oat crop," he said as he looked down the row of carrots she was working on.

"I've carried many pails of well water out here, but it really isn't enough to make the garden grow the way I would like it to," she said as she paused in her work. Looking up at the sky she sighed, "If only it would rain soon."

"The hay field isn't very good either, but I need to get busy and cut it with the binder. Next month I'll cut the oats and see how much feed we get for the animals for the winter," Jacob said.

In November, after the farmers were done with harvesting and pig butchering, the men were back to work on the well and brought dynamite to blast a deeper hole. Over the next weeks, as Helena prepared meals for them all, she often jumped in fright as she heard the big BOOMING sounds of the dynamite blowing dirt out of the well. Watching from the window, she and the children saw the men running for cover after someone yelled "Fire in the hole!" and then big clumps of dirt and rocks would shoot up into the air, landing on the yard.

As the weather got colder, the men decided to put the explosives inside the house to keep them from freezing. Helena watched in shocked silence as the men moved the boxes of dynamite under the kitchen stove! She was angry with them for taking such a risk.

Dynamite sticks drawing by NB

As the men were eating their noon meal, Helena walked into the kitchen to see Annie, aged four, holding sticks of dynamite.

"Annie!" she gasped, "No! Don't play with that!" Annie reacted by dropping the sticks and crying because she didn't know what she had done wrong.

Helena glared at the men seated at her table and as she began to tell them what she thought about the whole thing, Jacob walked into the house. Before the door closed behind him, a cat ran into the house and under the stove. Jacob saw the cat, grabbed a broom and began to poke at it around the dynamite boxes in order to chase the cat out!

"Jacob, DON'T!" Helena cried out with a terrified look on her face. "The dynamite is under the stove!"

The men saw how frightened she was. They got up from the table and took the boxes outside. Then they came back in to finish their meal.

Still shaking, Helena said, "I thought it was the end for all of us!"

"It won't blow up just by being dropped," one of the men said.

When Jacob and the men had gone back to work, she sank down at the kitchen table, put her head down on her arms and cried with relief that they were still all alive. What would have happened if a spark from the fire in the stove had landed on the dynamite?

When the first winter blizzard blew into the area, Jacob and the other men stopped working for a few days and then got back to going deeper into the ground using the dynamite. Helena tried to come up with meals to serve these men and worried about them getting tired of noodles with gravy or sauce, or fried potatoes with eggs. There just wasn't a lot of variety of food to serve, but she had canned fruit from the past summer so could give them desert for some meals.

As winter moved along into January, the men decided to wait with the rest of the work on the well until spring. It was too cold, too windy and the days were getting too short.

Grandpa Julius Comes to Visit

CHAPTER 57

After a long cold January and February, the weather began to be calmer and sunnier, but it was still fairly cold. Helena was again expecting a baby in spring and looked forward to the snow melting and the weather warming up so that the children could play outside and she could plant her garden, once the baby was born.

As she was baking bread one afternoon, she heard a team of horses drive up to the farm house. She rubbed a spot of frost off of the kitchen window and saw a man climb out of a sleigh. The sleigh turned around and left while the man walked to the door of her house. The visitor knocked on the door and as Helena opened it and he took off his Russian fur cap, she gave a surprised squeal of delight!

"Papa!" she said as she gave him a hug." I didn't know you were coming!"

"I've been to a church Brotherhood meeting at the village of Neuanlage and the men just dropped me off here until tomorrow when we go back to Aberdeen," he said.

"Come – take off your coat and boots and warm up near the stove!" she told him.

"Annie, Julius, come see your grandpa!" she called.

"Lena and Jake are at school," she said as she turned back to her father. The other two children came up shyly, hiding behind Helena but she pulled them out to greet their grandfather. When her father saw little two year old Julius, his namesake, he smiled and held out his arms.

"Ah, kyleena Yoolyis (little Julius) – come sit with me," he said as he picked up the little boy and sat down in a chair. As he cuddled the little one, he grinned at Annie and got her talking about what she had got for Christmas a few months before.

As the smell of fresh bread filled the room, Jacob walked in from working outside and welcomed his father-in-law. Sitting down at the table for fresh bread, butter and a cup of coffee, the adults visited until Jacob said, "I have to go to town to pick up the children." He rose from his chair, put on his outdoor clothes and after saying "Aufwiedersehen (see you later)," he left for Osler.

Lena, Annie (with hat), Jake, and their dog Pup. See the windmill in the Background.

"How have you been feeling, Papa?" asked Helena as they continued to visit. "Mama wrote that you have a lot of pain some days."

"Yes. I don't always feel very well. The pain in my chest and stomach are hard to take sometimes. My legs also ache, but the last few days have been better, so I wanted to go to the church brotherhood meeting."

When Jacob returned, Lena and Jake got reacquainted with their grandpa. He soon had them laughing while he tickled them and played with them. He left the next morning when the other men picked him up for the trip back home. Helena was so thankful for his visit but she was concerned about his health.

Unexpected News

CHAPTER 58

Early on the evening of April 3rd 1930, the telephone rang and Jacob got up to pick up the receiver. The telephone operator said, "I have a call from Aberdeen."

"Hello?" a voice said. "This is Helena's brother Julius calling. I have some bad news. Our father died last night. Could I please speak with Helena?"

"Yes, here she is," Jacob answered. Turning to her he motioned for her to come to the phone.

"It's a call from your brother Julius. Your dad died last night."

"No!" she whispered in disbelief as she reached for the receiver and stood to speak into the voice piece. "Hello Julius – what happened?"

"Papa went to Aberdeen for seed grain and said that if it got too late he would stay with the Jacob Schellenbergs for the night. He didn't come home, so we didn't worry about it," her brother said.

"This morning several men brought his body home with Papa's sleigh and horses, saying that they had met him on the sidewalk at the bar the evening before. Papa had been speaking gibberish and they couldn't understand him so they thought he was drunk. They put him on the sleigh thinking the horses would take him home, but they forgot to untie the horses."

"What? They left him alone all night to freeze?" Helena asked. Knowing she couldn't talk on the phone very long, she asked when the funeral would be.

"The funeral will be on Saturday, April 5th, here at the farm." Julius said. After assuring him that she would try to be there, they said their goodbyes and hung up the phone.

"How could he be gone?" asked Helena. "He was just here a month ago." She got up slowly and walked over to Jacob who hugged her while she cried.

The next morning after the older children were at school Helena spoke her thoughts out loud,

"How could those men have left him like that? And if he wasn't making any sense why didn't they take him inside somewhere to see if anything was wrong? He hasn't been well for a long time – surely they knew that! I just pray that Papa was ready to meet God."

"I don't understand it either and I'm sorry your Papa is gone, Helena, but do you think it is wise for you to travel all that way? You're going to have another baby in a month," Jacob said.

"I have to be there! This will be so hard for Mama and my sisters and brothers. I'll be careful, Jacob, and if we all keep warm enough, it should be all right."

"I'm also concerned about the river ice road. The weather is turning warmer and we don't know when the ice will break up. But all right. We'll try. I've just finished building the new closed-in sleigh so we should be warm enough." Jacob replied.

That afternoon he phoned to Blumenheim to tell his family about the death of his father-in-law and asked if one of his brothers could stay at their Osler farm on Friday night and do the milking on Saturday.

Friday evening, his brother Isbrand spent the night and early next morning he helped Jacob get the milking done quickly so the family could leave early for the funeral.

Inside the house, Helena woke and dressed the children, packed buns, cold sausage and coffee for the trip while six stones heated up in the oven.

"I see you're almost ready?" Jacob said as he brought in a pail of milk. Opening the oven door he said, "Good. You've heated stones. That should keep us warm most of the way."

His brother walked in and after sitting down to breakfast, Jacob bowed his head, thanked God for the food and prayed that He would keep them safe on the trip.

"It's very cold out this morning, so I think the river ice road will be safe," Jacob said as he reached for another piece of bread to eat with his porridge. Turning to his brother he said, "Isbrand, we won't be coming home this evening, so please get the milking done tonight and tomorrow morning. We can take you home on Sunday." Isbrand nodded between gulps of hot coffee.

"Papa," asked Jake "May I take my little wooden horse along?"

"I want to take a doll," Annie said.

"Yes – you may each take something to play with. It will be a long drive."

Helena tended to the pail of fresh milk. She strained it and poured some into a bottle which she wrapped in a thick towel.

They bundled up warmly and climbed into the brand new sleigh. Jacob put the heated stones in gunny sacks and laid them down so they all had a stone to put their feet on. Sliding the front window open a bit, he snapped the reins on the horses backs, called "Giddy-up!" and started out.

It was still quite dark out so the children sat quietly, listening to the clip clop sound of horses feet and the jingling of harnesses. As they drove east toward the river, the sun began to rise in glorious shades of bright red, orange and yellow. Sitting in the back, the children could now see one another in the morning light and began to blow their cold breath at each other, giggling at the foggy air they created.

Soon they arrived at the steep river hill that descended down to the ice road. Jacob tried to keep the horses walking slowly on the way down and when they reached the river ice, he held the reins firmly as the horses snorted their disagreement about walking on to the ice. Snapping the reins and calling out to them, they started over the river. Many sleighs had driven there through the winter. It had been a good solid road to drive on.

Lena scratched the frosted window in the back so she could see outside and Jake and Annie took turns looking out, too. Soon they were on the other side of the river and travelling up the hill on the way to Aberdeen. As the children chattered and played in the back, Helena and Jacob talked quietly at the front of the sleigh.

At the livery stable in Aberdeen, they stopped so the horses could be given some hay and a drink of water. Helena took the children to the outhouse and then they were off again.

"I'm hungry, Mama!" little Julius said as he stood behind his mother.

"Are you all hungry?" she asked.

"Yes! I want a bun," said Annie.

"May I have some sausage?" asked Jake

"I'd like sausage and a bun!" said Lena.

Helena rummaged in the lunch bag and gave them each something to eat. Then she picked up the milk bottle and turning around she said, "Here, you can each take a sip of milk. I'll hold the bottle so it doesn't spill."

The stones were cooling off by now and the little ones were willing to snuggle back into their blankets. Julius was soon fast asleep.

The family arrived around noon and found the house full of the family, and many other people. The house was not big, but everyone crowded in. Helena found her mama, sisters and brothers and there were many hugs and tears. Her sisters had made a big dinner for everyone and after spending the afternoon together, Grandpa Julius' body was taken to the village of Edenburg for the burial the next day. Helena and Jacob drove to her sister Anna and David Buhler's place for the night. It was closer to the village where the funeral was to take place and closer to the river ice road for their trip home.

'Caboose' built by Jacob. Used in Winter for travel and in summer to house baby chicks until old enough to mix with the rest of the chickens.

A Terrifying Ride!

CHAPTER 59

After the singing and preaching was done at the funeral, the women set out the buns they had brought and made coffee for everyone.

As the day wore on, the sun shone brightly, warming up the temperature and melting snow. Jacob and the other men gathered outside for a while to chat and smoke. Watching the water dripping off the roof, he wondered how the river road was holding up.

"Are you going back today?" someone asked him. "If you are, I wouldn't wait too long because the ice and snow are melting fast. You want to get over that river before the ice breaks up."

That was enough to increase the anxious feeling he already had. He didn't want to hurry Helena because this was a very hard day for her, but they really needed to get home.

Finding Helena, he urged her to get the children ready because the weather was getting quite warm and he wanted to get over the river. She was disappointed but she agreed. The thought of the ice breaking was alarming for her. They needed to get home for chores too.

They said their goodbyes. Again heated stones were wrapped in sacks and the children were bundled up. They were on their way home again.

The snow became slushy and splashed around the horses' feet as they trudged along. On their way down to the river, Helena gasped.

"Jacob, look! There is water standing on the river ice!" She looked over at Jacob who wore a shocked and worried look on his face. "We can't go across – it's too dangerous!" she said.

"We have to get across! Otherwise we have to go around through Saskatoon and it would take days to get home!" he answered. "The ice is still several feet thick – it can't have melted that fast!" Their four children stood and peered over their parents' shoulders to see the water on the ice.

Urging the horses forward, they neared the edge of the river. The horses balked and wouldn't move. Taking the long reins, Jacob whipped their flanks and yelled at them to move. They bucked and neighed in fear, but he kept at them until they moved forward. It was all he could do to control them as they drove through the slushy snow and water. The horses screamed and fought, their eyes wild with fear, but continued on.

In the sleigh, Helena sat tensely gripping the dash of the sleigh with her hands and praying. There were cracking sounds around them.

"Jacob! We're going to break through the ice!" The children felt their parents' fear and stood behind them looking at the water and watching the frightened horses.

It seemed a long ride, but the river was not very wide and soon they were over on the other side.

"Ho!" called Jacob as he pulled on the reins. He sank back against the seat in relief while Helena quietly sobbed. As she turned around and saw the children's anxious faces she calmed herself and said, "It's all right. God brought us through. Thank God!" The horses were still nervously prancing and trying to move forward.

"Here, take the reins Helena," Jacob said. "I want to go calm the horses."

He slowly got out of the sleigh, talking calmly to the nervous horses as he walked toward them. He stroked their quivering backs and moving to their heads, took their halters firmly in his hands, still quietly talking and rubbing their faces gently. Slowly their wild-eyed look changed and they stood still. He walked back to the sleigh, brought out some hay and held it out for them to munch on. Hearing a loud, cracking sound echoing around him, he turned toward the river to see pieces of ice breaking apart.

No Eggs – No Meat – No Butter

CHAPTER 60

As the weather turned warmer in spring, Jacob hired a young man to help him with finishing the cooling house and building a fence.

Helena had run out of eggs, meat and butter. Every day she wondered what to make for meals. After serving fried potatoes for a few meals in a row everyone was getting tired of them and needed something more filling.

"Jacob," she said one morning after Lena and Jake had left for school. "All we have left are a few potatoes and a bit of flour and milk. That won't fill you or the hired man. The cows won't have their calves for a few weeks yet, so there isn't enough cream to make butter. What are we going to do?"

"I don't know. I have no money left," he replied in a discouraged voice as he walked out of the house and to the pasture. Catching one of the horses, he hitched him to the buggy and drove away.

Helena saw him leave but didn't know where he was going. As the clock ticked away the time, she got worried as it neared dinner time and Jacob was still not back. *(The Mennonite people called their noon meal medach (dinner)which meant 'mid-day', and the evening meal oventkost (supper) which meant evening meal)*

"It's nearly noon. What can I make to eat?" she asked herself and prayed for an answer.

"I'll walk to the Dycks and ask if I can borrow some butter and then I'll make milk soup. That will have to do for now." Taking the baby carriage outside, she put Julius inside and calling Annie she said, "Come, we're going for a walk."

She pushed the carriage down the road towards the neighbours' farm. It was a quarter of a mile walk. When she got there, she asked if she could borrow some butter.

"Mama isn't home right now, but I'll tell her you asked," said one of the Dyck girls.

Thanking her, Helena turned the carriage around, took Annie's hand and started back home. She still had no answer as to what they could eat at noon.

A half hour later Mrs. Dyck drove up in her buggy, and getting down, walked to the door. Helena answered the knock on the door and invited her in.

"The children told me you needed some butter so I made some as soon as I got home. Here it is. I hope it is enough," She gave Helena a pound of butter wrapped in some clean wax paper.

"Oba, danke shoen!(Oh, thank you)," exclaimed Helena with a smile.

After Mrs. Dyck left, she hurried to make some tiny dumplings while she heated milk on the stove. Soon the milk soup was bubbling. She set the table.

"Annie – please call the hired man to come and eat," she said. Little five year-old Annie ran out to where the young man was pounding a fence post into the ground. Soon they were back in the house and sitting down to eat. Jacob was still not home.

He arrived later in the afternoon. He hitched both horses to the wagon and then walked into the house.

"I went to several places to see if I could find a bit of work to help us through the next while, but I couldn't find any," he told Helena.

"One of the men told me that there is a need for scrap metal and I could probably sell it in Osler. He told me where to take it, so I'm going to load up all I can find on the yard. We have a lot of old iron junk around here and hopefully I can sell it. I'm also going to check the town garbage dump for iron."

He collected as much scrap metal as he could find and took it to Osler. He was able to sell it and then was able to buy what they needed. He longed for a better way to earn money and hoped they could make it through until the cows had their calves. Then they would have a lot more cream to ship.

Short-term Angel

CHAPTER 61

On May 2, 1930, a little baby boy was born. He was small and weak with a frail cry. The midwife gently washed him and said, "You need to get a doctor to see this little one. There is something wrong."

As Jacob watched Helena unwrap the little one to count his little fingers and toes, they saw that there was something wrong with his back. His legs were not kicking as they should be. His colour was not good either – instead of a red rosy face like most newborns, his skin had a faint blue tone.

"I will call the doctor in Warman and ask if he can come on the train and see him," Jacob said. Arrangements were made and the doctor came over. He checked over the baby's body and said, "This little one will not live very long. He's a blue baby." Helena began to cry.

After the doctor left, they sat holding the little boy and hoped that maybe the doctor was wrong. In any case this baby would be loved and his name would be 'Daniel'.

The work on the well and wind-mill had started up again just after baby Daniel was born and continued through until fall.

In spite of all the work of feeding the men who came back to work on the well and the busy months that followed, Helena felt blessed to look after this precious baby boy. She kept him warm, gently rubbed his body with ointment and talked to him. There might be something wrong with his back and legs, but he had the brightest, intelligent, happy eyes! He smiled most of the time and his brothers and sisters loved him.

In the month of October things began to change for little Daniel. After catching a cold he just could not get well and wasn't eating enough. He became weaker and weaker and cried a lot. Helena didn't know what to do for him. He seemed to be in pain. She carried him for hours on end because it seemed to comfort him, and put him down only when he fell asleep. This went on for several weeks and one day in early November, she put him down in the baby carriage beside the table and sat down to eat with the family.

Suddenly she was aware that it was very quiet. She stopped eating, and meeting Jacob's eyes they both turned to look at the baby and realized that Jesus had finally come to take him home. He had stopped breathing on earth, but he would be completely well in heaven.

Jacob, Helena and the children were very sad at losing Daniel. They let their family members know and had a small funeral. They buried Daniel's body in the Osler cemetery. Their little angel boy had only lived six months.

Water!

CHAPTER 62

When the crew of men had dynamited deep enough, they found water! They put a long pipe in the well, deep down in the water, connected a pump to it and began working on setting up a windmill.

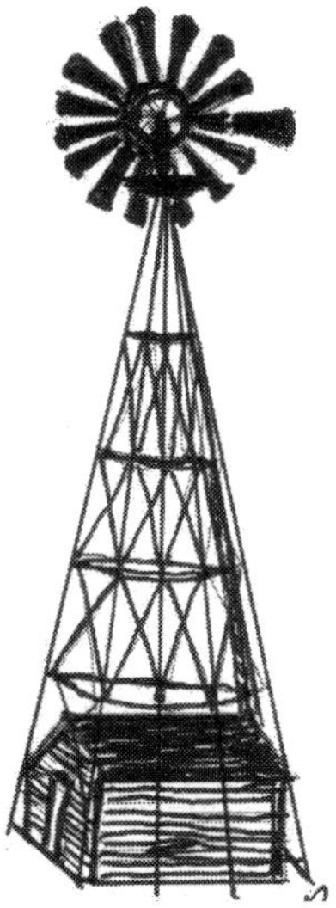

Drawing of windmill by NB

As the metal parts of the windmill were being set up, the children watched from a distance as it was built higher and higher. A steel ladder was bolted on it and then at the top, a wooden platform was built for the men to stand on as they put up the big wheel with the wings that opened and closed by a strong wooden lever beside the pump on the ground. The big day had finally come. There were pipes leading from the well into the cooling house trough.

"All right, everyone!" the foreman who had built the well called. "Here we go!"

The family and workers all gathered round as he released the lever of the pump. They looked up at the windmill to see the wings open up and the wheel turn in the direction of the wind. The pump started up while the big wheel high up on the platform turned in the wind.

Watching from in the doorway of the cooling house, Jacob waited with excitement. Suddenly there was a gurgling sound and water gushed out of the pipe and into the trough!

"Here it comes!" he shouted. There were smiles and laughter and hand shaking all around. The children ran to their papa and asked if they could see the water. Jacob picked Julius up while the other three crowded near the trough.

Mr. Driedger walked up to Jacob with a big grin, slapped him on the shoulder and shook his hand saying, "Jacob – someday you and I are going to be rich!"

Helena smiled as she walked into the cooling house. What a luxury! They had all the water they needed now.

That evening when the men had left and the children were in bed, Jacob and Helena again walked to the windmill and looked up. Wondering what the water tasted like, they went into the cooling house, cupped their hands and had a drink. It didn't taste very good. A few days later when the water was tested, they found it was great for the cattle but it was not good for people.

"Well. That is a disappointment," Jacob said, "but we can order water from Saskatoon for drinking. The milk truck can bring our milk cans back with water in them. At least we don't have to haul water for the cows. We'll still have to haul water and melt snow for washing clothes. In the spring we can haul water from the pond in the neighbour's field."

As fall turned into another winter, the Friesens often commented on how wonderful it was that they didn't have to haul water or melt snow for the cattle. Jacob piped the run-off water from the cooling house trough into the cistern in the barn where he hauled up pails of water to bring to each cow and horse in the barn. Each animal had to be given fresh food and water twice a day. And every day Jacob shovelled the manure out of the barn to keep the building clean.

The daily chores kept the family busy. Each morning the milk truck returned their cans from the day before filled with water, and picked up fresh cans of milk to take to Saskatoon. The Saskatoon water was used for drinking and cooking.

However, Lena and Jake and their mama, Helena, still carried many pails of snow into the house after school and dumped the snow into the barrel by the stove where it melted. This water was soft and good for washing clothes, dishes and little faces.

The chickens were laying a lot more eggs by this time so the children had to gather them after school. Helena carefully wiped the eggs with a damp cloth, and put them into a basket for Jacob to take to town in exchange for flour, sugar, coffee and other supplies. They were thankful for the things God had provided.

A Sewing Machine and Christmas Dresses

CHAPTER 63

In the evenings, the children played by lamp light after doing their chores and listened as their father taught them the High German language. Jake, Lena and their father were learning English as well. Helena only spoke to them in Low German but she was beginning to understand the English. Jacob was pleased with his children's accomplishments at the English school and also of their ability to read and write the German Script letters he was teaching them.

"Education is very important for you," he often told them. It wasn't long before Annie and Julius picked up English words as they played with their older siblings.

While Lena and Jake read their school books, Annie sat at the table drawing pictures. She loved drawing and colouring. Little Julius had a wonderful imagination. He occupied himself for hours with tooth-picks or buttons that became imaginary people he moved around in games against each other.

In the evenings Helena sat by the table with a lamp nearby. She was busy mending, sewing, knitting and crocheting while the children played and learned. She smiled as she watched her children. They were her joy. Christmas was coming soon and she wanted to have gifts for them all. She thought about what she could make for presents but she'd have to work on those things after the children were in bed.

Glancing at her mama who was busy with a needle and thread, Lena said, "Mama, the other girls in school are all getting new dresses for the Christmas Concert. May I have a new dress too?"

Papa Jacob looked up from his German book and met Helena's eyes. "We'll see if I can sell enough eggs and milk to pay for some new cloth," he said. A few days later he walked into the house after a trip to Osler to sell eggs and milk.

"Look what I found at the store," he said to Helena. He unwrapped a parcel and there was some pretty green and red plaid cloth.

"Oh – that looks very nice," Helena said. "How much did you get? Is there enough for two dresses? I'd like to make one for Annie too." She measured the material and smiled. "I think there will be enough!"

"Here's some blue cloth that I thought would look nice for shirts for the boys," he said as he pulled the fabric from under the plaid. Helena agreed. She wondered aloud how she would be able to get all that sewing done by hand.

One cold, blustery day in the middle of December, Jacob returned home from Osler and drove the team of horses near the house. Helena heard him call "Ho!" and looked out of the frosty window to see why he had driven up to the house instead of going to the barn with the animals.

She watched as he pulled something off of the open sleigh. It seemed heavy. He lifted the bulky box and carried it to the house. Helena hurried to open the door so he wouldn't have to set the box down. Putting it down on the kitchen floor, he closed the door and took off his gloves, hat and coat. Turning, he smiled and said, "Open it."

Treadle sewing machine (Osler Museum)

With a questioning look at him, she began pulling off the cardboard box to reveal a beautiful treadle sewing machine!

"Oh!" she gasped in delight. "This is wonderful! Where did you get it?"

"I ordered it from the catalogue when I was at the Osler store last week," he answered. "There is a book of instructions on how to use it in the drawer on the left side. It is in English, but if you can't understand the diagrams, I'll translate for you."

"This is the best Christmas gift! Thank you!" she said. "Sewing the Christmas dresses and shirts shouldn't take so long now! I used your aunt's sewing machine when I worked there before we were married. Maybe this one will be the same."

That evening as the children excitedly inspected the new machine, she called them to her as she held a measuring tape. "Lena, please stand still while I measure how long I have to make your dress. You have really grown this past year. Then I will measure the rest of you too," she said as she glanced at Jake, Annie and Julius.

The next morning, after the oldest two were off to school, she eagerly cleared the dishes off the table and spread out the plaid cloth. She had a pattern from the girls' old dresses and now just had to make them a bit longer and a bit wider.

After cutting all the pattern pieces, she sat down at the sewing machine and looked at the diagrams. She was surprised that she could read some of the English instructions and soon understood how to thread the needle. She practiced sewing on an old piece of cloth. It wasn't long before she got the rhythm of how fast to move the treadle with her foot. How exciting it was to watch a machine making even, neat stitches – much neater and faster than she could by hand!

As she sewed the pieces together, she ironed them with sadirons which were heating on the stove, so the seams would be smooth. In those days, people didn't use electric irons like we do today. Helena used heavy, metal irons. She heated them on the stove, slipped the cool wooden and metal handle onto one of them and used it until it had cooled too much. Then she'd put that one back on the stove to heat and slip the handle onto a hot iron, and so on, until her ironing was finished.

By the time the day of the concert rolled around, Helena had made two dresses and two shirts. Seeing their oldest children standing on the stage in their new clothes made Jacob and Helena smile.

Annie and Julius watched in wonder as the candles on the school tree were lit. The light of the candles made the shiny tree ornaments sparkle. There was a man with a candle snuffer on a long pole, who continually watched the candles on the tree. He put them out one at a time as soon as they burned down. The school room was packed with children and parents and there was only one door to get out in case of fire, so the candle snuffer man had an important job.

The youngest two Friesen children could hardly wait until the end of the concert when all of the children would be given paper bags with an orange, nuts and candy!

After the church concert on the 24th, the children put plates on the table for the next morning when they would find their gifts. New zocken, hankies, and socks were put on the plates along with one toy – a whistle, a ball, a box of crayons and a spinning top. There was a colouring book they would all share.

On Christmas Day the children woke early to play with their toys and then the family got ready for church. That afternoon there was the usual Friesen family Christmas celebration in Blumenheim.

The next few days of holidays were spent enjoying their toys and treats. New Years Day would be another special day and some relatives might come for faspa.

New Years day of 1931 saw Helena busy making neeyausch kuken (new-year's fritter) dough. She added lots of raisins as she mixed it all together. The children all begged for some of the dried fruit and each of them received a small handful to eat as a snack.

Since she had the dried fruit out already, she decided to make pluma mousse (fruit soup) and fried ham for their noon meal. The kitchen smelled good as the family waited for it to be done.

As she fried the ham, she glanced over at the fritter dough in her 'bahk-kum' (dough tub) and found the dough had risen quickly. Turning the ham over in the frying pan, Helena washed her hands and punched down the dough to let it rise again and then tended to the meat again. Yeast dough must rise, be punched down, rise again, be formed into bread, buns – or fritters and be allowed to rise one more time before it is baked or fried.

Jacob walked into the house for dinner and commented, "Daut rickt shoen (That smells good)," as he took off his boots and overalls and went to wash his hands. The family sat down to thank God for their first dinner of the New Year.

"I think my brother David and his family might come for faspa this afternoon," Jacob commented between bites.

"Oh, that's good!" Lena said. "I was hoping some children would come over to play."

After getting the children to clear the dishes and wash them, Helena heated the lard on the stove so she could fry the fritters. As soon as it was hot enough, she cut small pieces of the risen dough and dropped them into the fat. She watched them puff up. Once they were golden brown on both sides, she put them on brown paper to cool.

"Please, may I have one?' asked Julius. The others also crowded in close, each asking for one.

"Yes, but move away from the stove!" she said. "Hot fat might spatter you. Lena – get the sugar bowl and put some into a dish. You can dip your fritters in the sugar."

The children were soon gathered around the table taking turns dipping their treats in the sugar and enjoying the yummy taste. When all the frying was done, Helena put the fritters in the clean dough tub and covered them with a tea towel. Then she set a big pan of sunflower seeds in the oven to roast.

She brought out a pail of sawdust and spread it on the living room floor for people to spit out their sunflower seeds. Soon the jingling of horses' harnesses was heard and their cousins arrived.

Bahk-kum (photo of a friend's dough tub)

Dust and Thistles

CHAPTER 64

The next months seemed to fly by as spring returned. As the snow melted Jacob felt hopeful again. Maybe there would be enough moisture from the melted snow in the ground to seed another oat crop. The last year's crop had not been good. There wasn't enough feed for the cattle and he had to buy some hay. He hoped there would be lots of nutritious grass for the cattle this year.

Potato planter built by Jacob and still in use.

Helena wandered through her garden checking to see if her fruit trees and other trees had buds on them. She had carried many pails of water to them in the fall and soaked the ground around her trees, gooseberry and currant bushes and was happy to see that they were growing. Tiny leaves would soon be sprouting on the branches. She lifted her eyes to the sky and whispered her thanks to God.

The third week of May was garden planting time. Jacob ploughed the garden for her and then went back to seeding his oats.

Helena seeded her carrots and other vegetables, cut up the old potatoes, carried the potato planter to the garden and planted them. She put three old sprouting carrots from the year before into the ground. These carrot tops would turn to seeds in the fall. The garden took a week to put in because of all the other farm work.

As Helena fed her chickens she heard several hens making peculiar 'cluck, cluck' noises. She knew those hens wanted to be mothers to baby chicks. Jacob helped her build a low square box out of boards, divided it into four runs and covered it with chicken wire. She made new straw nests at one end of each run. At the other end was a dish of water and some grain. She carefully arranged six fresh eggs in each nest and then placed a clucking hen in each run. It didn't take long and the hens sat down on the eggs. In 21 days Helena expected to find baby chicks.

As the time came for the chicks to be hatched, Helena took a bowl of warm water and reached into the nests under the mother hen. She removed the eggs and put them into the water. If the eggs floated and bobbed on top of the water, she knew there were babies inside and she quickly put them back under the warm mother hen. If the eggs dropped to the bottom of the bowl, she knew they were rotten and she threw them out onto the garbage dump in the pasture.

A few days later, the baby chicks hatched out of their shells! Once the chicks were all hatched, the mother hen went out in her run to scratch the ground and look for bugs and seeds to eat. Her babies followed her and learned to find bugs too. In the evenings they all crowded under her wings to keep safe and warm. A few weeks later the hen and her babies were allowed to roam around the farm yard.

Soon the summer sun grew hot and the wind picked up. Jacob and Helena watched in dismay again as the black soil blew off of the seeds in the field and in the garden.

"Jacob, we can't lose the garden. We didn't have a good one last year and we need that food. I'm trying to carry pails of water, but since we're having another baby in fall, I just can't carry all that water."

"I'll see what I can do," Jacob answered. Over the next few days he traveled around to several garbage dumps and scrap heaps, finding different lengths of pipe and water hose. Bringing them home he put them all together and made a very long pipe all the way from the wind-mill well to the garden. He dug paths around the plant rows in the garden soil to make a tiny creek that snaked back and forth across the whole garden.

As the water was turned on, Helena breathed a sigh of relief as she watched the little 'creek' fill with water. Her garden was being watered! She was determined to keep those vegetables growing.

Out on the field, there was a lot of green showing. Jacob was hopeful but when he walked out to look at it, it was mostly Russian thistle weeds. The hay field was full of it.

"This won't be a good crop year," he said to himself. "Oh God, how am I supposed to feed my family and my animals?" he prayed.

Jacob worked on repairing the hayrack and other equipment as well as building a small shed for a black-smith shop. He welded together a small stove to heat metal so that it could be bent and made into horse-shoes, hoes, rakes and other tools needed for farming.

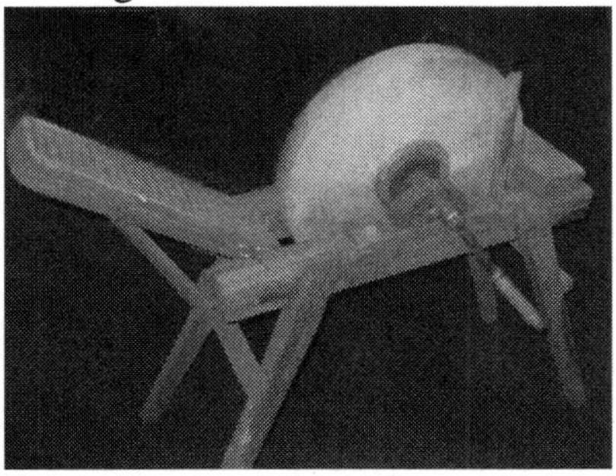

Grinding Stone (Rosthern Museum)

He bought a grinding stone so he could sharpen knives, scissors and garden tools. Then Jacob let it be known in Osler that he had a small blacksmith shop and would be glad to make horse shoes for the farmers' horses and sharpen tools. This way he earned a bit of extra money.

Summer turned to fall and harvesting and the children helped bring in the potatoes and carrots. They spent a lot of time rubbing sunflower seeds out of the sun flowers so they could be dried and roasted into knackzoat. Annie started school that fall so only three year old Julius was home with his mama during the day.

"Well, I guess the only cattle feed I'll have is Russian thistle and oat straw this year," Jacob said as he came into the house for a cup of coffee one day.

"I wish we would still get rain," Helena sighed. The black dirt blown around by the wind seeped into every crack of the house and she was constantly wiping dust of off window sills, furniture, the kitchen table and chairs, everywhere! Sometimes the dust and wind storms were as bad as a snowy blizzard: it was hard to see where one was going. The dust got into their eyes as they walked and muddy tears streamed down their faces as their tears tried to wash the dirt out of their eyes.

Taking the horses and binder out in the field, Jacob cut all the hay and oats along with the green thistles and had Mr. Peters come over with his feed chopping machine. It had a long hose that went up to the hayloft of the barn and as the thistle, hay and oats were chopped the feed was blown up into the hayloft through the hose.

Jacob went to Osler one evening to visit with the men at the store. Everyone was suffering with the drought. They found out that the Government of Canada knew about their problems and was going to help. The farmers would all get food relief stamp booklets, one for each child - according to how many people were in their families. Trainloads of food would be coming to all the small prairie towns and people would have to go to the train station when the food came in and trade their food relief stamps for the food.

"At least we'll have more food to eat," said Helena when he told her about it. "We can be thankful for that!"

Jacob's food stamp book

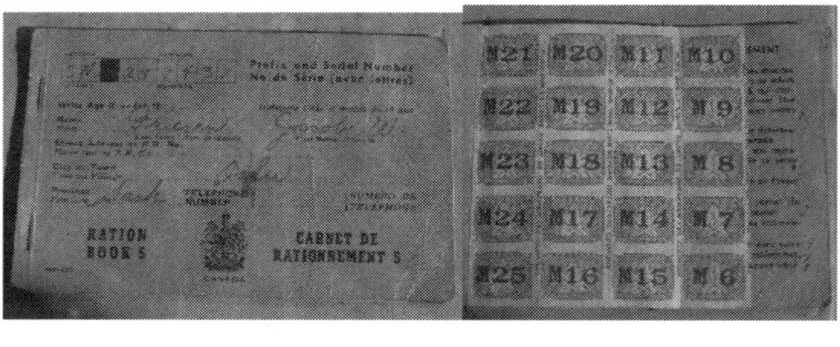

Baby Tena

CHAPTER 65

Helena prepared for another baby and on October 4th 1931, Lena walked Jake, Annie and Julius to the Nicolei Dycks farm to wait for the baby to be born. Later that afternoon they returned home and found a beautiful baby girl in the cradle. Their new sister was named Katherina – but they all called her 'Tena'.

Helena and Jacob were so thankful to see this little girl so healthy and strong. This time there was no bad news about the baby not living long and they all enjoyed her. Lena, as the oldest child, was often called on to carry the baby around after school when their mama was busy. All the children loved to gently rock the cradle until Tena fell asleep.

News came that the trainload of food had arrived at the Osler station. Jacob hitched up the horses and wagon and drove out to collect his share.

As he showed his food stamps to the one in charge, he was given several boxes of goods to take home. Thanking the man, Jacob loaded up his wagon and moved aside for other farmers to receive their food.

"Here's the food from the train," he said as he carried the boxes into the house. Helena kissed baby Tena and put her down in the carriage and helped Jacob to unpack.

"Canned milk?" she said as she opened the box of cans. "We have our own milk, but I can use that for cooking and baking."

"This is heavy," Jacob said as he pulled out a large round package. Opening it up, he found a large round of cheese.

"The man at the station said that the milk and cheese came from Ontario. There are apples and turnips from British Columbia and fish from eastern Canada."

As they dug deeper they smelled something strong and smoky. "What is that awful smell?" asked Helena. Jacob pulled out the last box and opened it.

"It's smoked fish! But it's hard, dry and dark looking. It looks like it has spoiled," Jacob said.

They put the fish aside. After a few days, Jacob came home from the store with a bag of flour and said, "Everyone's fish smells like that. People in eastern Canada eat it that way. I guess we will try as well."

"What do I do with it?" asked Helena. "Maybe I will have to soak it for a few days and then cook it." However, no matter how she tried to prepare it, they were not used to eating fish like that – they were used to catching them fresh from the river. She could not coax the children to eat the dried fish. Even Helena felt sick to her stomach when she ate it.

When the cold of winter came again, Helena was home with just Julius and baby Tena. All of the children needed new clothes because they were growing so fast. She had been saving all the cloth sacks that the flour came in and decided she had enough to make clothes out of them.

She washed the sacks thoroughly and put them out on a snow bank for the sun to bleach the lettering that the flour mill had stamped on them. Each day for several days, she put them out in the sun and then using her lye soap and some bleach she bought, she let the sacks soak for a day until the rest of the lettering was gone.

"What are you doing?" asked Lena one day as the children returned home from school.

"I'm going to make you girls some slips and dresses from these flour sacks," replied Helena. "What colour would you like your dress to be?" she asked her girls.

"I want blue!" Annie said.
"May I have a red one?" asked Lena.

"I'll see if I can find the dye in the store," Helena answered.

She kept busy with sewing, mending and knitting again that winter along with the usual farm work. The winter seemed long but the snow made the dried out land look beautiful and again brought the hope of better things to come.

Fun at the Farm

CHAPTER 66

There was always something to see and do on the Friesen farm. Spring brought the excitement of a new colt running after its mother; new calves bawling, jumping, and running around the calf pen; and the joy of fluffy baby chicks, and puppies and kittens in May and June.

At the end of May the children began checking the farmyard and barn. Mama cats were very careful about hiding their babies until they were older. The first week or so the kittens could not see because their eyes were closed.

"I wonder if we have any kittens," Annie wondered.

"Let's check the hayloft!" Jake said, and they all ran into the barn. Their papa was there, busy cleaning out the manure and straw while the cows were grazing outside.

"May we go up to the hay loft, Papa?" asked Lena.

"Yes you may, but let me help you so you don't fall."

"I don't need help!" Jake said, but found his papa's hand firmly on his back as he climbed the ladder to the hayloft. Soon Lena, Jake, Annie and Julius were all up in the loft searching in the straw and behind walls looking for kittens.

"Don't come down without calling me first," their papa said. "It's more dangerous to come down than to go up."

The children promised and suddenly Lena put her finger to her mouth and said, "Shhhh!" They were standing close to a pile of straw near one wall and as they stood quietly for a minute they heard faint mewing sounds. Lena carefully moved some straw and they found a mama cat and her kittens. The mama cat did not look pleased. Her kittens were still so little and delicate. As Jake moved in closer she hissed at them all.

"She's going to scratch you, Jake," Julius said as he crouched down for a better look. The tiny kittens were moving about but their eyes were still closed. They were too small to play with and so the children decided to go back down to the main level of the barn.

"Papa!" called Annie. "We want to come down now." Papa was there to quickly help each child down safely.

"We found the kittens, Papa, but they still have their eyes closed," Julius said.

"That's good. You children are wise to wait to play with them. If you go look in the room behind the horses' stall, you will find that Pup has her babies too! But don't go too close to her because she will bite you to protect her puppies. When they are older and playing around the yard she won't mind you picking them up," Jacob told them.

They ran into the small room behind the horses' stall and found Pup lying on some old horse blankets. There were five squirming little balls of fur. The children stood back and looked at the tiny puppies.

"I want the black one with the white ear!" said Jake.

"No! I want that one!" Annie stated, but she was out-voted by her big brother. She chose a light brown puppy as hers instead.

"Look at the white one with brown spots," Lena said. "I think I want that one."

Julius took his time looking over the two that were not claimed and decided he would choose one later. After seeing the puppies, they scampered off to the kitchen to ask for a glass of milk and a cookie. Sitting at the kitchen table, they told Helena all about the new babies they had found.

Lena wandered off to the garden while Annie stayed inside to draw a picture and Jake bounced a rubber ball against the barn wall. Julius found a nice shady spot behind the house where he pulled a handful of nails out of his pocket. He scratched a ball diamond shape in the dirt and stuck a nail at each base and some farther out. These were his baseball players. He took a tiny rock for the baseball and had another nail 'hit' the ball out in the field. In his imagination his team players ran the bases, making one run after another. Jacob walked by and smiled at his son's concentration on the game.

Hail Storm

CHAPTER 67

That spring Jacob decided to cement a much larger outside trough for the cattle to drink from. He built forms to make sides for the trough and after mixing gravel and cement with water, poured it between the forms to make the walls. It took several days to build the forms and mix and pour the cement, and a few more days for the cement to harden. Finally the day came when he connected a pipe from the cooling house trough to the outside trough. The windmill turned and water pumped out. It didn't take long for the cattle trough to fill. The cattle had lots to drink.

The summer work in the garden, yard and fields kept them all busy. With the water from the new well, Helena's flower gardens were beautiful. The fruit trees were beginning to bear some fruit. She looked forward to plums, gooseberries and currants. She would dry some for pluma mousse and make jam with the rest. She also looked forward to a better vegetable garden.

Their neighbours, the Nicolei Dycks, moved and another family, the George Heins, moved onto that farm. Now there were more children to play with.

The summer was very hot, windy and dusty again and one evening as they walked back to the house after milking, Jacob pointed to the sky. "Look! There are dark clouds moving our way. Maybe we will finally have some rain!"

Helena stopped to watch for a while and then said, "Jacob, those clouds are moving very fast and they're very dark. I think there might be a bad storm coming." As she turned the crank of the cream separator in the kitchen, she kept looking out the window. It was only seven o'clock in the evening but it was getting very dark outside.

Jacob got up to light a lamp and then walked out on the porch step, looking up. The wind was getting stronger. Dust blew around the house and big bunches of dry Russian thistles were rolling across the yard. Little flashes of lightening kept appearing in different parts of the sky. The dark clouds were so big it looked like they were almost touching the ground.

Suddenly there was a bright flash of lightening and a loud clap of thunder! Rain began to pour down on the dry ground, making puddles everywhere. Jacob hurried inside.

"Papa! What's that noise on the roof?" asked Lena as she ran into the kitchen from the living room. They all heard it. It was the deafening noise of large hail stones pounding the roof and walls of the house. There were flashes of lightening and crashes of thunder all around

"Children!" called Jacob. "I want you all in the kitchen near the door! If lightening strikes the house it will catch fire and we have to be ready to run outside!" Fearfully, they all crowded close to the door.

The storm passed. The sun came out and Jacob and Helena walked outside. They dreaded what they would see. They walked to the garden and saw the fruit knocked off the trees. All the vegetables plants were pounded down and full of holes. They realized that everything was gone.

Helena cried softly and Jacob put his arm over her shoulder, fighting tears himself.

They walked to the fence that separated the cattle yard from the oats Jacob had planted. They saw nothing but broken bits of the plants. They looked at the dents on the house walls and shingles made by the hail stones.

After putting the children to bed, they sat at the kitchen table and sadly talked about what they would do now.

"Well, it is early summer and all the vegetables that grow underground will probably be all right. They will get new leaves," Jacob said with a sigh. He got up to get a bowl of cereal for night lunch.

"I suppose," Helena answered. "If the roots have not been uprooted by all the sudden rain, the other plants might come back as well and we might get some vegetables. At least we'll have the food stamps to trade for food from the train boxcars at the station and for things like flour, sugar and coffee at the store." Then she added with a shake of her head and a rueful smile, "If only they wouldn't send us that fish!"

At this Jacob smiled a bit and said, "Well, I've heard of some farmers using the biggest dried fish to cover holes in their shingles!" They both chuckled at that idea. It was good to be able to find a bit of humour in the situation.

As the summer days went by, quite a few of the vegetable plants grew new leaves and because of the wet ground they were able to do well. There would be lots of potatoes, beets and carrots. The fruit trees would have to wait until next summer to bear fruit.

Out in the fields, the Russian thistle grew quickly with all the sudden moisture in the soil. Some of the oat and hay crop plants tried to grow again, but they never grew tall or had grain kernels. Jacob cut down the green thistle and the rest of the crop and had Mr. Peters bring down his feed chopper again. He was thankful that he was able to store up some food for the cattle for the winter, even if it wasn't quite enough.
(Hay is nutritious stalks of green grass. It is food for the cattle and horses. Green Russian thistle had some nutritious value. Straw is

dried stalks of crops with the seeds cut off. It makes warm bedding for the animals, but it has very little food value left in it.)

Hayrack drawing by NB

Jacob also needed lots of straw for the winter, both to mix in with the chopped thistle and for bedding for the animals. He hitched up his big hayrack and travelled to farms where there was extra straw for sale. For some of the straw, he had to go across the river on the ferry to buy straw from farmers near Aberdeen. Nobody had much extra straw to sell. He had to buy small loads from many farms to fill up his hayrack so that he would have enough.

After harvesting was done in 1932, Helena received a letter from her sister Maria, telling her that she was to be married to William Martens on November 6th. Helena groaned with disappointment as she remembered that the river road across the ice would not be thick enough to travel on at that time of year. She would miss another family wedding! She wrote to her sister to tell her she was happy about the news but would not be able to come.

Going Fishing

CHAPTER 68

On a warm fall Friday evening Jacob suggested they go fishing at the river the following morning. He was hungry for a good fish fry. Helena agreed. It would be nice to have some variety in their meals. She prepared some things to take with them and then was up early in the morning.

While the children and Jacob did the milking, she packed bread, a jar of canned chicken, some pickles, cookies and jars of water to drink. At breakfast Jacob told the children, "Your mother and I have decided we're all going fishing today, so find a hat and a jacket and we'll leave as soon as we've had our breakfast and have the food packed in the wagon."

"Where is the net to catch grasshoppers?" asked Julius.

"It's hanging in the lean-to at the barn. Jake – you can go get the horses when you're done eating, and Julius, you can find the fishing lines and the box of hooks, too. They're in the room behind the horses stalls. Just be careful with those hooks and don't open the box! I don't want you getting your fingers poked."

Lena and Annie helped to get the food packed and soon they were on the wagon. Ten year old Jake was allowed to drive for a while. He snapped the reins to make the horses trot down the road. The sun was hot and they were glad for their hats and jackets. No one wanted a sun burn and no one wanted to feel the grasshoppers landing on their arms as they drove.

Julius stood at the side of the wagon, holding out a long pole with a gunny sack for a net at the end of it. "Look, I've already got a lot of hoppers for bait," he said as he watched the insects fly right into the net.

When they got to the river they unhitched the horses and tied them to the wagon with long ropes so they could graze while the family fished.

Jacob found strong willow branches and cut them for fishing poles. Pushing them about a foot deep into the sand near the water, he then tied a fishing line at the top of each pole along with a couple of tiny bells. On the other end of the line he tied a hook. Julius grabbed a grasshopper from the sack and gave it to his papa. Jacob poked the hook through a grasshopper for bait.

Next he attached a little piece of iron called a 'sinker' on each line next to the hook and after telling everyone to stay out of the way, he swung the line round and round above his head and then let it fly out into the water.

Julius, Jake and their father each settled down on the sand beside the fishing poles at the edge of the river. They waited for the bells to ring telling them that the fish were biting.

Helena laid blankets down for everyone to sit or lie down on and settled on one herself. It was quiet and restful at the river: the sound of the waves lapping at the edge of the water; the birds chirping in the bushes and the happy sounds of her oldest two girls talking while they waded along the sand looking for clam shells. Two-year-old Tena slept beside her on the blanket.

They had all taken off their shoes and socks. The sand was cool and damp under their feet. It was fun to try to make shapes in the sand. Suddenly they heard the tinkling of little bells.

"I've got one!" shouted Julius. He began pulling in the line. Jake's pole began to shake and those bells rang too. Jacob got up to help Julius pull the line to the shore. The fish fought hard to stay in the water but they pulled it up on to the sand.

"Oh! Look at this one!" Jake said as his fish tugged and pulled away. Soon both boys had their fish lying on the sand. They were both Gold Eye fish and both a good size.

"Fill that big pail with water from the river and throw the fish into the pail," their father told them while he pulled his pliers out of his back pocket and removed the hooks from the fish's mouths.

The cold lunch was eaten at noon and they spent a good afternoon fishing and relaxing. As the sun rose higher in the sky they decided they had enough fish to clean. Jacob and his boys had all caught fish and were happy with their catch.

"All right," their father said, "Let's get everything packed up and head home for chores."

That evening, after chores were done, Jacob told Helena he was going into town to visit with the men at the store.

"What about all these fish we were going to clean?" Helena asked.

"I'll do that when I get home," he said. Helena was tired and hoped he wouldn't be too late because once Jacob had removed the fish scales the insides had to be cleaned out. Then the fish were put into a bowl of cold well water so they would stay fresh until the next day.

After the children were asleep and it was getting close to 10:00 o'clock in the evening, Jacob finally walked in the door. Helena looked up and saw he was not walking very steadily and his hands shook when he hung up his coat. She could see he had been drinking and could smell the alcohol. Jacob did not often drink alcohol and if he did, it was just a little. He saw the disappointed frown on her face. He knew all about her alcoholic father and how hard life had been with him.

Awkwardly he sat down and began scraping the fish scales off. After quietly watching him for a while Helena's frown turned to an amused smile. He kept dropping the fish and his hands couldn't hold them steadily enough to get the job done. Soon Helena's shoulders were shaking in silent laughter at her husband's clumsy efforts.

Jacob looked up at her and she couldn't hold her laughter quiet anymore. He looked so embarrassed and she laughed 'til tears ran down her cheeks.

"Heah! (Here)," she giggled finally, "Go schlopen (Go to bed)! Eck voa dit dounen. (I'll get this done)." Jacob got up and staggered over to the sink.

"Just one thing," Helena said, "If you want to get drunk, you sleep in the barn."

Jacob stared at his usually submissive wife for a moment, grabbed his barn coveralls and walked out to the barn. He never drank again.

An Early Christmas Gift

CHAPTER 69

As the weeks of November moved on and the snow was fell, covering the bare and dusty ground with a lovely white blanket, Jacob and Helena discussed the possibility of butchering one of their pigs. The pigs were not very big, because there wasn't as much food for them to eat but the family needed meat for the winter.

"Why don't we get it done the second week of December?" Jacob said. "By then everyone else will have finished with their butchering and we could ask people to help us."

"That's getting close to when our next baby is due," Helena answered. "But I think we could plan for butchering. I don't expect the new baby until the end of December."

The decision was made and neighbours were asked to meet at the Friesen farm on December 11th. The day arrived with a snow storm blowing in, but neighbours began arriving early in the morning anyway.

Helena was busy heating water on the stove and preparing food to feed all of those people. While she was visiting with some of the women who had come to help, she suddenly realized that something was happening! Her baby was coming earlier than she had expected!

"Jake!" she said to her ten year old son, "Get your coat and hat on and go to the barn. Tell Papa to come in quickly." Jake put on his coat and ran to the barn.

"Papa, Mama wants you to come to the house right away," Jake told his father after running into the barn.

"Now?" asked Jacob.

"Yes!" Jake replied. Excusing himself from his neighbours, Jacob hurried into the house and found Helena standing near the stove holding her stomach. He understood why she had wanted him to come inside.

"Lena, come and help get little Tena dressed. All of you children, get your coats, hats and mitts on. You're going to visit the Heins for a few hours."

"Why? We want to help with pig butchering!" Lena answered.

"Just hurry!" he said and walked out of the house to the barn. The women who had come to help quickly came to the rescue and helped get the children dressed.

"My wife is going to have her baby so we won't be butchering this morning," Jacob told the men when he got back to the barn.

"I wonder if one of you would go to the neighbours to see if they could come with the car. We need to get the doctor from Warman." The men looked at each other.

One of them said, "Jacob, no one will venture out in this blizzard with their car. They'd get stuck on the road. You'll have to phone Mrs. Dyck at the Post Office and go get her!"

"I'll have to hurry," he said. He turned to another neighbour. "Mr. Hein, would you mind taking my children to your house for a while?" Mr. Hein agreed right away. Jacob hurried to make the phone call. He hitched the team up to the cotta and drove off toward Osler.

Inside the house one of the women stayed until Jacob arrived with Mrs. Dyck. She and her husband decided they would wait until the baby was born in case she was needed to help.

When Mrs. Dyck walked into the bedroom, the baby was already born! The little one decided not to wait for anyone! When the children returned from the Heins' a few hours later, they welcomed another pretty little sister. Jacob and Helena named her Justina, but she was always called 'Christine'.

New Clothes from Old Clothes

CHAPTER 70

Helena rested in bed for a week and looked after her new baby. Jacob's cousin Agatha Wiebe came to help with the housework and children.

It was getting closer to Christmas so Lena and Annie began pestering their mother about new dresses for the school concert.

"I'm sorry," Helena said, "but we don't have the money to buy fabric to make new dresses this year."

"But my Sunday dress is too small!" Lena complained.
"Mine has a hole in it," added Annie.

Sighing, Helena sent a silent prayer to God for help and said, "We'll see what we can do." For the girls, this was almost a promise so they walked away hoping that somehow it would still happen.

As Jacob climbed into bed that night, Helena lay quietly staring at the ceiling before putting out the lamp light. Sensing something was bothering his wife, Jacob turned toward her.

"What's wrong?" he asked.

"The children all need new clothes. The girls are begging for new dresses for the school program and I looked at Jake's and Julius' pants and they're way too short. The children have all grown so much. I need to make new clothes but we don't have money for them," she said.

After a moment Jacob answered. "I heard Mr. John Driedger is going to Saskatoon tomorrow. I'll see if I can go with him and have him stop at the Salvation Army store. They often have big bags of old clothes for twenty-five cents. Maybe there'll be something in the bag that you can make over."

"Or maybe there will be some children's clothes in the bag that fit right away. That's a good idea," she said as she turned over to get some sleep. Morning would come too soon and she needed rest.

Jacob got his ride to Saskatoon and while the children were in school, Helena kept Tena and Julius entertained and the baby looked after while she waited for him to get back.

Just after Lena, Jake, and Annie returned from their walk home from school, their father arrived home, carrying two big bags into the house. The children immediately crowded around to see what he had brought.

Helena moved the meat she was frying to a cooler part of the stove and watched as Jacob opened the bags. He removed several dresses and coats and soon the children were all pulling clothes out and dropping them on the floor.

"Don't put them on the floor!" their mama said. "Put them on the table so we can see them."

"Look! Here's a red scarf," Lena said. As they emptied the bags they found shirts that fit their papa, one that fit Jake, some pants that fit Julius and many big dresses and big pairs of pants.

"Red suspenders!" Jake said as he pulled them out.

"There are no dresses for me," Annie said sadly.

"Oh, but there will be!" her mama said as she held up a pretty women's size cotton dress. "I can make you children dresses, shirts and pants from a lot of these clothes! But if I am going to get all of that done before Christmas, you children will have to help a lot more with chores when you get home from school!"

There were smiles of relief on the children's faces as they promised they would help. Jacob's cousin Agatha came back for a few days to do the cooking and cleaning so Helena could work on the clothes.

On the day of the concert at school, Jacob was very happy with the wonderful clothes Helena had made out of old clothes as he watched his precious children on the stage at the concert. Soon the concert was over and the children eagerly waited for their gifts and candy bags.

Lena received a book called, "Lassie", a story about a dog; Jake got a baseball and glove and when Annie's name was called she gasped with delight as she opened a box and saw a beautiful porcelain doll in a long pretty dress! She had never had a doll of her own before. Helena and Jacob smiled at the excitement on her face.

At home after the concert, the family gathered around the pot-bellied stove in the living room, eating their treats from the candy bags. Helena and Jacob listened to the children's happy chatter.

"Mama, the teacher said my new dress is very pretty!" Annie said.

"My best friend really liked my dress too!" Lena added.

"And you boys looked very handsome in your new shirts and pants," Jacob said as he bounced two year old Tena on his lap. "Those red suspenders looked good too, Jake," He added.

As Annie held the box with her doll in it, Helena said, "Let's put your doll up on the shelf in my bedroom so it doesn't break. I'll get her down for you when you want to play with her, but you'll have to be very careful." Annie agreed and watched as her mother lifted the precious box up on to the shelf. Then it was bed time for them all.

As Helena read her Bible that night before going to bed, she came to the seventeenth verse from second Corinthians chapter five, "Therefore if anyone is in Christ, he is a new creation; the old has gone, the new has come."

She smiled as she thought, "God makes us new when we believe in Christ. Our old sins are forgiven and we've been made new. That's what the Bible says. Kind of what I did – making new clothes out of old ones!"

Making Shoes to fit Horses Feet

CHAPTER 71

During the cold winter months, Helena pulled out several old sweaters from the clothing bags Jacob had brought home and washed them. When they were clean, she began to carefully unravel the yarn. After school the children saw what she was doing and offered to help.

"I'll give you each a sweater and show you how to start," she said to Lena and Annie and Julius. "Here is the end of the yarn. Now just pull gently and wind it into a ball."

The children enjoyed pulling the sweaters apart. "My ball of yarn is bigger than yours!" one of them said, and soon they were trying to wind the yarn faster! They often dropped the yarn ball and laughed as they quickly bent to pick them up before they could unwind too much.

"What are you going to do with all this yarn?" Annie asked.

I'm going to knit new sweaters for you children, using the old yarn."

"But the colours are not the same," Lena said.

"They are close enough in colour that I can dye the finished sweater a new colour and it will all look the same," Helena replied.

The next few months were busy as they waited for spring. Again Jacob and Helena wondered if this would be a better year for rain, but as the snow melted, the sun shone warmer and warmer again and after planting their crops and garden the rain still did not come.

Jacob needed to earn more money because the money they received for shipping cream was not enough. He was glad his blacksmith shop was getting busier all the time. When people ploughed their fields, the plough shares *(sharp metal plates that cut the ground)* sometimes broke on the rocks and stones. They needed to be fixed so farmers brought their tools and broken machinery parts to him.

Besides tools, people brought their horses' shoes to him for fixing and re-sizing. Jacob often wandered around junk yards to pick up scrap iron and other metals that he could use to make things. He also found quite a few used horse shoes and brought them home.

In his blacksmith shop he heated the open stove with coal and pushed air into the bottom of the stove with a bellows, causing the fire to become very, very hot. He tested a piece of metal by holding it in the fire. When it turned red hot, he knew the fire was hot enough. Holding a horse shoe in the fire with long metal tongs, Jacob waited until the shoe was a bright red fiery colour all over. Then he knew he could bend it any way he wanted.

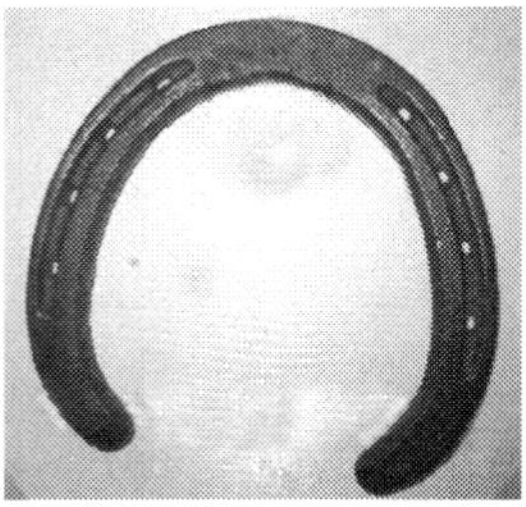

Photo of horse shoe
By NB

He laid the red hot horse shoe on a heavy, flat iron surface called an 'anvil' and began pounding the hot horse shoe into the right shape with a heavy hammer, stopping once in a while to bend it into place. When it cooled down, he held it in the fire again until it was red hot and soft enough to work with again.

Farmers in the area often drove their teams of horses to the Friesen farm and stopped near the blacksmith shop.

"Jacob, my horse 'threw a shoe' again today." (*That meant the horse shoe had come off a horse's hoof*) "Could you please make a new one for him?" they would ask. "He also needs to have his hooves clipped."

Standing next to the horse, Jacob lifted the horse's hoof to measure the size and shape. With the horse's hoof between his knees, he scraped out any dirt that had collected there and cleaned each hoof carefully.

"Hand me that hoof clipper in the corner," he said to Jake who was standing near him, watching. Jake ran to get the clipper and brought it to his dad. Looking at Jake he said, "Horses need their nails clipped too, right?'

Out of junk metal he found, Jacob made one clipper for hooves and one for clipping horns off of the cows' heads. Farmers clipped horns off the cows' heads because it made them less dangerous to the farmers and to each other. Jacob kept a bag of flour in the barn which he used to coat the spots where the horns had been removed. The flour stopped the bleeding.

After shaping the new horseshoes, he plunged them quickly into a pail of cold well water. The heat made the cold water hiss and spray. He left them there until they were cool enough to use. Then he picked up each horse hoof, put the horse's leg between his knees and nailed the shoe on with tiny, sharp pointed square nails.

The horseshoes didn't hurt the hooves. They kept the horse's feet from getting sore and their hooves from breaking and cracking – just like shoes do for our feet. The sharp pointed nails didn't hurt the horses because they didn't go into the fleshy part of the hoof – only the grown-out 'toenail' part. The horses didn't mind getting new shoes. They were used to it.

Paying Jacob and thanking him, the farmers left. They were glad that the horses would not have sharp little rocks digging into the bottom of the fleshy part of their feet anymore, as they clip-clopped down the dusty dirt road, in their fancy new shoes!

A Little Girl's Tears

CHAPTER 72

While Jacob was busy with his blacksmith shop, milking cows, and feeding pigs, Helena looked after her garden and the family. Everyone had to help.

"Lena," her mother often called. "I hear Christine crying. Get her out of the crib and change her diaper. Then you can bring her outside in the carriage."

"Jake, take this bundle of carrot and beet greens and throw them into the pig pen. Then you can pull up the pig-weed at the edge of the garden. The pigs enjoy those as well."

Yes, there was work but also lots of lazy summer playtime. Running to the pond in the neighbours' field and watching the tadpoles swimming around, was a great past time for them. Around the pond were bushes with many song birds. Ducks swam around with their ducklings following them. This was a special place.

"I'll race you home!" Lena called as she turned for home.

"No, you won't!" Jake answered as his long legs soon outran his older sister. Annie and Julius followed, but Annie had to stop and admire the buttercups and blue bells growing in the tall grasses of the field.

When Annie walked into the house, she called her mother and found her in the bedroom. Helena had just changed baby Christine.

"Mama, can you please get my doll down from the shelf? I want to hold her for a while."

"Yes, I can do that," her mother replied as she reached for the box. She opened the box for Annie who gently lifted the pretty doll and held her carefully. Just then two year old Tena ran into the room and saw the doll.

"Mine!" she said and reached for the doll.

"No! You'll break her!" Annie said as she turned away from her little sister. Tena began to cry and screamed loudly, "Mine! Mine!"

"No! Get away! You can't have her!" Annie told her.

Helena was trying to nurse the baby and found the screaming and fighting too much and with a sigh she said, "Oh, Annie – just let her hold it a bit so she stops screaming!"

"She'll break her," Annie said.

"No, she won't," her mother said, "Just help her hold it."

Carefully Annie lowered her doll to Tena's arms. Two year old Tena grabbed the doll eagerly and then it happened. Crash!! She dropped the doll, whose head shattered on the floor.

"No! No!" sobbed Annie as she knelt beside the broken glass. "You said she wouldn't break it." Helena sat shocked and so sorry she had given in to a two-year old's demands.

"I'm so sorry, Annie – but leave the glass alone, you'll cut yourself. No, Tena – don't touch it!"

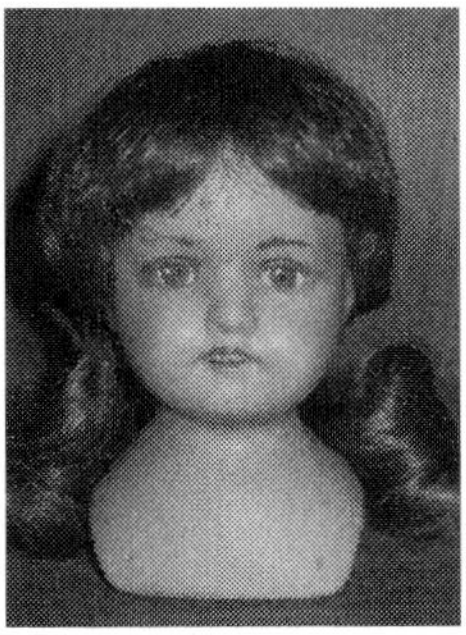

Similar to Annie's Porcelain doll's head (this doll belonged to Annie's aunt Marg which was given to Nettie Balzer)

The other children had come running when they heard the crying and as Lena saw what happened, she said, "I'll get the broom and sweep it up." She felt like crying too.

For a long time Annie could not forget the loss of her precious Christmas gift and often looked at her mother with sad disappointment in her eyes. Helena saw the hurt in her little girl's face and felt heartbroken for her. She wished she could afford to go and buy another doll and somehow make up for what had happened.

Grasshoppers!

CHAPTER 73

Helena finished knitting sweaters and mittens for the children from the yarn they had pulled from the old sweaters. She went to the Osler store with Jacob one day and found several different colours of clothing dye and bought them. A few days later, brightly coloured sweaters hung on old sheets over the backs of the kitchen chairs to dry.

Lena and Annie proudly wore their sweaters to school. They loved how warm they felt wearing them, and they were so pretty and bright! There was enough yarn left to make another for little Tena.

The spring rains of 1935 brought hope that this year, for the first time in seven years, there would be good crops and lush gardens. As spring turned to summer, the bright green blades of oats and wheat growing in the fields brought a smile to Jacob's face. After walking through the fields to check on the plants, he returned to the farm yard and found Helena in the garden.

"Look at all the flowers on the fruit trees!" she said as she pointed to the loaded branches. "Smell the perfume of the flowers! It fills the air."

Glancing at the neat rows of vegetables growing nearby, Jacob commented, "The rest of the garden looks good, too."

"I'm so thankful. We can look forward to a better harvest this fall," she said.

All summer they waited for more rain but it did not come. The crops had a good start so they were able to keep on growing for a while. Then they stopped growing.

One very hot, windy day in August, they noticed a dark cloud in the west.

"Rain is coming!" thought Helena. But the cloud moved very quickly and as she weeded in the garden she soon heard whirring sounds. Grasshoppers began landing on the ground! Hurrying as fast as she could, she ran for the house. Helena called to the children, "Gote em hoose enen!(Get into the house!) There are many grasshoppers coming!"

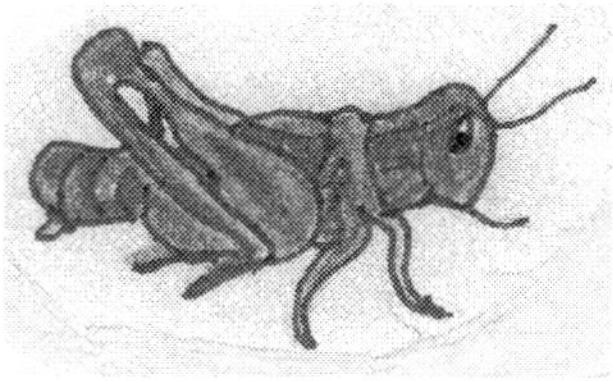

Grasshopper
Drawing by NB

Jacob heard her calling and walked out of the barn. He looked toward the west in disbelief! He, too, hurried into the house. Soon the air and ground was covered with grasshoppers. Over the next few days some of them moved on, but not until they had eaten the leaves off all of the plants in the field and the garden.

There would be no crops to feed the cows for the winter and now there was no grass left in the fields either! The cows looked skinny and tired. Jacob's beautiful horses stood with their heads hanging, their ears forward and their ribs began to show.

Every farmer in the area was facing the same problem: what to feed the animals. Jacob soon found out from meetings with other farmers at the Osler store that there would be shipments of hay coming from other provinces.

As Jacob and Helena sat talking in the evenings Helena wondered if the hay shipments would be enough.

"No," Jacob said. "There won't be enough hay for all of us farmers. We may have some Russian thistle by the fall to harvest but not a lot of hay. Farmers in the Melfort area are still doing well. They weren't hit with the grasshoppers. Some of those farmers are willing to keep our cows in their pastures and barns through the winter, but that is 200 miles away. How do I get them to Melfort?" he mused.

"But how do we ship cream if all the cows go to Melfort?" asked Helena.

"We'll keep a few here and maybe the hay we get will be enough for them and for the horses."

In the fall, Jacob and another farmer took their horses and wagons and herded the cows all the way to a farm near Melfort. It took many days to get there and they had to stop for the nights to feed and water the animals. The men curled up in blankets in the wagons for the night.

After being promised the cows would be well looked after, the men returned home to look after the remaining animals. They phoned around to see if they could buy extra straw and hay.

With all of the added stress, Helena missed her mother and family very much. She phoned her mother and family and asked if it would be possible for them to come for a visit. They planned to come on a Sunday, a week later. Helena looked forward to seeing her mother and siblings again. A few days later she received a letter in the mail.

*Aberdeen, October 11, 1935 (*translation of actual letter*)*

Dear Children,
Since we can not come on Sunday after all, I will quickly write to let you know the situation here. It is so busy here now that it just didn't suit to go. Tomorrow there is an engagement party at the David Quirings. So it wouldn't suit the John Buhlers to go either, since their son Peter is the bridegroom! And on Sunday is also Jacob

Loewen's silver wedding anniversary. We are all invited – but postponing doesn't mean it's hopeless. If the weather is nice again, we will come some day other than on a Sunday. That is if I feel well enough. This cold weather is not good for my health. Then I have a lot of pain.
So I will close for now and go to bed. The girls went to walk Annie Martens part way home and they have not come back yet.
Well – good night from your Mother.

Helena was disappointed, but she understood.

Grandma Banman Dies

CHAPTER 74

With winter coming and four children now in school, Helena tried to keep up with mending and knitting along with the usual work. The children were growing so fast it was hard to keep up with finding things to fit them. Lena was now fourteen; Jake and Annie would turn twelve and ten in December and Julius was six.

At home, four year old Tena and two year old Christine became close sister-friends. Helena found it easier to get work done because the two girls played for hours.

The days went by too quickly with all that needed to be done before Christmas. Jacob brought home more bags of old clothing from the Salvation Army and Helena was busy trying to find things she could make over into dresses, pants, shirts and especially, warm coats. She was also sewing baby clothes because another baby was expected in January.

Helena kept up with writing letters to her mother who was not feeling any better. Helena was very worried about her. Every day she prayed for all of her family: her own children; her mother; and other family members. The second week of December of 1935 Jacob brought another letter from Aberdeen. This time it was not written by her mother but her sister Agenetha.

December 13,1935 (translation of actual letter)

Dear family.

Since we received your letter today, I will answer it right away. Mother is much worse and has not been out of bed since Sunday. Each day she gets worse. Jacob Klassens are here today. We are relieved when someone is here with us. David Buhlers were here on Saturday. Well – I will sign off for this time.
Greetings from your sister,
Agenetha.

Good morning. Today is Saturday. Mother is not better. She wants to get dressed and sit in a chair for a while because she gets so very tired from lying in bed all the time. I think she is asleep right now. When she awakes I will help her get dressed.
Agenetha

That was the last letter before a phone call came seven days later on December 21st. Helena's mother had died of tuberculosis – a serious disease of the lungs.

Several days later the whole family was packed into the cotta and the horses started off for the river road and on to Aberdeen and the Banman farm. Jacob did not make the horses hurry. The animals were not as strong as they had once been because they didn't have enough good food to eat.

The children brought a few toys and books with them for the long drive and sat wrapped in warm wool quilts, resting their feet on hot stones. They tried to keep occupied. Lena read stories to the younger children. All of the Friesen children loved to read and listen to stories.

"Papa," Jake asked at one point on the trip "will the ice road be thick enough to travel on?" He remembered the scary trip when they had returned from his grandpa's funeral.

"Yes, Jake," his father said, "It will be thick enough. Besides, the river road is not as long now. There hasn't been enough rain for several years to fill the river, so the river is much lower and narrower now."

Jake leaned back against the wall of the sleigh and relaxed, listening to the harnesses jingle and the steady clop clop of the horses' hooves, while Lena continued to read.

An hour and a half later the horses turned into the Banman driveway to find many other sleighs and cars parked near the barn.

Walking into the crowded house, Helena still felt like it was empty because her mother was not there anymore. She knew Mama was in heaven with Jesus, but everything felt different, not just to her, but to all of her brothers and sisters.

In the bedroom, Mama Banman's body lay in a home-made casket lined with white cloth. The funeral was that afternoon. After the funeral the body was carried outside and the family gathered around for a picture. Many of the Mennonites took "family" pictures with their dead.

That night all the family members prepared for bed. The little cousins Tena and Chris's age were closely lined up in the schlopebenk and the rest slept on couches, floors and on Mama Banman's bed.

The next day the whole family drove down to the Edenburg cemetery to bury their mother next to their father. From there, with a heavy heart, Helena and her family returned home to Osler.

Another Angel

CHAPTER 75

A few weeks after Mama Banman's funeral, while the older children were at school and the little girls had been taken to the Hein farm, Helena and Jacob welcomed another little boy into their family. It was January 11th, 1936.

This time, the doctor from Warman was called and he drove to the farm house to help Helena. When the little boy was born, the doctor was very quiet as he looked the baby over. Handing the baby to the mid-wife who was helping, he called Jacob into the bedroom and turned toward Helena.

"What is wrong? Is the baby all right?" she asked. Somehow in her heart she knew things were not all right.

"This baby has the same problems as the other little boy you had - the one that didn't live. This little one will probably not last longer than six months, either. I am so sorry."

Tears streamed down Helena's and Jacob's faces. The baby was brought back to her after being bathed by the midwife and Helena held out her arms to hold him close. He looked up into her eyes and she was reminded of baby Daniel's bright and alert eyes. She was filled with love for him. She un-wrapped the baby and saw that his legs and back were the same as Daniel's.

"What shall we name him?" asked Jacob. "I was thinking of naming him Edward."

"I like that," Helena answered softly as she gently stroked the little one's face. "Let's see what the older children think of that name."

"I'll phone my sister Anna to see if she can help for a week," Jacob said "I'll bring the little girls home from the Heins after the others come home from school. Lena and Annie can do the work until Anna comes."

He picked up the receiver of the telephone and listened to see if the line was busy. No one was talking, so he turned the crank on the right side of the phone and rang his parent's number.

"Hello?" Anna answered.

"Hello – it's Jacob. We've just had another baby boy and wonder if you have time to come and help Helena out for a week. I could pick you up this evening."

"Yes, I can help out, but I will see if one of our brothers can take me to your house," she replied.

At supper time a team of horses pulled a sleigh into the yard and the children's Aunt Anna stepped out.

For the next week, Helena had help as she rested, mostly in bed, taking care of little Edward. He was just as contented a baby as Daniel had been and again she felt such love and joy in taking care of his every need.

In June, baby Edward became ill and just as it had been with Daniel, he cried a lot. Helena and the older children took turns carrying him to comfort him whenever he was awake. Knowing he would not be with them much longer broke Helena's heart. One day as she carried him, he relaxed and stopped breathing. He was six months old and died in July of 1936. Another angel-boy was now with Jesus. The family buried him beside his brother Daniel.

Family members came to the farm house for the little funeral. While the people sang hymns, Helena sat on a chair holding two year old Christine on her lap. As the tears streamed down her face, she often wiped her eyes with her handkerchief. Each time she tried to dry her eyes, little Christine reached up and yanked the handkerchief out of her hands.

After trying to make her stop several times, Helena suddenly began to giggle uncontrollably and her shoulders shook with laughter. She was embarrassed because people were looking at her, wondering how she could laugh at her son's funeral. She knew it was just nervous laughter and that her little daughter wasn't being naughty, she just needed some attention.

Grasshopper Poison

CHAPTER 76

During the winter of 1936, while Helena was looking after baby Edward, Jacob became very concerned about his cows in Melfort and decided to take a train trip to Melfort to check on them.

He was shocked to discover that the farmer had not looked after the cows properly at all and several of them had died! Also, now the farmer was claiming two of Jacob's cows as his own! There was nothing Jacob could do until spring when he could bring his cattle home, so he returned to Osler, worried, disappointed and discouraged.

"I'm going to talk to the other farmers who took cattle up there and make a plan to bring our cattle home as soon as the snow is gone," he told Helena. "I don't know what we can do about the cattle the farmer now claims are his."

As the snow disappeared, the farmers headed back to Melfort with their horses and wagons and after a week they returned from slowly herding the cows all the way back to Osler.

Jacob only had five cows left of the herd he had taken to Melfort. Spring had come and there was some grass growing so the cows were left outside to graze. Some of them had calves and soon there was more cream to ship again. Jacob borrowed money so he could buy oat and wheat seed to plant and soon the planting season began. He was also busy fixing farmers plough shares and making potato planters. It was easy to use and word about the planter spread. He didn't make a lot of money, but every little bit helped.

When a farmer brought him a broken plough share, he dug a shaped hole in the ground and placed the broken pieces together in the hole. Then he poured molten metal over the pieces. Once it was cooled, Jacob took the metal piece out of the ground. He heated it, smoothed out the metal with a hammer, cooled it again and sharpened the ploughing edge. The plough share was fixed.

As the weather kept getting warmer, the crops grew, the gardens began to grow well and there was rain. "Things are looking better now, aren't they?" asked Helena one evening.

"Yes they are, but I 'm worried about grasshoppers. The insects laid a lot of eggs last year. If they all hatch, we may have more problems than last year," he announced.

A letter appeared in Box 52 at the Osler Post Office one day, as Jacob picked up the mail. Every farmer in the area had received the same letter.

"Notice to all farmers," it read. *"Due to the large grasshopper problem last summer, the government will be shipping grasshopper poison on the train box cars in two weeks. When the young grasshoppers hatch in the fields you may spread the poison around. They'll eat it and die.*

"Please be advised that the poison will come in gunny sacks of sawdust mixed with poison. Do not spread it on your vegetables. Do not handle it with your bare hands. Keep it away from children and animals"

When Jacob returned home, he went to his blacksmith shop to work. The children walked home from school and, hearing him hammering in the shop, went to see what their papa was doing.

"What are you making?" asked Julius.

"I'm making little shovels with long handles," he replied.

"May we play with them?" asked little Tena who had followed the older children to the shop.

"No, these are for spreading grasshopper poison out in the fields," her papa told her. "The poison is very dangerous and I want you children to stay far away from it."

Soon the day came for him to pick up the bags of poison. Hitching the horses to the wagon, he drove to the Osler railway station and picked up his bags. Again the farmers were reminded to be very careful with it.

After school that day, Jake heard his father call him when he got home. Dropping his books and grabbing a cookie, he walked to where his dad was standing in the big wagon. Julius followed Jake to see what their dad was doing.

"Here, put on these coveralls and old gloves and grab one of the little shovels I made. You can help me spread the poison. Just be very careful not to get in on yourself or on your clothes."

"Giddy up!" Jacob called as he snapped the reins on the horses' backs. "Open the gate to the pasture, Julius, and close it after I am through."

Running ahead of the team, Julius opened the gate and swung it wide for the wagon to get through. Then he quickly closed it before the other horses or cows could get out.

Out in the field, they looked down. "Look at all those little grasshoppers! At this rate we'll have more than last year!" Jake said.

"Well, let's spread this stuff around on the ground and hopefully most of them will die," his dad answered.

Standing on opposite sides of the wagon, the two of them threw shovels full of poison around on the ground while the horses kept moving forward. After going back and forth all over the fields, making sure the horses didn't walk in the poison, they went home again and Jacob stored the rest of the bags of poison far away from animals or children.

While eating supper one evening, Jacob said, "When I was in town today, I heard that one of the farmers that picked up poison the same day I did, sat on the sacks on his way home. He died yesterday."

The children all looked at their dad with surprise and shock. Jake was glad he had listened to his dad and had been very careful in handling the poison.

"Now you know how dangerous it is," he continued, "You know that you should never, ever, play with it." As the children solemnly promised to stay away from the poison, their mother added, "Now let's hope and pray that the insects will die from it so we'll have garden vegetables and crops."

An Old Summer Kitchen And a New Washing Machine

CHAPTER 77

Summer kitchen at Osler farm. Drawing by NB.

A few yards away from the house on the Friesen farm stood a little shack with two windows and a door. Inside stood a coal and wood cook stove, an old table and lots of shelves. This little shack was used every summer to cook the family's meals. This way the big house would stay cool on hot days.

Washing machine at Rosthern Museum

In the summer, the laundry was also done in this little house. The first washing machine Helena used was made of wood and leaked a lot. It had a handle in the middle which had to be rocked back and forth until the clothes were clean.

As he and Helena waited for the crops and garden to grow, Jacob decided to work in his blacksmith shop and make his wife a new washing machine. He took his wagon to all the local scrap metal heaps again and found angle iron and strap iron, parts from different machines, a large piece of galvanized steel and a clothes wringer from yet another machine and brought the parts home. At home in the blacksmith shop he worked at welding the galvanized steel into the shape of the washing machine tub and with the strong iron he had found, he made a frame for it as well as for the lid.

After welding all the parts together and making an attachment on the lid handle that made contact with the gyrator (the piece that moved and washed the clothes) he set it on iron legs he had made, put wheels on them and attached the wringer to the top and side of the machine. Helena had a new washing machine!

Lena and Annie enjoyed helping with the laundry with this new machine. It was still hard work to move the handle on the lid, back and forth 100 times for each load of wash; but at least the machine did not leak water.

Sad iron at Osler Museum

Besides washing clothes, the girls ironed them as well. A fire was built in the stove and the heavy sadirons were set on it until they were very hot. The girls picked up a handle that clicked on to the irons and then smoothed out all the wrinkles on the clothes. Everything had to be ironed: the dresses; shirts; pants; sheets; pillow cases; tea towels and even the handkerchiefs. Ironing in the hot summer, in a hot kitchen was not easy.

There were two things the girls, especially Annie, did not like doing: rinsing dirty diapers before washing them; and rinsing slimy handkerchiefs after people had blown their noses into them. They didn't use Kleenex or tissues in those days. Everyone used cloth handkerchiefs and they weren't thrown in the garbage. They were washed once a week.

Everyone had to help with the chores and garden weeding, but in the evenings, after chores and dishes were done, it was play time! Lena, Jake, Julius and Annie loved to play catch or baseball in the lane between their farm and the neighbours' farm. Sometimes their papa played with them.

Another favourite game was called 'Anti-I-Over'. Two of the children stood on one side of the house, and two on the other. They took turns throwing a bouncy sponge ball over the roof of the house to each other. As they threw it, they yelled "Anti-I-Over!" If the ball didn't go over the roof and bounced back down they yelled "Pigs tail!" Then the two on the opposite side of the house knew that the ball had not gone over. Meanwhile the two whose ball had not gone over the roof, raced each other to find it and take a turn. Many summer and fall evenings were spent just having fun!

Hoping for Flowers

CHAPTER 78

With the garden and the crops growing, and more grasshoppers hatching, Jacob and Helena watched the ground anxiously.

"If only the potatoes and fruit trees could finish flowering before the grasshoppers eat the leaves, we'd still have potatoes and some fruit," Helena thought. "The carrots and turnips should still grow. I'll be thankful for that." She spent a lot of time praying that summer, the summer little Edward died. Not just for the baby, but for God to provide for the rest of her family.

Soon it was time for school again and the house was quiet with only Tena and Christine at home. Helena picked the few gooseberries and other fruit that didn't get eaten by the hoppers. It wasn't easy working in the garden with those insects jumping all over her!

"I hate those grasshoppers!" Annie said as she stomped into the house one day after school. "They jump into my hair and into my shoes and under my dress!"

"And then she screams until I help her get them out!" commented Lena.

"You don't like them either!" Annie said.

"No I don't – my socks are full of squished grasshoppers. I wish that poison would kill more of them!" Lena replied as she removed the dirty socks from her feet and turned to shake her shoes upside down outside.

Helena's hopes and prayers for the vegetables to flower were answered and in spite of all the insects still flying and hopping around, the potato harvest was good. There were carrots and turnips, too, but not many beans or peas.

The month of September was potato picking time. It was a big job for the whole family. When the children were all home on a Saturday, Jake and his dad dug up the potatoes while the girls picked them up, put them in pails and dumped them into gunny sacks on the stone boat when their pails were full. When the sacks on the stone boat were filled, a horse was hitched to it and one of the children led it to the house.

On the west side of the house, there was a little trap door on the wall of the foundation. Jacob opened it and inside was a tin slide which led into the potato bin in the cellar. One by one the sacks were emptied. The rumbling sound of potatoes sliding and bumping down into the cellar was a happy sound for Jacob and Helena. They would have food for the winter.

Tasty Baked Potatoes and 'Prips'

CHAPTER 79

The winter of 1937 passed quickly and soon it was late spring. On a Saturday, Jacob called the children outside.

"We're going to clean up the yard," he said. Handing the oldest four children rakes, he got them raking the yard, beginning at the house. "Tena, you can help pick up the garbage that has blown around in the winter."

As they got busy even little Christine followed Tena around picking up garbage and tossing it into the pile on the yard. With their father helping them, they soon had a big pile of leaves, grass and other garbage.

"I'm going to burn this pile," he said. "Jake, you can go to the house and get six potatoes out of the potato bin and push them under this pile. When the pile has burned down completely, the potatoes will be roasted and we'll dig them out so you can peel them and eat them with salt!"

Jake walked to the house and soon was back with six potatoes which he pushed into the pile before his papa lit it. They all watched as the fire grew bigger and after a while all that was left was red hot glowing ashes.

"Are they done yet?" asked Julius.

"Not yet. Wait until the ashes cool down a bit." After a few more minutes of waiting, Jacob said; "All right, I'll get them out with the rake. They'll still be very hot."

He raked the potatoes out of the ashes and put them on stones to cool off. Soon they were able to pull off the black, sooty peel. They sprinkled salt on them and enjoyed a treat for all their hard work!

As summer returned, so did the grasshoppers but there were not as many as the year before. Still, because of the hard years there was not much money for all of their needs.

Coffee grinder
Osler Museum

One day Helena wanted to grind coffee beans and realized there were only a few beans left. She knew there was no extra money so she walked to the barn where Jacob kept the wheat seeds. She filled a small bowl with seeds and went back into the house and roasted them until they were very dark and hard. Filling the coffee grinder with roasted grain, she ground them and put some into the kettle of boiling water. She knew other people who had done this many years ago. This coffee was called Prips.

At supper time she poured a cup of prips for Jacob. He took a sip of it and looked at his wife in surprise.

"We're drinking prips now?" he asked.

"Yes. We're out of coffee beans and I know we don't have enough money to buy extras like that. It doesn't taste too bad, does it?"

"Well, it's not coffee but it's hot and with a little cream it will do until we can afford to buy real coffee beans," he said. "I'm just thankful we are still eating. God is still taking care of us."

School Desks and Kitchen Cupboards

CHAPTER 80

"Helena, I've been asked to build desks for the school in Osler," Jacob told her one day when he returned from town. "The school board will pay me to make them."

"Thank God for that! We can use the money," she said.

A double desk
Photo from Osler Museum

Soon Jacob came home from the lumber yard with new wood and a plan of how to build the desks. Some of them would be single desks for one child to sit in and some would be double desks to hold two children. He measured, drew the patterns, sawed the wood, shaved the edges and sanded all the pieces so they'd be smooth. Using angle iron he found at a scrap heap, he made frames in his blacksmith shop for some of the desks.

The double desks had a shelf under the table top for school books. Other desks were built with a drawer below the seat for the books. The children enjoyed watching him work and once the desks were all built they were varnished so they would have a smooth shiny surface.

It took several weeks of hard work, but Jacob delivered the desks to the school in Osler and everyone was happy with his work.

Possibly one of the wooden desks made by Jacob, presently at the Osler Museum.

"There are quite a few pieces of plywood left from the desks," Jacob said at dinner one day. "I'll ask the school board if I can buy the leftover lumber. You've been wishing you could have better cupboards for a long time, Helena, so I'm going to build some."

He began building the cupboards at the end of June. He asked Helena for suggestions about how many shelves she wanted to have. Helena also asked for a pull out bin to keep the flour in. Jacob built the cupboards along the south wall of the kitchen, both top and bottom units, leaving a space for the kitchen sink next to the countertop. Helena painted them white, and looked forward to putting all her dishes and food stuff into them.

When the work was finished, she concentrated on another important event; she was looking forward to a new baby.

Another Daniel

CHAPTER 81

On July 9th, 1937, Jake and Julius were told to stay outside and work in the barn while Annie took Tena and Christine to the Heins. Lena was away babysitting at another farm.

Jacob picked up the telephone and listened first to see if anyone else was using the line. Then he turned the little crank to dial the operator.

"Hello, could you please connect me with the doctor in Warman?" he asked. The doctor answered and Jacob continued, "This is Jacob Friesen from Osler. My wife is going to have another baby and we're wondering if you could come out to the farm as soon as possible."

"I'll be there," the doctor said and hung up the receiver. Jacob walked to the bedroom to tell Helena that the doctor would be coming.

Soon a car arrived on the Friesen yard and the doctor got out and hurried into the farm house. About an hour later a tiny baby cried for the first time and Helena was relieved to hear him cry.

"This boy looks fine to me," the doctor said. "He's strong and healthy-looking, and right now he looks a little angry at being brought into this world. Jacob – pour some warm water into the wash tub and we'll get him washed and wrapped up."

Once the little one was wrapped up in a snugly night shirt, diaper and warm blanket, he stopped crying and looked around at his new surroundings. Jacob placed the baby in Helena's arms. She smiled into his face and talked softly to him as he gazed back into her eyes. He was quiet and seemed to be thinking, "I've heard that voice before!"

"I have always wanted to name one of my boys, 'Daniel', after my uncle Daniel Blatz. I know we already had one Daniel, but he is with Jesus now," she said after the doctor had left.

"We named Lena 'Helena' and her older sister had the same name and she is also with Jesus. Why can't we name this one 'Daniel' too?" asked Jacob.

"Well, the first Helena didn't live. Our first Daniel lived for six months. I also wanted a boy named 'Peter', after my brother. What do you think of adding a second name? His name could be 'Daniel Peter'."

The name sounded good to Jacob, so that was what he was named. Soon the baby became 'Danny' to his older brothers and sisters.

The older children were busy with weeding, farm work and for the girls – washing many diapers! Another new baby meant a lot more laundry but it was nice to be able to hang it all out to dry on the line in the hot summer months.

Soon there were choke cherries and pin cherries to pick, along with the gooseberries, plums and currants. The older children and Helena stood on step ladders with fruit aprons tied to their waists. The aprons had a big pocket into which they put the ripe fruit, later dumping it into pails.

Then came the canning and making of jams and jellies. Helena picked as much fruit as she could before the end August. It was a very tiring month just after having a baby.

Helena with sisters Susanna and Agenetha, on one of her birthdays.

The second last Sunday of August, Helena and her girls had been busy all morning, making the fried chicken, potatoes and salads. When the rest of the family returned home from church, the boys picked tubs full of ripe watermelons and muskmelons.

Soon the honking of horns was heard as Model T Ford cars motored down the driveway and stopped near the house. The farm yard was again filled with the Banman brothers and sisters and their families, for their 'once a year' gathering on Helena's birthday. Many teenage and younger cousins ran through her garden and all over the yard. She loved having them all.

White-washing the Barn

CHAPTER 82

In August, the milk inspector travelled to the Friesen farm and looked over the cooling house and the barn. Jacob knew he was coming and he and his boys had cleaned the gutters and swept the floor.

After a careful inspection, the man said, "Mr. Friesen, you need to put lime on your walls to disinfect the barn before you ship any more cream. You can get the lime from the store in Osler and mix it with water. The directions are on the bag."

The lime was like a white paint. Because it was white and clean, painting lime on walls was called 'white-washing'.

Jacob drove his team to Osler to pick up the bags of lime and some big paint brushes. The next morning after the cows were milked and let out to pasture, he cleaned several big pails and filled them with water.

At breakfast he talked about the big job they had that day. "I bought four brushes, so Lena, Jake, Annie and Julius can paint the inside walls of the barn. I have work in the blacksmith shop today, so you'll have to do the painting. You'll need to sweep and scrape any hard dirt you find on the walls before you paint."

The oldest four got busy that morning scraping dried manure off the walls, and sweeping off the cob webs and dust.

"My wall is ready," Jake said as he stirred the lime and water paste in the big pail. He dipped his big brush into it and began to spread it on the wall.

Soon all four were busy painting the lime on the walls.

From left to right; summer kitchen; house, well (behind mower wheel), outhouse in background just behind white horses; cooling house for milk, and part of windmill structure beside it.
FRIESEN FARM YARD NEAR OSLER

When they couldn't reach the higher parts, they stood on the little milk benches so the top of the walls could be painted, too. It was hard work, but gradually the walls changed from dirty grey to bright white.

"Dinner is ready!" Tena called as she ran to the barn to tell them to come and eat.

"Good! I'm hungry and tired," Julius said. At nine years of age he couldn't keep up with the older ones, but he was really trying. He tired out sooner and needed help to reach the highest spots.

They all scrubbed their white lime covered hands in the sink and gathered round the table for their fried potatoes and eggs.

Helena smiled as she looked at the smudges of white in their hair and the spots they'd missed on their faces and arms when washing. "So how much have you managed to paint so far?" she asked.

"We have two walls finished," Lena said between mouthfuls.

"The hardest part is the small area between the stanchions and the wall," Annie said. "That space is so narrow, it's hard to paint."

"Julius can do that part," Jake said. "He's small. If he reaches as high as he can, the rest of us can do the higher parts."

"I'm not that small!" Julius said as he glared at Jake. He didn't like being reminded that he was small for his age and was wishing he would grow faster.

They worked until it was nearly milking time and it was finished. The barn was bright and clean looking. Now their father could phone the inspector to come back and check the work and they'd be able to ship cream again. The children were pleased with their work and Jacob praised them for a job well done.

The grasshoppers that summer were not gone, but there weren't as many as the year before and there was a better crop so harvesting kept them all working hard until late in fall.

In October, the family enjoyed travelling to two weddings. On October 3rd Helena's brother, Peter, married Mary Fehr and on October 30th, her sister Agenetha, married Aaron Neufeld.

Skiing

CHAPTER 83

Snowy blizzards blew into November and December of 1937. The snow piled into high snowdrifts that reached up the sides of the barn and up the north side of the house. Some storms lasted several days and with the white-out conditions there were times when Jacob strung a rope between the house and the barn in order for him and the children to be able to find their way back to the house.

The children took the horses and cotta to school and put the horses into the school barn while they were in class. If the storms were too bad, the school was closed and the children stayed home.

Lena wasn't in school this year. She had been asked to be a kyaikshi (maid) at a farmers place near Osler, so Jake, Annie and Julius were busy with school work and the chores at home.

As the snow continued to fall, it was hard for the horses to plod through it, but Jacob and Helena were encouraged.

"It may be hard to travel," Jacob said, "but with this much snow we could have a much better year next spring and summer. There will be a lot of water when the snow melts and soaks into the dry ground."

As November turned into December, Jacob spent quite a bit of time in his blacksmith shop where the heat from the little furnace warmed up the room. The snow piled around the building helped to keep it warm. He was busy building something for Christmas while the children were away at school. He bent and hammered red hot steel into two long, flat, narrow pieces. He also used his hand saw, plane and hammer to work with wood. He looked forward to seeing the children's faces at Christmas time.

Helena kept busy with the usual housework, meals, baby Daniel Peter and her little girls, Tena and Christine. She also sewed on her treadle machine after the children were in bed.

"How's your work in the shop going?" Helena asked her husband.

"I'm almost finished. Now I just have to do some varnishing while the shop is warm and I'll be done in a few days," he replied.

The Christmas concert at the school was another exciting event for all of them. Helena had again managed to make some new clothes out of old ones and some new clothes out of new materials. The children again felt special as they stood on the stage singing carols. This year Lena wasn't singing at the concert, but Jacob and Helena could hear Jake, Annie and Julius singing right on key.

Tena and Christine took it all in with shining eyes. Tena looked forward to the next winter when she would be in school, too.

On Christmas Eve, after the church concert, they gathered around the stove in the living room and shared their candy and nut bags.

"It's time for bed," Helena said. "Clean up your peanut shells and candy wrappers. Then put your plates on the table."

The next morning they gathered round the kitchen table before going out to milk the cows. There were treats on each plate, but only a few gifts on Tena's and Christine's plates. Lena, who was home for Christmas, Jake, Annie and Julius, looked around at their parents. Jacob stood looking back at them with a mysterious smile on his lips. Then he walked to the bedroom and pulled something out from underneath the bed.

As he walked into the kitchen, the older children's eyes widened and they broke out in big smiles.

"Skis!" they all said. Jacob grinned as one by one they took turns strapping their feet onto the skis.

"I made them for you all to share," he said. "Right now it's milking time, so let's get that done and after breakfast you can all take a turn at skiing."

It was a sunny day as the Friesen children pulled on their warm winter coats, hats, boots and mittens and went outside to try out their Christmas gift. In the garden they found a huge snow bank sloped up to the trees.

"Let's climb up there and slide down!" Julius said. They walked up to the top of the bank and took turns sliding all the way down, laughing when they couldn't keep their feet close together on the skis and went tumbling into the snow instead.

Inside at dinner time their cheeks were rosy from the cold fresh air as they talked and laughed about trying to ski. These were really cross-country skis and not made for skiing down hills, but they enjoyed trying it both ways. Listening to his children and seeing how much they enjoyed his gift gave Jacob a wonderful feeling deep down inside. All his hard work had been worth it!

A Painted Floor

CHAPTER 84

The melting snow in spring left small ponds of water standing on the yard. Hard snow drifts became slushy and watery and many times the children's feet slipped down through the soft snow into water underneath as they made their way home from school.

Of course, as the ditches filled, it was a big temptation to see how deep the water really was and after pouring the water out of their boots, they put them back on and walked home with squishy socks and cold wet feet. In the evening, several pairs of sopping wet boots stood near the kitchen stove and on the open oven door. The children hoped the boots would be dry by morning.

As the days became warmer and the snow all melted into the dry ground, it was seeding and gardening time. Jacob and Helena looked forward with hope that this summer and fall would produce lots of wheat, oats, and garden vegetables and fruit.

Once the crops and garden were planted, Helena looked forward to fixing up the inside of the house. It had been a long time since the floor boards had been painted. The walls needed new wall paper, too.

The family used the summer kitchen for cooking and meals again to keep the big house cool and clean.

One day Jacob took Helena to the hardware store in Osler to pick out the paint for her floors. She chose three colours: dark blue, red, and green. In the evening, with Jacob and the children's help, she moved the kitchen table, chairs and benches into the living room. Then after Annie swept the floor, Helena washed it.

The next morning as soon as the children left for school, Helena opened all the windows wide and painted the floor a solid dark blue colour. It was almost dry by the time they returned from school but they were not allowed to walk on it until after chores and supper were done.

That evening after everyone was asleep; Helena painted another coat of the dark blue colour. She was tired, but happy with the way it would look once she was done. By morning the floor was dry enough to carefully step on it to go outside.

Now came the fun part! Sitting in the summer kitchen after feeding her family, Helena took two wooden blocks, some gunny sack material, some nails and a small hammer and began creating a lovely flower on one block and leaves on the other. She folded the gunny sack pieces over and around to make raised flower petals and leaves and used tiny nails to keep the flowers and leaves in place.

Another lovely, hot morning dawned and Helena put the baby carriage and diapers out in the summer kitchen. After feeding baby Daniel Peter, she put him to sleep in the carriage.

"I'm going to start painting the pattern on the floor now, girls," she told Tena and Christine. "If the baby cries, you can take him for a ride around the yard in the carriage."

"May we watch you?" asked Christine.

"Yes – for a little while and then you need to go outside to play." Kneeling down at one side of the kitchen floor, Helena took her red paint, dipped the block of flower petals she had made into it and carefully stamped the flowers evenly across the floor.

"When will you do the leaves?" asked Tena.

"That will happen tomorrow, after the flowers are dry. Now go outside to play and watch the baby so he doesn't climb out of the carriage when he wakes up."

Working quickly and carefully, Helena soon had the whole floor done and took her supplies outside. She cleaned her hands and after feeding the chickens and gathering eggs, she made dinner on the summer kitchen stove.

The next morning she carefully stamped all the leaves. She stood near the door, looking at the finished floor with a satisfied sigh. It looked like 'bought' linoleum. It was fresh, new and clean! She was glad the floor was finished and would have time to harden well before the children were out of school. In the meantime, they were not allowed to walk on it any more than was needed.

"Now I have a new floor for when my relatives come in August!" she thought.

The second last Sunday in August the Banman clan arrived in time for Sunday dinner. The cars and wagons lined up near the house. All of Helena's brothers and sisters were there along with the many nieces and nephews. Around 20 cousins milled around the house, yard and gardens.

Helena made her famous fried chicken, coleslaw and potatoes. The Banman clan loved coming to her house for their once-a-year family time. The sisters commented on Helena's lovely floor.

As they visited, her brother Julius walked up to her to introduce his girlfriend, Anne Fehr.

"Helena, we'll be married on October 16th. Do you think you can come to the wedding?"

"We'll try, Julius. The ferry should still be running over the river, so I hope we can go."

October 16th, 1938 the Banmans were together once again as Julius and Anne were married.

The Last One

CHAPTER 85

One day in early December of 1938, Helena and Jacob gathered with other family and friends to butcher pigs at his brother Wilhem's farm. Helena did not feel well at all and was not in a good mood. She felt too tired to get up so early to go pig butchering.

While working in the kitchen helping her sister-in-law set things up for the meat that would be coming in soon to be made into sausage, Helena peeled potatoes for the noon meal for all the people. She quietly went about her jobs, listening to the other women instead of joining in the visiting. She felt sick to her stomach and when the meat was brought in, the smell of it was too much for her and she hurried to the outhouse to throw up.

Helena's sister-in-law watched her quietly and while the other women were busy preparing food she put her hand on Helena's shoulder and said, "You are not feeling well. Are you all right?" Tears gathered in Helena's eyes as she said, "No! I'm not all right! I'm going to have another baby. We already have seven children and it's been so hard to raise them and keep them fed and clothed. My other three babies died. I thought we were done with this – I don't want to have another baby."

Looking around to make sure the other women were still busy with their work, her sister-in-law led her into another room. "I know it's hard, Helena," she said. "But don't say that. The day will come when you will be so thankful to have this child. Just wait – you'll see that I'm right!" As the months went by, Helena began to feel better and the first time she felt the baby kick, she smiled. She was starting to feel happier about having this last baby.

Spring brought the new kittens, puppies, baby chicks, new calves and colts. The gardens were alive with new flowers on the fruit trees and in the garden. Spring rains soon had the yard, fields and gardens growing with crops and vegetables.

One day at the end of July, Annie took Danny, Christine and Tena to the Hein farm. On the way Tena said, "I wonder if we'll have a boy or girl."

Annie looked at her sternly and said, "What makes you think there's going to be a baby?" Children were not to speak of such things. Tena fell silent.

Helena with baby Nettie

So another baby was born. The doctor lifted the little girl for Helena to see and after she was washed, wrapped in a soft blanket and placed in Helena's arms, her heart filled with the same love she had always felt when holding her new babies. She was thankful to God for a healthy child. It was July 29th, 1939. Her parents named the little baby girl Agenetha, but the family called her Nettie.

Postscript

Jacob lived to be 62 years old. He passed away from cancer in 1958. Helena lived to be 102 years old. She passed away in 2001 having lived in three centuries. Their lives had many ups and downs but many wonderful times as well. Through the years their faith in God and their understanding of Him deepened. They were sure of what they believed and the old uncertainty of being told that you can't be sure you'll be accepted into heaven was gone and replaced with a new joy.

Helena sold the farm in 1959, the year after Jacob died. She bought a house in Osler and for the first time in her life enjoyed the use of electricity. She bought a new electric stove that had been damaged in shipping and paid $100.00 and 100 chickens for it.

Helena became very busy with her church and her friends. There were many quilting bees with her friends and as long as she was able, she made a quilt for each grandchild and great-grandchild. For some time her family was scattered in four different countries: Jacob (Jake) in Japan; Helen (Lena) in Mexico; Julius, Tena and Christine in the USA; Anne, Dan and Nettie in Canada. The children moved through the years as well and except for Helen, ended up in three different provinces in Canada. Even though her children and grandchildren were often so far away and she missed them so much, they were still her joy.

In 1967 she married Mr. John M. Dyck of Osler. Her life became even busier as she accepted another large family as her own. Helena and John Dyck had 15 years together before he died in 1982.

Jacob and Helena's Children

Helen (Lena) married DeForrest Metcalf and they lived most of their married years in Texas. They had no children. Helen was a missionary in Mexico before her marriage, taught Spanish and worked in a book store. She loved to play the piano and guitar.

Jacob (Jake) married Junko (pronounced "June-ko")Okada in Japan. They were missionaries. They had three children: Jonathon, Andrew and Helene. They had five grandchildren. Both Jake and Junko played the violin, were involved in church planting, and raised their children.

Anne never married. She was a teacher for many years and was a talented artist. She loved to travel.

Julius married Genevieve Lembeck. They were teachers. They had two children: Joel and Roslyn. They had two grandchildren. They enjoyed singing in the Oratorio choir in Saskatoon. Julius loved to write and published many articles, and raised his children.

Tena married Raymond Dell. He was a pastor. They had five children: Byron, Ruth, Jane, Bradley, and Dawn; fourteen grandchildren, and nine great-grandchildren. Tena was involved in music, taught in a private Christian school and helped her husband in the ministry and raised her children.

Christine married Lorne Albertson. He was a pastor. They had four children: Dale, Linda, Marilyn and Amy; seven grandchildren and six great-grandchildren. Christine taught piano, was involved in music and helped her husband in the ministry and raised her children.

Daniel married Ellen Bergstrom. They were both teachers. They had three children; Eric, Timothy and Jana; They had nine grandchildren. Dan loved to write, played the piano and the saxophone and raised his children.

Nettie married Joseph Balzer. They had five children; Verdeen, Karen, Nolan, Carmen and Noreen; eight grandchildren and one great-grandchild. Nettie played piano, became a church secretary, worked in Women's Ministry and raised her children. When she retired, she wrote two books.

Photo taken in 1949
Back row left to right: Daniel, Tena, Anne, Jacob(Jake), Julius
Seated; Nettie, Christine
Front row;Helen (Lena), and parents Jacob and Helena

The Friesen Farm near Osler

Farm yard with remodelled house. It was obviously a good year for crops. Note the big bale and straw stacks behind the barn.
The summer kitchen was moved from the front of the house to the far left of the picture. The cooling house is next to the windmill and the chicken barn is at the far right.

Helena's Parents

A BIT OF HISTORY

JULIUS BANMAN was 13 years old when his parents, John and Agenetha Banman and their family emigrated from Chortiza, Russia to Winkler, Manitoba, in the year of 1889. Julius was born in Russia on September 16, 1876. He had three brothers, Peter, Jacob and Solomon who also emigrated with his family. There were five older brothers, one of whom (Wilhem) died at the age of one year in 1855. There is no record of the death dates of the other four: Johan; Heinrich; Franz; or Kornelius and there is no record of them coming to Canada. There was also a sister, Anna, who did not emigrate, however, her son, John, emigrated with his grandparents and uncles. There is no recorded date of Anna's death.

While in Russia, Julius' father had been employed as a tailor, making men's suits. The Banmans were Mennonites whose ancestors had immigrated to Russia from the Netherlands on the invitation of Catherine the Great to settle land she had won in a war with Turkey. In the Netherlands, the Mennonites endured intense persecution at the hands of Catholic political rulers. It was this persecution that drove them to different countries in Europe.

During the Crimean war, the Mennonites were not comfortable with the situation in Russia and sent people to Canada and the United States to see if there was land they could settle on. The Banmans ended up settling in the Winkler, Manitoba area, in the village of Kleefeld. Several sections of the province were designated for Mennonite settlements. Kleefeld was located on the

West Reserve. The ocean voyages were very difficult for them all. Food was scarce and some people died on the ocean trips. After that there were the long train and wagon trips to their final destinations.

Helena's great grandparents, Henry Banman and Margaret Vogt in Russia

Settling in a new land was more difficult than they had imagined. In Russia many of the Mennonites had been quite wealthy and had servants to work for them. Now they faced living in sod houses, breaking new land for farming and shortages of food when they had been used to plenty.

HELENA KLASSEN was born in Russia on April 4, 1875, and emigrated with her family on June 23, 1876. She was only a year old. Her mother (Helena Buhler) married a widower named Andreas Blatz. He was her first husband and he brought three children from his first marriage to this family. Together they had five more children, but two of them died when they were babies. Then, Andreas Blatz died in 1873 and his wife Helena married Peter Klassen, another widower, who brought three children from his first marriage. Peter and Helena had another three, one of whom died at the age of three. That still left a big family of 11 children. Helena Klassen was one of the youngest.

Helena Klassen's family also settled in the Winkler, Manitoba area, arriving 13 years before the Banman family. Living in a village made it easy to get to know other young people and as Julius and Helena saw each other at church and with other young people, they became interested in each other.

When they decided to get married, people warned Helena that Julius had a problem with alcohol, but she didn't think it was that important. They were married on February 9, 1897, in the village of Kleefeld, where both the Banmans and Klassens lived. A year later their first baby, Helena, was born on August 22, 1898 and a year and a half after that her sister Agenetha was born on March 14, 1900.

Helena's parents, Julius Banman and Helena Klassen near the lake at their farm south of Aberdeen

In the Mennonite families, it was the custom to name the first baby girl that was born after her mother, and the first baby boy after his father. That was why Helena Banman had the same first name as her mother and grandmother and why she named her own first baby girl, Helena (Lena).

(There is no picture of Julius Banman's parents, John and Agenetha(Driedger) Banman)

Jacob's parents, David Friesen and step mother Maria Janzen. (David was blind) Pictured with Jacob's parents are his sister Justina, and Maria's son Jacob Janzen.

Jacob and Helena at their Osler farm house

Maps

Helena's great-grandparents came from the Chortitza colony in the Ukraine. Jacob's great-grandparents were also from the Chortitza area.

On the following page is a map of the southern region of Manitoba where the West Reserve for the Mennonites was located. The villages of Kleefeld and Neuendorf are shown, as well as the town of Winkler from which the Banmans took the long train ride to Aberdeen Saskatchewan. Also shown, is the village of Blumengart, where Jacob's grandparents settled and where he was born.

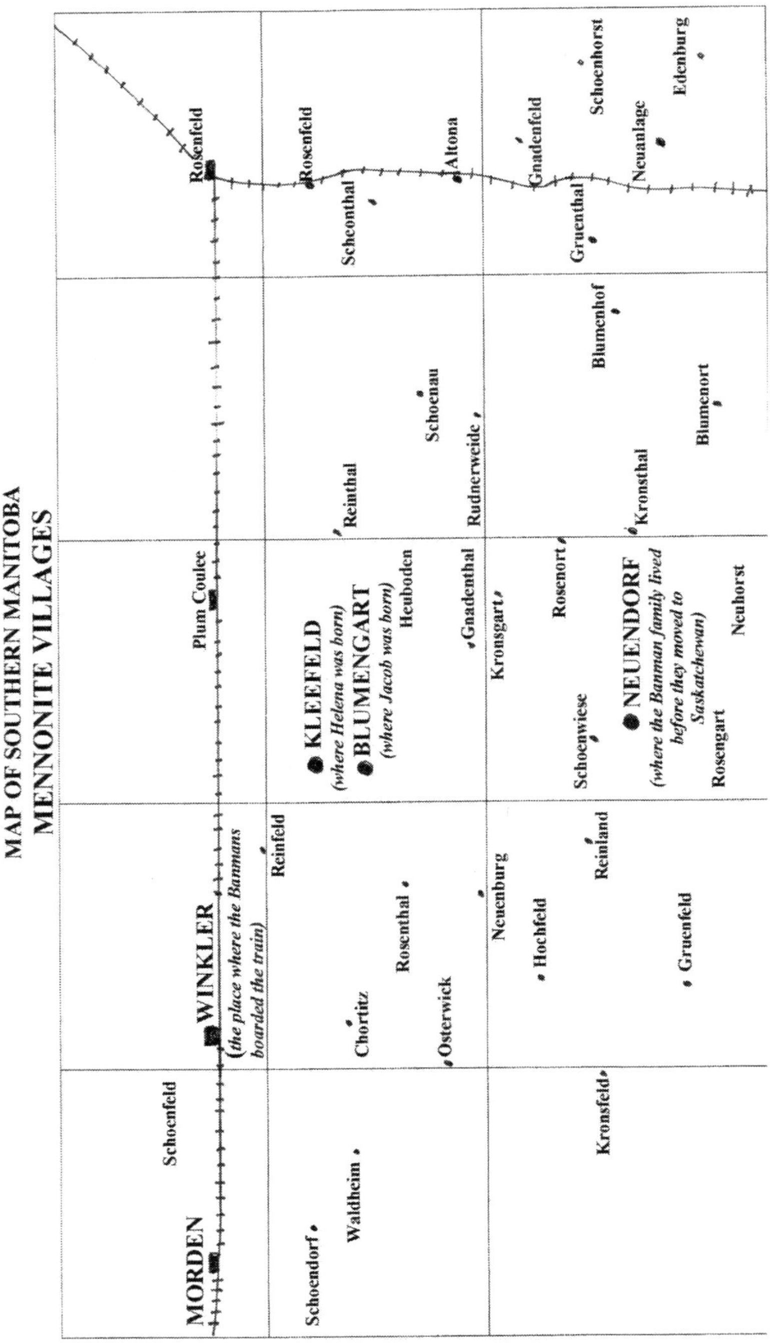

The last map is of the Saskatchewan River separating Aberdeen,

the Banman farm, Edinburg and Olgafeld on the east, from Blumenheim, Kronstahl, Neuanlage, Reinland, Rosenfeld, Osler and the Friesen farm on the west.

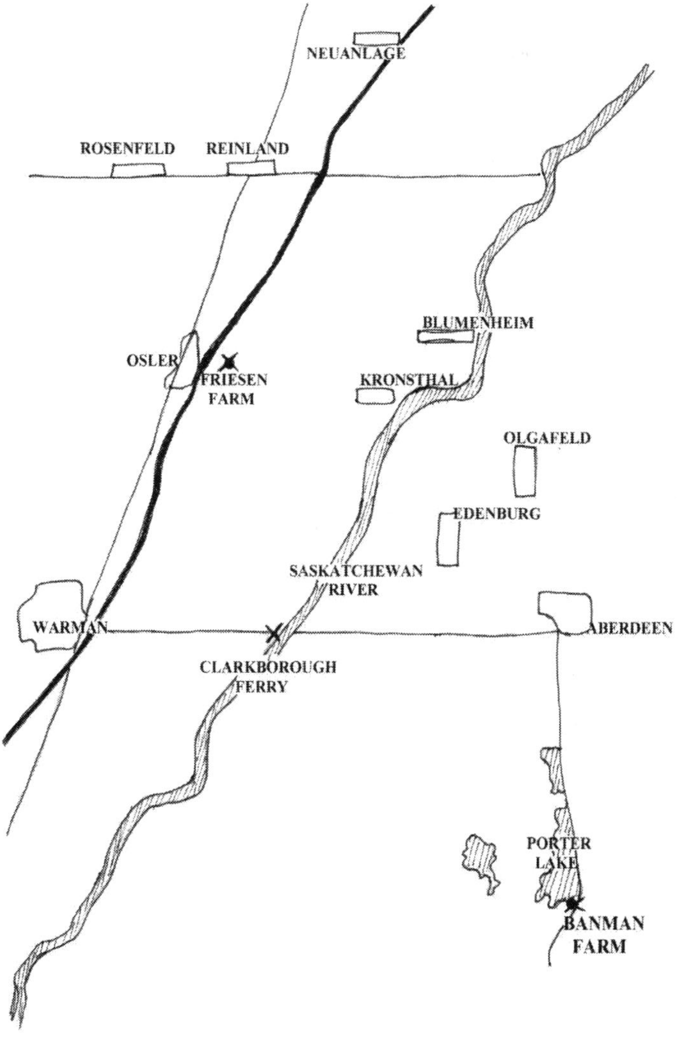

A Few of Helena's Recipes

Schmaunt Kuken (Cream Cookies)

3 eggs	2 cups white sugar
1 teasp. Vanilla	2 cups thick sour cream
4 ½ cups flour	1 teasp. Soda
4 teasp. Baking powder	

METHOD: Beat eggs, add sugar. Mix soda with cream and add to first mixture. Add vanilla, then flour and baking powder. Mix all together and roll out to ¼ inch thickness.
Bake at 350 degrees just long enough for the cookies to start to brown at the bottom. The top stays white.

Paepanate (Peppernuts)

4 eggs	½ teasp. Nutmeg
1 cup powdered sugar	1 teasp. Soda
4 cups flour(approx.)	½ teasp. Salt
¾ teasp. Cinnamon	grated rind and juice of 1 lemon
½ teasp. Cloves	¼ teasp. Black pepper

METHOD:
Beat eggs until frothy. Gradually add powdered sugar, lemon juice and rind. Sift flour. Measure and add salt, soda and spices. Sift again. Add sifted dry ingredients to egg and sugar mixture. Beat until medium soft, smooth dough is formed. Chill dough in refrigerator. Divide into 6 parts. Cut off small portions and form into fingerlike sticks, rolling with flat part of hand. Lay sticks in parallel rows and cut across, making pieces the size of a small marble. Place pieces cut side up close together on a greased baking sheet. Bake at 425 degrees until they begin to turn a light golden brown.

Peppernut Buns (Helena made these more often than the

peppernuts)

1 ½ cup shortening	2 cups white sugar
1 cup brown sugar	6 cups warm water
¾ teasp. Black pepper	1 teasp. Salt
1 ½ teasp. Cinnamon 2	2 teasp. Yeast.

METHOD:
Dissolve yeast and 2 teaspoons sugar in 1 cup lukewarm water. (taken from amount in recipe) Mix all ingredients with about 6 cups of flour; then gradually add flour to make a soft dough. Cover, let rise one hour. Knead. Let rise until double in bulk and knead again. Let rise until double and shape pieces of dough into very small buns. Set close together in pan greased pan, sprinkle with sugar and let rise. Bake in 360 degree oven for 30 to 35 minutes.

Chicken Noodle Soup
Cook one chicken for about two hours, until meat is tender. Add two sprigs of parsley, five bay leaves, two small sticks of cinnamon, one teaspoon of while black pepper kernels, one Star Aniseed and one small piece of whole ginger. Salt to taste. When almost done, prepare your noodles. Place noodles in soup tureen and add soup stock.

Home-made Noodles
1 egg ½ cup milk
¼ teasp. Salt Enough flour to make a hard dough. Roll out to 1/8 inch thickness. Spread lots of flour on top of it and roll up. Then snip into small strips, with knife or scissors, and put in boiling water until done. Drain and add to soup stock.

Vereneki

½ cup milk	2 egg whites
½ teasp. Salt	flour to make dough hard enough to roll.

Make a soft dough. Roll out on floured surface and cut into rounds.

Filling: 1 package dry curd cottage cheese
½ teasp. Salt
2 egg yolks
Blend cottage cheese, salt and egg yokes. Place a spoonful of the

mixture on dough rounds. Fold dough over and seal edges. Drop into boiling water and boil for 10 minutes. Serve with sour cream or cream gravy. Rhubarb or strawberry sauce is also good instead of gravy.

Pluma Mousse

1 ½ cups raisins	½ cup dried apricots
1 cup dried prunes	½ cup sugar
¼ cup dried apples(cut up)	Three pints of water

METHOD:

Add water to dried fruit and cook till almost soft. (15 to 30 minutes) Add ½ cup sugar during last five minutes of cooking. Make a paste of 3 cups of milk, ½ cup flour, ¼ cup sugar, and ½ teaspoon salt. Add thickening to fruit and stir until done. Serve warm or cold.